PRAISE FOR PIGNON SCORBION & THE BARBERSHOP DETECTIVES

"Rick Bleiweiss's *Pignon Scorbion* has quirky, wonderful characters and all the elements of a great (and fun) detective story. I totally loved reading this novel!"

—HEATHER GRAHAM,
New York Times bestselling author of over 150 novels

"Fans of Hercule Poirot and Sherlock Holmes will love *Pignon Scorbion & the Barbershop Detectives*. Get ready to be transported back to Edwardian England in this rousing tale of camaraderie and cerebral detective work. In an era before computers and DNA matching, an inspector's intellect ruled the day. With no detail missed, no stone left unturned, Bleiweiss has crafted a detective who can crack even the toughest cases with flair!"

—ANDREWS & WILSON,
bestselling authors of *Sons of Valor* and *Tier One*

"Shades of Sherlock Holmes, Hercule Poirot, and Perry Mason—Chief Inspector Pignon Scorbion is here! Kick back, put up your feet, stow away your cares, and prepare for some good old-fashioned fun. You are in a barbershop in a small English town, circa 1910, with Scorbion and his eccentric group of deputies. Follow the threads of clues as one by one they emerge in murders and mysteries, even a traveling circus. Using inductive reasoning worthy of his predecessors, Bleiweiss's writing is crisp yet evocative, and the story is a breath of fresh air which readers will love. I loved this book. It was a refreshing escape."

—PAMELA BINNINGS EWEN,
bestselling author of *The Queen of Paris*

"It's adorable. I frequently laughed out loud while also envying Rick's impeccable plotting. Hats off to him and his merry band of solvers. A superbly structured detective story in its own right, it's also a respectful, affectionate, and frequently very funny tribute to classic British detective fiction. It just might become a classic, itself."

—NANCY PICKARD,
New York Times bestselling and award-winning author of *The Scent of Rain and Lightning*

"Bleiwiess's debut novel is sure to delight fans of traditional mystery. The novel hearkens back to the golden age of mystery fiction, and Pignon Scorbion is a detective comparable to Hercule Poirot. His unlikely group of 'deputies' at the barbershop bring a fresh perspective to this fascinating mystery. I look forward to the next in the series!"

—AMANDA FLOWER,
Agatha Award–winning and *USA Today* bestselling author

"Extortion, theft, revenge, and murder fractalize into a dazzling kaleidoscope of crime in Rick Bleiweiss's *Pignon Scorbion & the Barbershop Detectives*. Taking over as chief police inspector of a not-so-sleeping English town circa 1910, Scorbion finds an unlikely investigative team in the denizens of Calvin Brown's barbershop. The subterfuge begins day one, but the action really heats up when a circus comes to town, touching off a three-ring spectacle of deception, detection, and deduction. Get comfortable in your favorite barber's chair, turn the sign on the door to Closed, and draw the window shades, because it's hard not to binge-read when the end of every chapter leaves you with another puzzle to solve. Bravo, Rick Bleiweiss!"

—ROBERT ARELLANO,
Edgar Award finalist and author of seven novels,
including *Havana Lunar: A Cuban Noir.*

"This charming tale of the eccentric Chief Inspector Pignon Scorpion, artfully told in the style of the detective stories of old, will be sure to delight fans of Christie's original Hercule Poirot series, as well as cozy-mystery and historical-fiction readers. I'll be looking forward to more cases being solved by this delightful cast of colorful characters in the barbershop!"

—NATASHA BOYD,
bestselling author of *The Indigo Girl*

"Bleiweiss's Pignon Scorbion, the new (circa 1910) chief police inspector of the British hamlet of Haxford, is a splendidly unique addition to the list of entertainingly eccentric investigators who use brain over brawn. With a deductive prowess and penchant for precise couture that are more than a match for his contemporary Hercule Poirot, Scorbion prefers to solve his mysteries (here ranging from proof of parenthood to pig theft to bloody murder) in a barbershop, assisted by a young newshawk (his Watson), a trio of amusing tonsorial artists, and a bookseller as bright as she is beautiful. Good company. Good fun."

—DICK LOCHTE,
Nero Wolfe Award winner and bestselling author of *Blues in the Night*

"The game is afoot, and the foot is firmly on the gas pedal in Rick Bleiweiss's pawky, Sherlock-like mystery, *Pignon Scorbion & the Barbershop Detectives*. Driven by its razor-sharp title character (and joined by an often-hilarious host of deputized barbers) this case-cracking tale takes plenty of thrilling, genre-delighting twists and turns without ever running off the road. Bleiweiss writes with a cleverness that pleases rather than patronizes, and the observational powers of the percipient Inspector Scorbion rival those of any classic literary sleuth. Perfect for genre diehards and newcomers alike."

—JAMES WADE,
Spur Award–winning author of
All Things Left Wild and *River, Sing Out*

"Rick Bleiweiss's book, *Pignon Scorbion & the Barbershop Detectives*, is fabulous. Written in the style of an Edwardian author, i.e. Conan Doyle, it captures perfectly the time frame. I've been reading European Noir books for ages, and this was a breath of fresh air. The police procedural part is spot on, with great characters and twists in the plot which kept the interest level at a maximum. Bravo, it's fantastic. Do yourself a favor and buy a copy."

—BILL BERGER,
music industry senior executive

"Bleiweiss transports us back to Edwardian England with a fascinating new detective who is quite accomplished at rooting out truths."

—D. ERIC MAIKRANZ,
author of *The Reincarnationist Papers*

"Bleiweiss's novel is a worthy addition in the tradition of Conan Doyle and Christie. Holmes and Poirot, please make room for Pignon Scorbion."

—REED FARREL COLEMAN,
New York Times bestselling author of *What You Break*

PIGNON SCORBION

& THE BARBERSHOP DETECTIVES

Rick Bleiweiss

BLACK
STONE
PUBLISHING

Copyright © 2022 by Rick Bleiweiss
Published in 2022 by Blackstone Publishing
Cover and book design by Kathryn Galloway English

Printed in the United States of America

First edition: 2022
ISBN 978-1-6650-4675-6
Fiction / Mystery & Detective / Traditional

Version 1

CIP data for this book is available
from the Library of Congress

Blackstone Publishing
31 Mistletoe Rd.
Ashland, OR 97520

www.BlackstonePublishing.com

This book is dedicated to my late cousin Saundra Shohen, a model, author, scriptwriter, organizer, editor, podcaster, health care administrator, humanitarian, rape-victim activist, AIDS activist, and educator.

Saundra was the most amazing, caring, brilliant, creative, beautiful (inside and out), accomplished, and wonderful person I have ever had the pleasure to know. The world is quite dimmer without her in it.

Saundra was more than a relative, she was a close friend who encouraged my writing and unselfishly edited most everything I wrote, including the earliest versions of this book.

Saundra, we did it! This one's for you . . .

To view the full cast of characters, visit RickBleiweiss.com

To unlock the last two levels of the
Pignon Scorbion Find the Hidden Objects video game,
enter the code HAXFORD

PREFACE

Billy Arthurson worked for a newspaper, the *Morning News*, from 1910 to 1930 in the small English town of Haxford, writing popular articles (which he later turned into full stories) about the exploits of the town's chief police inspector, Pignon Scorbion (pronounced Pin-yone Score-bee-on), a peculiar but brilliant detective.

Scorbion, a contemporary of Hercule Poirot, deductively solved cases much in the same manner that Poirot and Sherlock Holmes employed. Scorbion idolized Holmes and was overjoyed when, by the pure happenstance of attending the same function, he met and became friends with Dr. John Watson later in his life, after Holmes had passed away.

Billy witnessed Scorbion's case-solving abilities firsthand during a time when he, Scorbion, a female bookshop owner, and a group of deputized barbers solved a number of cases together in the town's barbershop, which they used as an interview room.

Billy's earliest stories and articles—which took place in 1910—are the basis of this book, in which you will be introduced to the great chief police inspector Pignon Scorbion, his tonsorial sleuths, and a memorable cast of town characters, "for your enjoyment, entertainment, astonishment, and delight," as Billy wrote in one of his articles.

CHAPTER ONE

The banging on the front door was so thunderous and insistent that to Cora Gromley it felt as though the furnace might soon explode. The stately English country house's cavernous, bare-walled rooms seemed to amplify the constant barrage of resounding thuds and booms. Even though she was in the kitchen on the other side of the house, the ruckus stopped Cora from serving her husband Mortimer's lunch, which she and their cook had only just prepared.

She turned to the cook. "Nellie, what *is* that ghastly pounding! Has something happened to our furnace?"

Nellie replied, "No, ma'am. Methinks there's someone at the door."

Cora considered that for a moment. "Yes, that could be it. But who would be acting in such a manner? Never in my fifty-two years have I ever experienced such commotion!"

Nellie closed the oven door and straightened. "Shall I go to the door and see who is knocking?"

Cora quickly replied, "No. I will find out what is going on and put an end to it. I find it terribly annoying and irksome." She untied her apron, laid it on the kitchen table, picked up a rolling pin, and strode through the dining room, living room, and library to the front of the house. She shouted, hoping that her words would get through the thick beams and slabs of the heavy wooden door. "Who is there? What do you want?"

When she received no reply, and the banging only intensified, she decided to open the door, armed with the rolling pin and the knowledge that there were others in the house who would come to her aid, should she need it.

She opened the door a crack. "Who is there, and why are you disturbing us so?"

She shrank back when a tall, scruffy, scowling young man of perhaps thirty-five years suddenly loomed in the open doorway, filling it with his menacing presence. He appeared to Cora to be very agitated and removed any doubt when he yelled, "Open the damn door. I want to see Mortimer Gromley. Now!"

When he started to push the door open, Cora put her weight against the other side and shouted back at him, "Stop that this minute, young man! I don't know who you are or why you are here, but you will not enter this house without first telling me why you want to see my husband so badly that you see fit to disturb our lunchtime and create such tumult."

The young man glowered at Cora and again tried to push his way in. He stopped when she brandished the rolling pin and commanded, "Let go now!"

Stepping away from the door, he hissed at her, "It is no matter that concerns you. It is something of great importance solely between me and Mortimer Gromley."

Cora was not having it. "*Everything* that concerns my husband also concerns me. If I allow you to enter, will you stand by this door until I fetch my husband?"

After the man nodded twice, Cora opened the door, took him by the arm, and positioned him next to the entry, holding the rolling pin over her shoulder, ready to wield it if need be. "Stay right there while I get—"

Before she could complete her words, Mortimer ambled down the stairs from their bedroom. Cora turned to him and said, "Did this hooligan wake you from your noontime nap?"

Mortimer kissed her on the cheek as he reached the bottom of the landing. "No, my dear, I was already awake. But I must say I was curious about all the racket." He looked around and spotted the young man in the room. "And who is this?" Then his gaze went to Cora. Seeing the weapon she carried at her shoulder, Mortimer asked, "And, why are you threatening him with a kitchen implement?"

Feeling safer with Mortimer by her side, Cora lowered her arm. "I have no idea who this young ruffian is, and he was rather brash in wanting to see you. In fact, he tried to force his way into our home."

Mortimer studied the squirming young man. "I have no idea why you desire so badly to meet me, but I am here now, so what is it, sir, that you want?"

The young man took a step toward Gromley, which brought Cora's rolling pin back up. Then, in an accusatory tone, he said, "Are you the same Mortimer Gromley who makes his living selling fine linens?"

Gromley answered, "While I no longer ply my trade or wares, yes, that is who and what I have been for the greater part of my adult life. And now that you know who I am, who, pray tell, are *you*?"

CHAPTER TWO

Chief Police Inspector Pignon Scorbion opened the door to Brown's Barbershop and perused the establishment. It felt and smelled familiar and comfortable, reminding him of barbershops he had frequented in other towns: a staggered black-and-white checkerboard tile floor, three barber chairs along the left wall in front of which were oval mirrors with lighting sconces hanging above them and ledges sitting below, on which were perched tools of the tonsorial profession—razors, combs, scissors, and antiseptic jars that leaked their pungent odors. The back wall was adorned with coat hooks, hanging barber capes, a calendar, a clock, a small shelving unit, and two brooms idly leaning near the frame of a door that led to a generous storeroom. There was a wall of windows to Scorbion's right, and a large window running the length of the front of the store next to the door, through which the morning light was streaming between the slats of half-closed blinds.

Though the person he sought was nowhere in sight, Scorbion walked inside, took off his bespoke charcoal-grey linen suit jacket, and placed it on an oaken coatrack that stood at the entrance with the same care and attention to detail that he unfailingly displayed in solving murders and other crimes.

Three of the men in the shop, lounging on the simple wooden

chairs that lined the front window, and a younger man sitting upon the barber's chair closest to the back wall, turned to look at Scorbion as he hung his coat. A fifth man was crouched on the floor, tightening a screw on the base of the middle barber chair, unaware of Scorbion's presence in the shop.

Scorbion's wiry, athletic body, accented by his formfitting starched white shirt and contoured grey slacks, cut an arresting figure, and to the men in the shop, he was probably the sharpest-dressed dandy they had seen in a year—possibly ever.

One of the men sitting on the chairs nudged the man next to him. "We surely don't see many peacocks like him this far from London, do we?"

The third man leaned over and murmured, "I w-wonder who he is. Haven't seen him around here. Qu-quite the fop, isn't he?"

Scorbion furthered that image by waving for the shoeshine man to come over to him.

Thomas—clad in his customary green shirt, brown-and-black-stained overalls, and leather apron—stood up from one of the chairs and brought his low stool over to Scorbion.

In a kindly but commanding tone, Scorbion asked, "What is your name, my good fellow?"

"Thomas, sir. Thomas Worth."

"Well, Mr. Thomas Worth, I am here for a haircut, a shoeshine, and to have my nails buffed. I implore you to take extreme care with these two-tone shoes that I am wearing. I have them specially made, and I have no doubt that they are unlike any other shoes you have ever worked on. I do not want to see the white polish in the black sections nor any black polish in the white parts. Can you do that, Thomas?"

Before Thomas could answer, another voice did. "Of course he can!" Calvin Brown, the overweight, grey-haired owner and chief barber of the shop, reprimanded his longtime friend as he slowly rose from the floor, screwdriver in hand.

Scorbion smiled as Calvin walked over to him.

"When I did not see you, I momentarily wondered if you had sold this establishment and set sail for the antipodes!" Scorbion mused.

Calvin cleared his throat and smiled. "No, my friend, I am here forever. I find this town much to my liking, and now that you are also here, it makes life all the more enjoyable." He turned to the two men on the guest chairs, who were clad in white, high-collared barber's shirts. "Barnabus and Yves, I would like to introduce you to our newest client, my good friend Pignon Scorbion. He has just come to Haxford to be our chief police inspector, and you will find his skills of observation, deduction, and crime-solving to be extraordinary. Pignon and I first met many years ago, in the village of Chamfield. I was apprenticing at a barbershop that happened to be centrally located within his jurisdiction, back when he was just a street copper. Through all the years we spent together in that village, Pignon would let no one but me touch his hair."

Scorbion picked up the story. "Calvin may have been in training, but even then he was the best barber I had ever met. And he retains that distinction today. We have remained in contact during all the intervening years after we both departed Chamfield for other destinations—Calvin returning here to Haxford, where he was born and raised, and opening this shop, while I served as a police inspector in two other localities. And now, through happy circumstance, I have been hired to serve this community, and we are together again. Bravo." He touched his brow and added, "It is my pleasure meeting you, Barnabus, Yves, and Thomas. I am certain I will be seeing you all on the occasions when I am here to have my hair cut, my nails buffed, my chin, neck, and cheeks shaved, and my shoes cared for."

Yves, a clean-shaven, rotund French transplant who was so short that he stood on a wooden pomade crate when he cut his clients' hair, gave a wave of recognition. Barnabus, who at forty-five was ten years older than Yves and a full three-quarters of a foot taller, gave Scorbion a thumbs-up. In doing so, he brushed against his long, plush ginger beard and caused it to crackle.

Scorbion then addressed the younger man sitting in the barber chair. "And you, my good fellow, who appears to be part of the clientele of this establishment. You who have not been identified yet, what is your name?"

"I'm Billy, sir. Billy Arthurson."

"And what do you do, Billy Arthurson?" Scorbion asked. "No, wait. Let *me* tell *you*. Swivel in that chair to face me fully."

Billy did as he was asked.

"From the grease on both your trouser cuffs," Scorbion related, "I would say that you work with machinery. But your shoes have none of that substance anywhere on them; they are clean and somewhat polished. So you do not work on those motorized carriages that have begun to invade our streets, or in some position with the railway. If you did, those shoes would be scraped, and dirty, and scuffed by cobblestones. If you would indulge me, lift up and rotate your hands for a moment."

Billy did as Scorbion instructed, turning them front and back.

"I see that you've tried to clean them, but some of the ink is still under your fingernails. And on your right sleeve cuff as well."

Billy bent his arm to see the cuff.

"Nice to meet you, Billy, the printing press mechanic for . . . ah yes! For the *Haxford Morning News*. If you worked for that ghastly rag that passes for an evening gazette, you would not be here in this shop at this time of day, would you?"

Billy stared, open-mouthed. Finding his voice, he said, "You're quite right, sir. I do keep the presses at the *Morning News* running. I have been working there since I moved to this town a half-year ago. Your deduction was superb."

"You flatter me, but it was nothing more than a bit of observation that anyone could have made."

"And yet, no one did but you, sir."

"You are quite right. However, allow me to inquire as to your age. You appear to be young, possibly not old enough even to enjoy a shave in this establishment."

Billy stroked his smooth chin. "My father is as devoid of facial hair as I am. It is a family trait. That has nothing to do with my age. But, Chief Inspector, as you once again correctly observed, I have only recently completed my schooling. The job at the *Morning News* is my first. I have always been good with machinery, so keeping the presses running is duck soup for me. But, my real ambition is to be a writer, which I also have a knack for. I'm hoping that working at the newspaper will give me a chance to do that one day."

"I like you, Billy," Scorbion said. "I appreciate ambition and intelligence, and you appear to have both, despite your youth and lack of stubble."

Calvin interjected. "As the paper is printed in the early hours of the morning so that the newsboys and other hawkers have it available when the town wakes and people depart from their homes, Billy is often here when I open, gathering the gossip that my clientele regularly indulges in. As you know, Pignon, men come here not just to have our duties performed on them, but also to socialize. And in the short time that I have known Billy, I have found your observation of him to be quite correct—he is intelligent, aware, and a keen observer."

Billy paused a few seconds to relish the compliments that Scorbion and Calvin both paid. "Chief Inspector Scorbion, may I ask you a question?"

"You may call me 'Inspector,' Billy."

"Thank you, Inspector, I will," Billy replied. "Might we learn the derivation of your names? Both your first and last are entirely new to me."

Scorbion responded, "That is something I will be delighted to divulge, but at some other time."

Calvin broke in. "Come sit in my chair, Pignon, and let me cut your locks and buff your nails."

"Gladly," Scorbion replied, as he walked to Calvin's chair and sat down.

Thomas then set his low stool in front of the barber chair and said, "I'll be very careful with your shoes, sir."

As Calvin began cutting Scorbion's hair, he remarked, "If I recall correctly, Pignon, you first wore those shoes to the opening night of *The Mikado* at the Savoy Theatre in London. Was that not in March of 1885?"

"You are absolutely correct, my friend, and I assuredly received my share of snickering and derision at that event for these singular beauties. And even now, twenty-five years later, I still elicit those identical reactions when I venture into that same metropolis wearing them. But it matters not to me. I stand immune to the sniggering of the dreary sheep who reside in our capital city, whose putatively fashionable costumes are indistinguishable and interchangeable. Fortunately, the good citizens of the towns where I have served have grown accustomed to my distinctive footwear, despite their utter uniqueness in all the world."

"That is true, Pignon," Calvin affirmed. "Everyone knows that they are as exclusively yours as your signature." Then he mused, "My goodness, 1885 seems like such a long time ago, does it not?"

Scorbion agreed. "It does. Time marches in lockstep, inexorably parading from one moment to the next, one day to the next, and eventually one year to the next with no regard to anything in its path."

Calvin momentarily stopped clipping and turned to the other barbers and Billy. "Speaking of that era, even when Pignon was just a constable, he could have posed for a fashion plate. He always kept himself in the best of conditions so that his clothes fit perfectly. His trousers were always creased, his shoes shined, his nails buffed, his shirts starched, and never, ever, a hair out of place on his head." He patted Scorbion's shoulder. "I'm glad to see you have lost none of your panache, and that you continue to have your suits custom tailored. You always look very stylish—something I could never manage with my paunch. But, enough of that—after I'm done with your hair, would you like me to use the emery on your nails?"

"Yes, Calvin, yes. You have a way of making my nails shine in a manner unlike any other I have ever encountered in an establishment of this ilk. It is another of the reasons that I am pleased to be here." As Calvin started on his nails, Scorbion added, "What has changed the most, I would assume, in the intervening years since last I saw you is that you are now married. During our time together in Chamfield, you were a confirmed bachelor, however your correspondence to me since has indicated a change in that status."

Calvin stopped working on Scorbion's cuticles and answered with a slight laugh. "Yes, I have been hooked. My belly attests to that. It is from the delectable meals that my better half provides me. Mildred and I have been married for just over two years now, but with no children—I'm afraid they are not meant to be for us. I will invite you to our home for dinner and you will meet her. You'll rather like Mildred. She is quite pleasant."

"I look forward to meeting her and sampling her culinary skills," Scorbion acknowledged. "Do any of your other men have spouses?"

"None of them. They are all footloose, although I would wager that both Barnabus and Yves would prefer to find someone to settle down with than remaining alone. Though I have never asked him why, Thomas does not seem to be as interested in the fairer sex as I was when I was twenty-five years of age. Billy is still a bit youthful to be involved in a relationship of any depth."

Barnabus stroked his beard. "Chief Inspector, a qu-question, if I may?"

"What might that be, Barnabus?"

"When your predecessor, Chief Inspector B-Benson, had his hair done, he would often tell us about a case that he had recently s-solved. L-learning about his cases was always a highlight for us whenever he v-visited the shop. I realize you haven't been in town v-very long, but I was w-wondering if you've had anything interesting happen since you've arrived in Haxford, or m-maybe something that took place in your last position."

Everyone in the shop fell silent to hear Scorbion's reply.

His answer surprised them.

"You ask what interesting cases I've encountered lately. None! My God. *None.* It has been so boring. No challenges. No criminal masterminds. I left my last position because the town was so lacking in crimes of any substance that I was stultified beyond all tolerance. I need intellectual stimulation. While I have all manner of weaponry available to me back at the station, I do not carry a truncheon, sap, or any other sort of deterrent upon my person. I have no need for them. My brain is my most formidable weapon. It has given me the ability to see and discern what others do not—the connections and contradictions that help me uncover those details that are not obvious, or even fathomable, to most. It is a brain that was built to solve cases. But not dull, uninteresting, little boring affairs—'my husband is missing'—where all that is truly missing is fidelity in the marriage. And those were the only manner of cases I encountered before relocating here. It was an answered prayer when Chief Inspector Benson made the decision to retire, and I am hopeful that there will be more fertile ground in Haxford for me to apply my intellect and skills."

Scorbion put his hand on his forehead in mock fatigue and sighed. "I am so tired from doing nothing. My brain grows flaccid with disuse."

The men were all stunned. Benson *always* regaled them with the details of his latest cases and how he solved them. Indeed, his stories were the spark in their humdrum existence. No one in the shop could believe that Scorbion had nothing interesting to tell them.

"I would give anything . . ." Scorbion paused. "I would *give these shoes* for an interesting case."

Calvin gasped. "But, Pignon, they're your trademark. There are no other shoes like yours in all Haxford—in fact, in all the British Isles. They are you, and you are them."

"That is true, my friend, but my mind is more important to me than my feet. My mind is currently devoid of anything that even comes close to engaging it, and it is keenly aware of that condition, whereas my feet are clad in this fine footwear, yet are unaware of it in any conscious manner. They walk in blissful ignorance of my frustration."

Thomas stood up from his stool and positioned himself directly in front of Scorbion.

"My rich uncle lives just outside town. He and my mum had a fallin' out, but I visit him and my aunt sometimes, and he just told me that somethin' strange happened to him. It might prick your interest, Chief Inspector." Then he added, a bit shyly, "And I won't be wantin' your shoes if it does."

Perking up as he leaned forward, Scorbion gave Thomas his full attention. "What has happened to your uncle, named . . . ?"

"Mortimer Gromley, sir, and Cora is my aunt. Noontime two days ago a tall, scraggly young man in his early to midthirties showed up at their house and pounded on the front door demandin' to be let in."

Thomas went on to describe in detail the events that took place when the young man arrived at the Gromleys' house, right up to the moment when he revealed to them why he was there. Thomas paused at that point and asked Scorbion, "Should I stop? Am I borin' you?"

Scorbion shook his head. "To the contrary, Thomas. This affair is quite intriguing. However, before you reveal the young man's identity—which I am quite sure I have already ascertained—can you tell me the ages of your aunt and uncle and the ages of their offspring?"

"Can indeed. He's turnin' fifty-nine and she's fifty-two. They never had no children. You really know who he is?"

"I do. And I believe I could detail the events that took place."

"No kiddin'!"

"It is my belief," Scorbion postulated, "that the young man emphatically stated he was your uncle's son. If that is so, and I were he, *I* would have said, 'I am your son,' so I assume that that is exactly what *he* said. Immediately following that revelation, your aunt and uncle would have undergone an uncomfortably short period of incomprehension, after which questions, and possibly anger, would have emerged. That would have led to your uncle's first comment to his purported offspring, most probably along the lines of, 'You are *what*? I have no son, young man.' And I presume that your aunt would have interposed with a statement similar to '*I* would know if he had a son, because I would have borne him—and I have borne no children.' This young man would then have told them the circumstances under which your uncle and his birth mother conceived him. His story most unquestionably included an illicit affair—possibly a one-time assignation—which resulted in the birth of a child of whom the father, your uncle, was never made aware. He would have had a handwritten copy of his birth record and would then have asked if his mother's name was familiar to your uncle, and if it sparked any part of his memory."

"Blimey, Chief Inspector, you got it right!" Thomas enthused. "Like you were there."

Scorbion responded nonchalantly, but with a tinge of excitement in his voice. "Thank you, Thomas, but that does not matter. The most important part is yet to unfold. The time to confirm or deny this young man's story has arrived. Tell me, what is the name of this possible heir to your uncle and aunt's fortune?"

"Jonathan Bentine."

"And have the inquiries looking into young Jonathan's allegation begun?"

"No, sir. That just happened two days ago. Auntie and Uncle tol' me about it right away, 'fore they did anythin'."

"The best advice you can give them is to let them know that you have brought the news of their situation to me and that I, Pignon Scorbion, your new chief inspector, will take the case on to determine the authenticity or fraud of Mr. Jonathan Bentine, possibly née Gromley. And I will do so right here in this shop, assisted by every one of you."

The men looked at each other with incredulity on their faces. Then Billy asked aloud what they all were thinking. "You mean you want us to help you solve the mystery of Mr. Bentine's identity and parentage?"

"Th-that would be th-thrilling!" Barnabus added.

"Yes," Scorbion confirmed. "You all will be my assistants. We will have a formal inquiry and together we will solve this case. Right in this shop, today—if Thomas can get his uncle and young Jonathan to come here and join us forthwith."

Billy looked bewildered. "But why here and not in a more formal setting with your sergeant?"

Scorbion replied at once. "I have only been in this town for a short period and have not yet had the opportunity to establish a full rapport with Sergeant Adley. Moreover, I do not wish to take him away from his assigned duties. On the other hand, my good friend Calvin and I have known each other for many years. I trust him and his judgment implicitly, and his observations benefited me in a number of cases when we were together in Chamfield, so I welcome his involvement. And the rest of you"—Scorbion gestured to the others—"appear to be bright, decent fellows."

Calvin affirmed, "I will vouch for my men, and for Billy as well."

"Therefore, I am quite comfortable having you all assist me in this inquiry."

As soon as Scorbion confirmed that, Thomas, whose excitement was obvious to everyone, turned to Calvin and asked that he be allowed to leave to find his uncle and Bentine and ask them to attend the hearing.

"With haste, please," Calvin replied. "I'm sure we're all curious to learn how this affair is resolved, and we will have customers to attend to so we must do this as expediently as possible. And, Pignon, thank you for the compliment, and for your trust. I have completed your nails, so you may now move."

Thomas departed to search out the two men, while Calvin turned the Open sign on the door to Closed and shut the blinds over the windows.

Under Scorbion's direction from his perch on Calvin's chair, Yves, Barnabus, and Billy retrieved and arranged the chairs and tables that were stored in the shop's back room. Soon, they had created a head table with six seats behind it. They placed another two chairs on the other side of the table, with a foot and a half of space between them. Scorbion instructed each man to sit on one of the six chairs behind the table, leaving the two center ones open for himself and Thomas. The two chairs on the opposite side of the table, he said, "are available for the witnesses, should they agree to participate."

Barnabus turned to Yves and, in his customary needling manner, asked, "W-would you like me to f-find a highchair so you can see over the table, like the b-big fellows?" In return, Yves gave Barnabus a one-finger salute and muttered, "*Casse-toi!*"

Billy put a pad and a fountain pen on the table in front of his seat. "Would you mind if I took notes, Inspector? Possibly I can turn this into a story for the paper and get a byline."

"Not at all," Scorbion replied.

Just as Billy was about to thank Scorbion, Gromley, a man of short stature (though taller than Yves by at least four inches), arrived. Bald at the crown of his head, he reminded Scorbion of a tonsured monk, if the monk happened to be wearing a black sack coat, waistcoat, and matching trousers. Scorbion introduced himself to Gromley, and before long, Thomas arrived with Bentine in tow.

Scorbion welcomed the lanky young Mr. Bentine, who was dressed casually in brown tweed trousers, a white shirt, and a grey cap that covered his sandy hair. He held a small, well-worn, brown leather satchel in his left hand. Scorbion showed Gromley and Bentine the two chairs on the opposite side of the table, while he and Thomas sat down on the other side with Calvin, Yves, Barnabus, and Billy.

"Let me start by thanking you both for coming today," Scorbion began. "You have a situation that I fully believe my associates and I"—he indicated the five men sitting with him—"will get to the very bottom of. We will today ascertain whether Mr. Gromley has a son of whom he was unaware, and if so, whether Mr. Bentine is that son—or whether Mr. Bentine's tale is an utter fabrication specifically designed for the purpose of fattening his bank account and ensuring his future. Before I begin this interrogation, do any of my associates, whom I hereby deputize to make this proceeding official, have any thoughts to share?"

All five shook their heads.

"Then I will start. Mr. Bentine, I assume you know that I am the new chief police inspector in this town."

"I have been told that."

"Good. Then you agree that this will be an official inquiry, no matter how unconventional the surroundings?"

"I do, sir."

"And you similarly confirm that you will relate to us only factual and faithful details and events?"

"I do again."

"And you, Mr. Gromley, do you agree as well?"

"Yes, Chief Inspector. To both conditions."

"Good. Then we shall proceed."

CHAPTER THREE

Mary Alice Bentine smiled as the handsome, well-dressed man, whom she assessed to be in his early thirties, approached the makeshift wood-plank stage where she stood. The pianist was placing his sheet music for "Greensleeves" on the rickety, slightly out-of-tune upright piano, for Mary Alice's last song of the evening. When the patron reached her, she held up her hand and gestured for the musician to hold off striking the first chord.

She leaned down to hear the man standing before her. He smiled and said, "You have a quite lovely voice, and you are a most attractive woman. In fact, I have been so taken with both your talent and your beauty that neither my ears nor my eyes have left you for a moment almost this entire evening. Would you do me the honor of dining with me when you have finished your performance? That is, if you have not already had your dinner."

Mary Alice found the tone of his voice refined and gentle, and his garments were not threadbare—quite the contrast to the typically rough, coarse sorts in overalls and sweat-stained shirts who tried to solicit her company every evening that she sang. "I do not usually accept invitations from men I am not acquainted with, but I am hungry, and you seem different from the others who frequent this tavern. I have one last song and then I would be pleased to dine with you."

The man smiled again and remained standing in front of her during her entire final song, after which he held out his hand and helped her down off the stage.

He led Mary Alice to a table in the center of the room, pulled out a chair for her, and pushed it in toward the table once she was seated. He took the chair opposite her.

"And now," she said, "I would like to know who it is that I am having the pleasure of dining with this evening."

He replied, "Mortimer Gromley," and handed her his business card, which read "Mortimer Gromley, Purveyor of Fine Linens."

After studying the card, Mary Alice asked, "What brings you to our small village, Mortimer Gromley? We do not have many establishments in need of fine linens. And, if you look around this room, I believe you will agree that not many people seem to have any good idea how fine linens are used."

He replied in a low, almost purring, tone. "People have the capacity to upgrade their lives, and there are occasions, such as weddings, when wares such as mine have a place in the overall scheme. I am trying to foster an awareness of the quality of my finer linens, and a market for them."

"Have you been successful in your endeavors?"

"I have only just begun in this fair town. In fact, I have booked my room at the White Horse Inn until this day a week hence. And may I say that I hope that you will allow me to dine with you every night that I am here."

The Grey Hawk Tavern's owner approached, carrying a dish towel across his arm. "Is this man bothering you, Mrs. Bentine? If he is, I will make certain that he never does again."

Mary Alice smiled. "Thank you for your concern, Phillip, but quite to the contrary. Mr. Gromley is most engaging and gentlemanly. I am very comfortable in his presence."

Phillip broke into a grin. "That is nice to hear. May I bring you both food or drink?"

Mortimer asked Mary Alice, "May I order for both of us?" When she nodded, he told Phillip to bring them the best meal the kitchen could prepare, and the best wine to pair with it.

While eating the sumptuous repast of lamb chops that soon arrived, and washing it down with copious glasses of alcohol, Mortimer told Mary Alice exciting tales of his travels to splendid cities and exotic countries across Europe while peddling his linens. She was captivated by his stories—and his charm, looks, and sophistication—and by the end of the evening, they were both overfilled with food and inebriated.

Mary Alice felt a degree of comfort and attraction that she had not experienced with a man in many years, and when he asked her if she would accompany him to a nearby rooming house and be in his company for the night, she took his arm and they walked the short block to the lodgings, where they spent the night in passionate intimacy.

After a few hours of sleep, Mary Alice was the first to awake the next morning. As they lay side by side, she delighted in seeing how his swarthy face glistened in the sun's rays that streamed in between the window's drawn curtains. He looked almost angelic, and she relished the thought of being with him every night of his stay.

When Mortimer awoke, they made love one last time and he arranged to meet her at the tavern that evening. He left saying, "I cannot wait to hear your mellifluous voice, and to share this bed with you again, my darling."

Mary Alice began to joyfully sob, and when the drops from her eyes trickled down her cheeks, Mortimer handed her a linen hankie to dab her tears.

When she arrived at the Grey Hawk for her performance that evening, Mary Alice thanked Phillip for being protective of her, but shared that she and Mortimer had truly enjoyed each other's company the prior night. She confided in him that the afternoon had felt to her the longest in her life, such was her eager anticipation of seeing Mortimer again.

During her entire performance, Mary Alice kept scanning the room, waiting for Mortimer to make his entrance. Just before she started her last set, she asked Phillip if he had seen Mortimer, but he shrugged his shoulders and said he hadn't.

At the conclusion of her last song, she rushed off the stage and fairly ran to the White Horse Inn. When she arrived, she was breathing hard as she approached the desk clerk. He asked her, "Are you all right, madam?"

"I am," she gasped. Then she blurted out, "Do you have a Mr. Mortimer Gromley staying here?"

"We did," the clerk replied. "However, he departed this morning."

Mary Alice could not believe the words that seemed to hang in the air between them. "No, he is here. He told me he would be lodging here all week."

"I wish it were so," the clerk replied. "He is a fine gentleman, and a good customer, but I'm afraid that his reservation ran only through last night."

"That can't be," Mary Alice cried out.

"I assure you, it can. Mr. Gromley's wife arrived this morning after visiting a relative in a nearby town, and shortly after they reunited, they left together in a carriage that took them to the railway depot."

Mary Alice began to cry and then she fainted dead away.

CHAPTER FOUR

Billy arranged his notepad and pen, eager to see how Scorbion would approach the teasing out of Bentine's story.

Scorbion, looking confident and ever the professional, began, "I ask you, Mr. Bentine, to relate to us the narrative you told to Mr. Gromley. Leave out nothing, no matter how small or insignificant it may seem to you."

"I will indeed. For all of my life, my mother, Mary Alice Bentine, had told me that my father, William Bentine, abandoned her to journey overseas six months before I was born, claiming that he, William, wasn't the fatherly type and wanted no part of parenthood. She also told me that a shipmate of his wrote to her two years hence and gave an account of how my father had been killed by natives in the Amazon region. That's what I have believed about who my father was, and what happened to him, for virtually my whole time on this earth. However, six months ago my mother took ill with the pox—"

Scorbion broke in. "I am most sorry for that. It is quite disheartening. A disastrous illness."

Bentine threw Gromley a hard look, which Gromley ignored. "Thank you, Inspector," Bentine said. "It was indeed disastrous. She died horribly within four months. But during one of her last lucid periods before her demise, my mother told me she had lied to me about my father. She said that it was important to her that she set the ledger straight and tell me the true story of who my father really was. Is."

Everyone in the shop was as quiet as the shop's dormant teakettle, hanging on to the young man's every word. Even Billy's pen stopped as he too awaited Bentine's revelation.

"My mother was a handsome woman," Bentine continued, "and possessed a beautiful singing voice. During my childhood, she supported both of us singing nightly at the Grey Hawk Tavern on Fordyce Street, in the town of Avens, where we lived. Every morning she would regale me with tales of various gentlemen's attempts to win her heart. She rejected them all, telling me that she was waiting for 'the right suitor' to appear. My whole life, I was under the belief that she never found that suitor and had remained celibate. But during that lucid moment, there on her deathbed, she told me a far different story."

A soft clatter came from the front of the shop as the day's post fell through the slot in the bottom of the door. No one gave so much as a glance.

"She finally confessed that she had strayed once. And that admission turned my world on its end."

Bentine then told his spellbound listeners of Gromley's approaching his mother in the tavern, of her spending the night with what she described as a gentle, handsome, swarthy, *single* man, and of how the next evening, when he did not meet her as he had promised, she learned that he was married and had departed town with his wife earlier that day.

Bentine continued. "My mother was crushed. And before long she realized that she was in the family way with me. She was so ashamed of what she had done that she told everyone I was the son of the adventuring father, William Bentine, whom she had actually had no relationship with at all. She wanted me to be treated like a proper child when, in reality, I was the bastard son of a married gentleman with whom she had had a single evening's liaison. One unfortunate evening."

Scorbion interrupted. "If the tale that your mother told you was accurate, then it was *not* an unfortunate evening. But for that alleged tryst, young man, you would not be here with us."

"That is true," Bentine admitted, "but it ruined men for my mother for the remainder of her life."

Calvin asked, "You stated that the gentleman was married. How did she learn that?"

Good question, Billy thought. He noticed the slightest look of appreciation on Scorbion's face as well.

"She went to find him at the White Horse," Bentine said. When she arrived, he explained, the innkeeper told her that the gentleman's wife had appeared there earlier in the morning, and that they had left together in a carriage that took them to the railway depot.

Scorbion asked, "May we safely assume that the name of the man in question was Mortimer Gromley?"

"Yes, sir, it absolutely was."

"And when did this infidelity and betrayal, as you have described it, occur?"

"I reached twenty-five years of age on the second day of this month, therefore, it was twenty-five years and nine months ago."

Barnabus waved his arm in the air to ask a question, but before he could speak, Scorbion said, "There is no need to raise your hand, my good man. If you have something to say, just speak up."

Billy appreciated Scorbion's openness to the participation of others, realizing that Scorbion's including them wasn't simply a courtesy, but rather that he appeared genuinely interested in a range of perspectives and questions. Billy scratched a note to remind himself that the next time he thought he had a good question, he should just interject with it. It made him think that perhaps informal detective work was excellent training for an aspiring newspaperman.

"Yes, well . . ." Barnabus slowly uttered, "M-Mr. Bentine, do you have any s-sort of evidence that could confirm the d-details of what you have related to us?"

"I do."

Bentine reached into the bag that he had set on the floor to the left of his chair.

"This is my record of birth." He handed a yellowing piece of paper to Barnabus, who carefully unfolded it, scanned it, and passed it to Scorbion.

"It lists your father as William Bentine," Scorbion observed.

"It does, Chief Inspector. As I said, my mother wanted me to be perceived as having a proper father. She confessed that after he left for sea, she appropriated Mr. Bentine's name and asserted that she was his wife, knowing that he had left no one behind who could dispute her contention."

Scorbion studied the document. "All appears normal: seven pounds, twelve ounces, twenty inches long, brown eyes and hair, male, birth date the second of June. Do you have any other supporting items or documents? Ones that more closely tie you to Mr. Gromley?"

Reaching into the bag again, Bentine removed a faded swatch of off-white fabric with his left hand. He gave it a shake, and everyone could see that it was a woman's linen hankie.

He handed it to Scorbion, who held it almost reverently. "One can immediately discern that this is linen of the finest quality," Scorbion said. "The lace and embroidery are delicate and intricate, in a manner that suggests it is French, and crafted by a superior artisan."

"My mother handed it to me just before her death. She said Mr. Gromley had given it to her at the conclusion of their intimate encounter, so that she could dab from her eyes the tears of joy she was shedding at having met such a wonderful man, with whom she believed she would be spending many more evenings."

Scorbion passed the hankie to Gromley. "Is this an example of your wares, sir?"

Gromley looked it over carefully. "I cannot be certain, Inspector. It is of the quality and feel of my merchandise, but I was not the only merchant selling these items. It may have been one of my samples. Or not."

Scorbion turned back to Bentine, "And you have another piece—?"

"It is Mr. Gromley's trade card, which he also gave to my mother that evening."

Bentine handed the card to Scorbion.

"Yes, it certainly does say 'Mortimer Gromley, Purveyor of Fine

Linens.'" Scorbion turned to Gromley and held out the card to him. "Would you please examine this as well and confirm its validity?"

Gromley took the card, looked at it, turned it over, ran his fingers across its surface, and then handed it back to Scorbion. "Yes, that was my trade card. But I gave out many hundreds of them. Possibly more."

"Ah yes," Scorbion replied, "you most probably did. But the question at hand is, Why did this one end up in Mr. Bentine's possession?"

Bentine reached back into the bag. "I have one other item."

He took out a small black-and-white glass plate photograph and handed it to Scorbion.

"Can I assume that the woman is your mother, Mary Alice Bentine, and the small child is you?"

Scorbion passed the photograph around the table.

"Yes. It was taken when I was four years old. You can see that we are standing in front of the Avens town sign."

Looking at the picture, Billy inquired, "What are you holding in your right hand?"

Bentine responded, "That was my favorite stuffed animal. She was a little bear."

Billy asked innocently, "Did she have a name?"

"If my memory serves me correctly, I called her Belle."

"Interesting," Scorbion interjected, "but unimportant to the matter at hand, as is your record of birth. Neither has anything to do with Mr. Gromley, and neither plays any part in confirming or refuting your tale. They go only so far as to establish your identity. May I ask, though, did your mother continue to use peroxide to bleach her hair throughout her life, as she appears to have done in this photograph?"

Bentine said, "I guess so. It is how I remember her."

"And of what stature was your mother?"

Bentine paused. "Oh, I don't know. Um, let me see . . . she was of average height and build. As she appears in the photograph."

"Thank you," Scorbion said. Then he turned to Gromley. "Regarding the trade card and the hankie, what explanation do you have for how Mr. Bentine came into possession of those items?"

"I have no explanation, Chief Inspector."

"Then may we hear an explanation from you regarding the evening with Mary Alice Bentine, which this young man has described in such detail?"

"Again, I have no explanation," Gromley stated. "It is a complete fabrication. Well, a small part of it is accurate. Avens *was* one of the towns I took lodging in during many of my trips selling my goods. And I did often go to the taverns there for my meals and some light amusement. I often lodged at the White Horse Inn, as well. But I have no memory of this young man's mother or the encounter he has described. Yes, on my travels I have had occasion to dine with all manner of people, including charming, youthful women, but I have been a faithful partner to my wife every day and night of our thirty-three years of marriage. I have not strayed. Not once, not ever. I contest Mr. Bentine's story, and I will do so until my last breath."

"So," the inspector declared, "we have a paradox that must be sorted out. *This* is the sort of conundrum that I live for and believe that I am singularly equipped to unravel."

"If I may, Inspector . . ."

"Yes, Billy?"

"How will we determine who's telling the truth and who's lying? We have nothing to go on. Just two men's conflicting words."

Scorbion waggled his finger at Billy. "This is where we will use our brains—all of us—to inquire more fully about their allegations and denials. Then we will sift through every piece of information they have given us, as well as all we have seen with our eyes and heard with our ears. We will look for those elements that are inconsistencies or outright fabrications. I advise you, there are always one or two vitally important details that are initially overlooked, but which, when uncovered, lead directly to refuting one side and confirming the other. The result is a conclusion of indisputable accuracy. It is our task to find those details. Those inconsistencies."

Calvin poked Thomas in the ribs. "He's good, is he not."

CHAPTER FIVE

The Grey Hawk Tavern was filled to bursting with regular locals who were bawdily celebrating the middle of the weekend. The din created by their shouting and carousing made it almost impossible for anyone to hear the songs that were being performed by the singer and pianist on the makeshift platform stage in a corner of the room.

An occasional scuffle would break out, especially near the dartboard, often a dispute over whether the thrower had stood the proper distance away. The men at the skittles table were less prone to arguing, yet still loud in their cheers when someone managed to knock over all nine pins, or groans when the furthest skittle didn't go down first.

Periodically, some member of the mostly male crowd, attired in overalls and brogans, would stagger up to the stage and ply the attractive singer with spittle-laden, bleary-eyed offers of drink, food, or undying love. The tavern's chucker, or on occasion the pianist, ever vigilant for such encounters, would see that the drunken admirer moved along.

The three men sitting at a table near the back of the Grey Hawk Tavern were deeply engaged in conversation, so much so, that they scarcely noticed the musical act, let alone what songs they were performing. From time to time, when a particularly favorite song was being sung, such as "Black-Eyed Susan," the one sitting with his back to the stage would turn and look toward the platform. On one of those occasions, he commented, "That singer is lovely." The other men lifted their heads to give her an appraising look, nodded in agreement, and immediately returned to their discussion of linens and train schedules.

These men—along with a plain, slightly built woman seated alone four tables from them—were the only patrons that evening who were attired in the finer clothes associated with merchants and brokers. The rest looked to be farmers, tradesmen, and laborers. The three well-dressed men were in their thirties and, unlike most of the men in the room, were clean-shaven. They each had a pint of lager on the table in front of them, which were constantly being refilled by the buxom waitress with a missing tooth and a grimy apron. She was being most attentive to these three, who were likely the biggest tippers in the place.

The man who had remarked on the singer's charms had consumed far fewer glasses of lager than his two companions and was far less inebriated than they were. When the singer began "The Riddle Song," he again turned toward her. At the same moment, a fight broke out among four brawny men at the next table. The barman and the chucker rushed to separate the brawlers, but before they could reach them, their pushing, shoving, and punching sent one of the belligerents staggering backward. He had the size—and agility—of an ox and went sprawling across the table where the three men were sitting. The wooden legs gave out under the sudden load, and the glasses flew up into the air, slinging their contents onto the two men who had not turned to look at the vocalist. The man who had turned her way had seen the big lummox teetering and managed to slide his chair out of the way so that none of the spilled beer touched his elegant three-piece suit.

Seeing what had occurred, the barman and the chucker inserted themselves between the fighters, while the waitress grabbed two bar towels and rushed over to the men whose clothes were now drenched in lager.

The men thanked the waitress for the towels and proceeded to mop themselves up as best they could. But it was useless, and they told their unsoaked companion that they would pay their bill, go to their lodgings to change into dry clothes, and then return to the tavern.

The dry man, who had been an apprentice to one of the other two, had not met the third man before that evening. He recalled the man saying that he would be departing the next morning. He suggested that they exchange cards, which they did, and then the two dripping men paid their bills and left.

The man who remained moved to a different table, closer to the stage, and waited a full hour for them to return. When they didn't, he assumed they had decided to remain at their lodgings. He stayed in the tavern until the singer had sung her last note. Then he approached the stage.

CHAPTER SIX

Scorbion turned first to Bentine, "We will get back to you shortly," and then to Gromley. "But for now, Mr. Gromley—"

"Yes, Chief Inspector?"

"If you deny having been with this young man's mother on the night in question, please recount to us, as well as your memory will serve, the details of any single journey you may have taken to Avens in that period of twenty-five to twenty-six years ago. Additionally, we ask you to describe how you spent your time while in the town's environs on that particular trip. Please include in your narrative the encounters you had with any women there."

"Unfortunately, I have no recollection of any specific trip that took me through Avens. I often stayed in the town before setting off for other parts of England. I took my meals and entertainment in a number of taverns. But no matter how hard I try to concentrate my mind, I cannot recall any specific visit there. They are merged together into one collective memory."

"Surely there must have been *some occasion* that stands out from a few of those trips. Is there truly nothing?"

"One or two events come to mind. But they may not be from the time period in question."

"Permit us to determine what might or might not be pertinent. Please relate whatever you might recall, no matter when."

"I once tripped over a small box in the street, one that apparently had fallen from the back of a wagon. I remember the incident because I went to a physician, Dr. Mayes, whose office was close to where I fell. He tidied up my bleeding knee and informed me that I was a lucky fellow that it had not shattered. However, he did say it was bruised, and that I must stay off it for a few days. I had to postpone the remainder of my trip and return home once the initial soreness left me."

Thomas noted, "That surely had nothin' to do with Mr. Bentine's mother."

Gromley continued, "You are most likely correct. But I did arrange a delivery of some of my finest linens to Dr. Mayes, and I included my trade card. It was my way of thanking him for seeing me, literally right off the street, with no delay."

"And you have another incident that remains in your memory?" Scorbion asked.

"I do, but it may have nothing to do with this affair, either. I was in a tavern one evening—I believe it might have been the Grey Hawk—and I do recall that an attractive young woman was indeed singing. But the event that made that night stand out was a fight that broke out between some drunken oafs at a neighboring table. One of the men was thrown so viciously that he landed smack on top of the table where I and two other colleagues were sitting. The table collapsed to the floor, and three pints of lager drenched me and one of my companions. I left for the White Horse immediately after the incident to change into dry attire. Once in my quarters, I considered whether to return to the tavern, but, owing to the lateness of the hour, I decided to remain in my quarters at the inn rather than returning to the tavern."

"If I may inquire, what were the names of your associates at that unfortunate occurrence?"

"Let me think for a moment." Scratching his head he continued, "Aha, I do recall. The other man who was showered in beer was Robert Garson. He and I met a number of times in Avens, where our travels often landed us at the same time. Garson was quite a likable fellow, though perhaps more handsome and gregarious than he was intelligent or successful. He sold linens of a far lesser quality than mine and had a hard time making his quotas. The bulk of his meager sales appeared to come from women who were more taken by his looks, stature, and charm than by the inferior merchandise he was peddling. On the other hand, *my* orders came from mercantile proprietors who valued quality. Unfortunately, I could not trade on my looks even if I had wanted to. My sallow complexion and short stature do not a successful lothario make."

"I fully understand," said Scorbion. "And do you have any recollection of the second man at the table?"

"I do not recall his name, but I will never forget the moniker he was known by: 'Choc'; c-h-o-c."

"A strange name indeed. Are you aware of why people called him that?"

"When I met him, he was relatively new to linens. He was accompanying Garson, learning from him. Garson had been training Choc, so that he could venture out alone when he went on his own route. In fact, Choc mentioned that he was setting out the very next day to cover four Eastern European countries not visited by either Garson or me. If memory serves, I believe he mentioned that some were countries of his heritage, and that he had visited them while tracing his ancestry."

"That does not explain the derivation of his sobriquet."

"I was curious about that as well, and so I asked him. His explanation was that before he came to the linen trade, he worked at a confectionery. His main duties were to stir and pour the chocolate. Hence, he was 'Choc' to all. In any event, I gave Choc whatever advice I could, but I'm afraid Garson was better equipped than I to tell him what he might do to succeed. You see, Choc was equally as handsome as Garson, and he would have sold a lot more linen by trading on his looks rather than his brains—the same as Garson was doing. Choc was no Newton, but he wasn't a Romeo either. He was rather timid and retiring. I wondered how, not having Garson's boldness, he might nonetheless make it as a peddler of linens. I never encountered Choc again. And after not venturing through Avens for a number of seasons, I lost track of Garson as well."

"It is an interesting coincidence," Scorbion observed, "that my father, too, was involved in the business of chocolate at one juncture in his life. It was a very rewarding venture for him—apparently much more so than it was for this man named Choc. Their both having been involved with that wonderful substance is just one of life's little oddities. But I digress. Let us continue, Mr. Gromley—"

"Excuse me, Chief Inspector," Gromley interjected, "but the man's name suddenly came to mind. Choc Ross—that was his full name."

"I am glad you were able to recall that," Scorbion said. "Now, in addition, do you have *any* recollection of this young man's mother, or of your meeting your wife in Avens as Mr. Bentine has described?"

"I do not recognize the woman from the photograph, nor do I recall ever dining with her, let alone bedding her. My wife's sister Eloise lived less than twelve miles from Avens, and we would often travel to that area together, go our separate ways, and then rejoin for the return trip home. That was a fairly common occurrence."

Bentine interjected. "How can you categorically deny what my mother told me on her deathbed? Are you asking us to believe that she would make up such a fantastic tale as she lay dying?"

"I am sorry young man, but I *do* categorically deny it, no matter when it was said to happen, and no matter what the circumstances."

Gromley then held up his left hand toward Bentine. "I have worn this wedding ring since the day of my marriage and have never taken it off, not even to bathe or swim. Yet you said that the man who courted your mother wore no ring."

Bentine swiftly responded, "I don't believe that you've never removed it. That's a convenient story."

Scorbion stopped the quibbling. "One of four things is a certainty: Mr. Gromley is not being truthful, or Mr. Bentine is lying, or his mother fabricated the story, or she did not recall the event accurately. To unearth the truth, we must dig deeper. Therefore, Mr. Gromley, would you consent to our asking Mrs. Gromley to join us, to summon back anything that she might have stored in the recesses of her memory regarding this situation?"

"Certainly," Gromley responded. "I have nothing to hide. In fact, I would rather she be a part of this proceeding so that I don't have to answer future questions along the lines of, 'And how many *other* young men will be coming to our door, claiming to be your son?' I want the truth ascertained so that we can put this to rest."

"Fine. Please go fetch her. We shall recess until you return."

Chapter Seven

When Gromley departed to get his wife, Scorbion excused himself, saying only that he was going to the police station and would return before the Gromleys appeared.

During the time that Scorbion and Gromley were absent, Calvin gathered the post and raised the window shades, saying, "Let's get a bit more sunlight in here."

When Scorbion reentered the shop, the Gromleys had not yet appeared, which gave Billy the opportunity to approach Scorbion and speak privately with him. "I have a number of questions I would like to ask you, as further background for the article I will write about this affair—or possibly save for later articles."

"You may ask me anything," Scorbion replied. He neatly hung his jacket on the coatrack. "However, I will only answer that which I am comfortable responding to."

"Mrs. Gromley coming here made me wonder if you are married? I don't think that most people in Haxford know much about you beyond your being our new chief inspector. Is that too personal a thing for me to ask of you?"

"While I *am* a discreet individual, and I *do* value my privacy, I see no harm in responding to that question."

Billy reached for a pencil and sheets of paper that he had brought with him to record what Scorbion was about to relate.

Scorbion gave him a harsh look. "This is for you, not the general populace. They may continue to languish in their ignorance of my personal affairs."

Billy set the pencil down on the paper.

"At one time, I had a wife, Katherine Walls. For a short while. Many years ago, when I was but a lad of twenty-two. After only six weeks of wedded nonbliss, it was apparent to both of us that our union was a dreadful mistake. She wanted children. I did not. She desired that I be at home with her more than I was, while I desired to spend the majority of my waking hours engaged in police business—which she had no interest in. She wanted tenderness. I am not built for that. My composition is more like iron than blubber. She was flighty and romantic; I, stoic."

"That doesn't sound ideal."

"It was not. Fortunately, we were able to have our union annulled, and once that action was completed, she relocated to Venice. When I saw her off at the train station, she told me that she was journeying there to live, as it was the most romantic environment she could think of, and after spending her time with someone as unemotional as I, she needed that sort of milieu to heal herself. In the ensuing years, we have stayed in touch solely by post and telegram, though on a number of occasions, she has written that she might try to find me and attempt to renew our relationship. Fortunately, the most recent letter I received from her was over five months ago, and in that missive, she made no mention of the matter. I am not desirous of seeing her again as we certainly are better as friends than we were as each other's spouse and companion."

"And you never wed again?"

"I did not. I discerned that I was not meant to be so entangled with another human being. Additionally, Billy, have you not witnessed that I have a number of eccentricities?"

"No offense, Inspector, but yes, I have."

"Eccentricities are not a good trait in a marriage."

"My mum and dad are quite unlike each other but they get along just fine, and I know of a number of people who have eccentricities yet also have good marriages."

"That may be true, Billy, however I believe that you will find that I have them to a greater extent than most. And have you not noticed that the more eccentric one is, the less likely it is that they are married? People's eccentricities are modulated by their spouses; they are softened, and the sharp edges are rounded off. It is generally a consequence of the compromises one must make when successfully living with another. So, when someone is quite eccentric, as am I, it is likely they are not wed."

"I never thought of it that way. But I'll be alert to that now when I encounter others. It is unfortunate though, because I know this woman, who is close to you in age, who's exceptionally sharp-witted and attractive, childless by design, an individualist like yourself, and very unorthodox. She told me that she's ending the relationship she has been in—much to the chagrin and protestations of the gentleman—and will be looking to replace him with someone who interests her more than he. I think you would enjoy her mind and her company—and she yours."

Scorbion raised his left eyebrow. "May I ask her name?"

"Thelma Smith."

Scorbion was quick to respond. "That is a most plebian name. Not the name of an intellectual, someone who might interest me."

Billy admonished him, almost in the manner that a teacher would scold a student. "It should not really matter what her name is. To evaluate her on that basis would be like judging Dickens solely on those horrid covers that wrap his books. Thelma is one of the most dazzling minds I've ever encountered. She would be a match and challenge for you. Someone you could enjoy engaging wits and ideas with. And she will be one of the most alluring females you will ever have the pleasure to cast your eyes on."

Billy's words and description intrigued Scorbion and he lightly grasped Billy's arm. "I must say, you *have* sparked my interest, Billy, so once you learn that she has ended her current relationship, please feel free to create an introduction so that I might meet this Miss Thelma Smith. In spite of her common name."

Billy gave a thumbs-up. "I will. Now, may I ask one other question?"

Scorbion released his grip on Billy's arm. "You may."

"What do you do when you're not conducting police work? Do you have any pastimes or other pursuits you take part in when you're not engaged in your cases?"

"I do, and this you can write about."

Billy picked up the pencil and prepared to take notes.

"I never missed the Sunday afternoon rugby contest at Landover Park in Dorby, and I will attempt to attend those played at Windsor Park in Brookdale. In point of fact, I participated in rugby matches up until I was ten years younger than I am at present. Those were the days that my legs were like a stallion's, not like a donkey's, as they are now. Other than that, I read, I enjoy viewing art—in fact, the only significant benefit that came out of the relationship I had with Katherine was the appreciation of art that I learned from her, that has remained with me to this day. I also will play the game of chess with Arnold Hill on the majority of Tuesday evenings. We have been acquainted with each other from when we both resided in Chamfield. And I have a snifter of brandy after supper most every night. As you can determine from that summary, I live a life of few extravagances and even fewer social contacts. Except, of course, in my position as chief inspector. I interact with many people daily in that role."

Before Billy could ask Scorbion any further questions, Calvin sighted the Gromleys rounding the corner and approaching the shop. As they passed through the front door, Scorbion welcomed Mrs. Gromley, and then introduced her to the other men, explaining the roles that each would play. He asked Barnabus to retrieve another chair and place it between the ones that Gromley and Bentine had sat upon. Once it was in place and everyone was seated, Mrs. Gromley positioned her chair slightly closer to her husband.

Scorbion began. "Mrs. Gromley, we all appreciate your being here today and agreeing to speak about this situation. As you are aware, Mr. Bentine has asserted that your husband engaged in one evening of passion with his mother, which resulted in . . . well, in Mr. Bentine himself. Your husband denies the allegation unequivocally. He admits to being in Avens on numerous occasions, but nothing more. We hope that you might shed some light on happenings in the time frame under discussion. It would have been twenty-five to twenty-six years ago, and you would have met your husband there after visiting your sister."

"My dear chief inspector, I have retained my memories to a greater degree than most my age, but I cannot possibly remember every visit I made to Eloise, or each rendezvous Mortimer and I had in Avens."

"Before young Mr. Bentine appeared at your home, were you aware of his mother, Mary Alice Bentine?"

Mrs. Gromley hesitated, then softly declared, "I was."

Mortimer Gromley instantly swiveled on his chair until he was squarely facing his wife. "You *what*?!"

"I knew of her, Mortimer."

"But how? I am astounded and at a complete loss for an explanation. How could *you* have known of her when *I* have not?"

Scorbion addressed Mrs. Gromley. "Please tell us the circumstances under which you came to be aware of her."

"Must I?"

"Unfortunately, you must."

Mrs. Gromley addressed her husband. "I'm sorry, Mortimer. You were never meant to know this." Then she turned to Scorbion, took in a deep breath, and exhaled. "I knew of Mary Alice Bentine because I had engaged Miss Abigail Speckler, of Simon & Abigail Speckler's Private Detective Agency, to follow Mortimer for the better part of twenty-four months. There were indications that he was not being faithful to me, but I needed to be sure before I said anything. Possibly, they were nothing, but I had to find out—learn the truth, as you are trying to do here."

"And what did Abigail Speckler determine?" Scorbion asked.

"I was relieved by her reports that although she had twice seen Mortimer having tea with attractive young women, both meetings appeared to be strictly aboveboard. One of the two young women was a buyer for her father's mercantile concern, and the other had brought him fabric samples for reupholstering my living-room sofa and chairs."

Calvin asked, "Was Mrs. Bentine one of those women?"

"She was not. Mortimer and Mrs. Bentine had no form of liaison, or interaction of any sort, during the time Miss Speckler was observing him."

Mortimer Gromley's face had turned a bright pink as his wife related the facts of her surveillance. "I—I . . ."

His wife stopped his spluttering. "Oh, Mortimer, you were away from home more than you were here. I believed you were faithful, but when you came home on one occasion, I found a long, dark hair on your shirt, and it did raise a question in my mind. I wanted to trust you and to believe you, but I had to be sure. I grant that you are no Adonis, nor are you a towering figure of a man, but your personality more than makes up for both—you are, quite simply, a delight. *I* fell victim to your charms, so why wouldn't others? I am not sorry for what I did. It gave me peace of mind and comfort during your extended absences."

"Your Miss Speckler would never have found me engaging in any activity that could have compromised our relationship, Cora. But I now understand that my constant traveling, combined with a gregarious nature, could raise doubts. I am sorry for ever causing you worry."

Scorbion spoke. "Mrs. Gromley, under what circumstances did you become aware of Mrs. Bentine, if she was not carrying on an illicit liaison with your husband?"

"Miss Speckler related to me that on one of the nights when she was observing my husband, a handsome young woman with a very beautiful voice was performing in the tavern where Mortimer and two other men were dining. Miss Speckler told me that she believed that if Mortimer were ever were going to have an affair, *that* woman would have been the perfect bait. Before my husband departed abruptly from the tavern in trousers soaked with beer, Miss Speckler had gone up to the woman and complimented her on her voice. That was when she learned the woman's name was Mary Alice Bentine. Miss Speckler specifically mentioned Mrs. Bentine's name in her report for that week, as an illustration of Mortimer's fidelity and loyalty to me."

Thomas asked, "Auntie, did you keep the reports? Do you still have them?"

"I do. And they will substantiate every detail I have related."

Scorbion asked, "Do you recall when this evening occurred?"

"I do not remember the exact year, though the reports would have that information. I believe that it took place in July or August, twenty-five or twenty-six years ago. That was the time period when I engaged Miss Speckler."

"And may I ask why you did not relate this to your husband when you learned the young accuser's last name?"

"Because, Chief Inspector, when I heard the name it sounded vaguely familiar, but I could not recall where I had heard it before. But after my husband left to meet with you here, I concentrated, trying to remember where I had heard the name, and it suddenly came to me."

Scorbion turned to Bentine. "And here we have some confirmation. Mr. Gromley tells us a story of being doused with alcohol and leaving the establishment where your mother was performing, which is corroborated by the observations of that very evening by an independent investigator hired by Mrs. Gromley. I postulate that that evening in early July, or one close to it, was the occasion of your conception, resulting in your birth nine months later, in April of the following year. If that is correct, then I state to you now, it is beyond unlikely that Mortimer Gromley is your father. Unless Mr. and Mrs. Gromley have conspired to defraud us with these mutually collaborating tales, an evening of unbridled passion with your mother does not fit Mr. Gromley's customary behavior. Abigail Speckler observed no infidelity by him on that evening or, it appears, on any other. I submit to you that, during the time when you could have been conceived, Mr. Gromley slept with no one other than his wife. Therefore, we can unequivocally conclude that no familial relationship exists between you."

Bentine shot out of his chair. He was angry. "They *could* be conspiring! You're just taking his side because he lives in this town. You're protecting your own."

Scorbion responded in a calm but stern voice. "Please sit down, Mr.

Bentine. There is no reason for such an outburst, nor for that accusation. I, Pignon Scorbion, will *never* subvert an investigation nor color the truth for any convenience, favor, or comfort. I came to this with an open mind, having no prior relationship with you or with Mr. or Mrs. Gromley. I have no stake in the outcome, I only wish to determine the veracity of the situation. I suggest you abandon such thoughts so that we may determine the truth of who your father is. I will compare the Gromleys' stories with Miss Speckler's notes upon their delivery to me tomorrow. The reports *will* affirm what both the Gromleys have related. I am as certain of this as I am of my own name."

Bentine sat down, but he did not relax.

Scorbion looked to the men in the room, "Billy, do you have any thoughts as to the identity of Mr. Bentine's father? Or you, Yves? Anyone?"

"Well, Inspector," Billy said, "I choose to believe that Mrs. Bentine did tell young Jonathan the story that he told us. I cannot fathom that she would have made up something like that."

Barnabus agreed. "It w-was too complicated and d-detailed an accounting to be totally contrived."

Thomas commented softly, "But who's his father? Could it be Garson or that Choc fellow?"

"Or the helpful doctor," Calvin added.

Yves concurred. "*Je suis d'accord.* Dr. Mayes had Gromley's linens and trade card. Surely, we must include him in our considerations."

Scorbion responded, "I think not. The good doctor was too prominent a local figure to be mistaken for Mr. Gromley. It is not a realistic probability. Let us assume for the moment that the Gromleys have not jointly lied to us. In that case, I am in complete agreement that the father could have been one of the other two men who were at the tavern with Mr. Gromley that night. They are our most likely suspects. But which one is the more probable gigolo? Is he Mr. Garson or Mr. Ross?"

"If I may, Inspector . . ."

"You may, Billy."

"Why are we limiting ourselves to just those two gentlemen? Why not include in the investigation *anyone* who might possibly have fathered Mr. Bentine?"

"An excellent question. Years upon years of investigating countless affairs of this nature enables me to tell you with a very high degree of certainty that someone who is obvious from the start is most often obvious for a reason. That is, he or she is most often the perpetrator. Or, in this case, the father. It will be most expeditious for us to examine those who are most obvious *first*, before widening the search to include every man who ever came into contact with Mrs. Bentine, or with Gromley. We focus on the obvious choices until we eliminate them or confirm them. If we remove them all, that will be the time to broaden the investigation. While it is true that I have achieved my greatest successes with those affairs that were *not* perpetrated by the obvious suspects, it is nonetheless equally true that in the majority of instances, the obvious one *is* the guilty one."

Barnabus asked Mrs. Gromley, "D-Did Miss Speckler report on the actions of any other g-gentleman your husband associated with in Avens?"

"Only a bit. She did mention how Mr. Garson—and to a much lesser degree Mr. Ross, the man my husband identified as Choc—appeared to woo attractive young women somewhat regularly. She reported that Garson was far more successful in his pursuits than Ross. Garson even approached Miss Speckler one evening, but she wasn't interested. She observed that Mr. Ross had less confidence—probably, she intimated to me, due to his gentle demeanor and inexperience in his occupation. She commented that his complexion reminded her of a dusky enchanter—but one who lacked self-assurance."

Scorbion waggled his pointer finger. "I suspected, early in my considerations, that Mr. Gromley was not the progenitor, but it has taken this unexpected revelation regarding Miss Speckler to fully confirm my conjecture. When I took my leave during the time that Mr. Gromley left to retrieve his wife, I walked to the police station and used our telephone to speak with the chief inspector in Avens. I asked him if either a Mr. Garson or a Mr. Ross, both linen merchants, had settled there. His response came as no surprise to me. However, I was quite astounded when he related to me the story of the town's first murder in many decades. A man and a woman were burned to death, their remains charred to the point that no identification was possible. Who these two were, and why they were put to death in that horrific manner has everyone in Avens baffled. The case is occupying all their resources, and I had a difficult time persuading their chief inspector to put his attention to our Messrs. Garson and Ross."

In spite of those details, Calvin could not contain his curiosity. "A horrid crime it is, Pignon, but what *did* the chief inspector say about Garson and Ross?"

"He affirmed to me that Mr. Garson does indeed reside within the limits of Avens and has been living there for over ten years."

Barnabus asked, "Why is t-that important, Inspector?"

"It is a matter of recognition. If the man who captivated and bedded Mrs. Bentine was not Mr. Gromley, yet she believed he *was* Gromley, then it was obviously someone who impersonated him. Someone who used his trade card and one of his fine linen samples to make her believe he was Gromley. A man who knew enough about linens to be convincing. I would assume it made him feel important and attractive to women to be perceived as a successful tradesman. He was probably rather like an actor playing a role. Living through Gromley's life and name, he could step outside his own personality and transform into someone else. But to make his plan work, he would have to make certain she would never see him again, or he would risk the threat of exposure by those who knew the real Mortimer Gromley. Which is why Dr. Mayes, known to everyone in Avens, would never have tried such a thing. No, permanently residing in Avens is *not* what the cad would do. And Mr. Garson apparently needed no assistance securing the affections of women, so he would have no need to impersonate Gromley. Therefore, I have eliminated Garson from consideration."

"So, the culprit was this man, Choc Ross?"

"That is my belief, Billy," Scorbion confirmed. "Gromley just told us that the man said he was to leave for the eastern countries the very next day, and he never again encountered Mr. Ross in any future travels to Avens. Therefore, the night that Mrs. Gromley said Abigail Speckler observed him with Mortimer Gromley must necessarily be the night that he and Mrs. Bentine had their tryst. A happy occurrence for us and for the truth. But I maintain that even without that coincidence, we still would have arrived at the same conclusion. It just may have been by a different path—possibly a much longer one. But no matter the road, it would still lead to Mr. Choc Ross being Jonathan Bentine's father, and to Mortimer Gromley having no culpability in the affair."

Gromley uttered a groan of satisfaction as he unfolded his arms from across his chest. His wife grasped his hand and squeezed it gently.

Scorbion continued. "I postulate that after the incident with the ruffians and the spilt drinks, both Gromley *and* Garson retired to their rooms, while Ross remained in the tavern with his clothes dry as a desert, as Miss Speckler reported. We can assume that he was smitten by the lovely diva, but his shy nature and lack of confidence kept him from making advances toward her. I can see him reaching into his pocket and pulling out the trade card that Mortimer Gromley had given him. It inspired an idea. If he could be *seen* as a successful merchant, he would have enough confidence to approach this woman who so attracted him."

Calvin spoke again. "Pignon, do you really believe he did that? Wouldn't it be too perilous to assume another man's identity? What if he encountered someone who knew the genuine Gromley?"

"Excellent questions, my dear Calvin. I truly believe he did. I presume that he did not consider any ramifications and acted on pure impulse and desire. Let us go inside the mind of this man who impersonated Gromley and claimed his identity, so that we can comprehend the occurrences of that evening. After finding Gromley's card and sample in his pocket, Ross had a moment of inspiration: by professing to be Gromley, he would achieve stature and importance in the eyes of the lovely songbird who had so mesmerized him. Knowing that he was departing shortly thereafter to commence his new career in those distant territories, and probably learning from Gromley that he, too, was departing the next morning, Ross recognized that he need only sustain Gromley's persona for one night."

"That makes perfect sense."

"Thank you, Calvin. I continue. He would have approached Mrs. Bentine during one of the interludes between her songs and introduced himself as Gromley, the wealthy, important, *unmarried* linen merchant. As we have been told, he was a man of handsome features and gentle manner, Ross doubtless won her over with his looks, his charm, and his station in life. I imagine that during the dinner they enjoyed together at the conclusion of her performances, he enchanted her, and next they left the tavern together in an inebriated condition. Adding to her already giddy state was the joy of having found a man such as he, especially after being so long without male companionship and for such an extended period as she went through that was lacking in intimacy. The nearby boarding house provided a convenient location for the venting of her passions while affording Ross the anonymity he required to sustain his guise as Mortimer Gromley."

"*Mon Dieu!* Do you believe he anticipated that he would get away with the charade?"

"My dear Yves, I have no doubt."

Scorbion continued as he paced to and fro. "Let us examine the events that transpired from the time the sun arose the next morning. First, as young Mr. Bentine has told us, his mother awoke to find sunlight glistening—that was the word he said she used—on her lover's face, making him look angelic. Again, her description. Certainly, Ross's swarthy complexion and exquisite features created that perception. It most definitely does not describe Mortimer Gromley. No offense, sir, but I would never allude to you as angelic-looking."

"No offense taken. I am who I am, and I look as I look."

"Thank you. I shall continue. Ross, still posing as Gromley, must next have created some excuse for having to leave shortly after arising, with a promise to return to the tavern that evening, knowing full well that he was departing Avens that afternoon. That evening, after he did not appear at the tavern, there is no doubt that Mrs. Bentine made inquiries as to where Mortimer Gromley was lodging. Once acquiring that information, she sought him out at the White Horse, the inn at which the real Mortimer Gromley had been staying. There she was told that Gromley, whom she believed Ross to be, had departed with his wife earlier that morning. She must have been shaken to her core by the revelation. And of course, the ultimate consequence of Ross's deception was the conception and birth of Jonathan Bentine, whom his mother mistakenly believed was the progeny of Mortimer Gromley. In fact, he was sired by Mr. Ross."

"Qu-quite the situation, Ch-Chief Inspector."

"Indeed, Barnabus. When Mrs. Bentine related her tale to her son, I am sure it was in part so that she could expose the truth and lift its weight from her breast. Additionally, she wanted her son to claim his rightful place with, and inheritance from, the successful linen merchant Mortimer Gromley, and have the station in life which she believed he was due."

Calvin spoke. "It rings true to me."

The others nodded in assent.

Scorbion turned to Bentine. "Young man, I would suggest that if you desire to be reunited with the man who planted the seed that conceived you, you should be as vigilant in locating Mr. Ross as you have been in determining the whereabouts of Mortimer Gromley."

Bentine shifted in his chair. "I don't care what you say or how you twist the facts to fit your theory, if my mother said that Gromley is my father, then he is my father."

Billy responded skeptically. "How can you say that? All that Inspector Scorbion has said makes perfect sense. And Miss Speckler was a firsthand observer. I would think that the most important task to you would be to find your father, no matter who he might be, not to challenge our chief inspector."

The others grunted in agreement.

Scorbion addressed Bentine again, "It is quite difficult to prove paternity. For the most part, we have to assess complexion, features, and mannerisms. And I must say, my dear young sir, that you look nothing like Mr. Gromley. Your hair is much lighter than his, your nose is squatter and shorter, your eyes more rounded, and you are of a significantly greater stature than he. Only your pale skin tone maintains any similarity. With no shred of doubt in my mind, I suggest to you that your most advantageous course of action is to cease this meaningless questioning of my conclusions. They will lead you nowhere. Instead, leave here, and begin a search for your real father. That will accomplish your goal of joining up with your one remaining parent."

Thomas turned to Bentine. "Your mother was right when she tol' you it was a Mortimer Gromley who bedded her and helped conceive you. It just wasn't *this* Mortimer Gromley. It was a Mortimer Gromley bein' portrayed by Choc Ross."

Scorbion nodded. "Very good, Thomas . . ."

Before Scorbion could complete his thought, Bentine stood up, gathered his materials, and put them back into his bag. "I am aggrieved by what has taken place here. You don't definitively know that was the evening of my conception. It could have been some other day. But none of that matters as I can see that you are all against me and set on asserting that Mr. Gromley is not my father. You have proven nothing to me. I will return to my lodgings and put my thoughts together. Before I depart for Avens, I will diligently work to uncover whatever else I can in Haxford that will prove that *this* Mortimer Gromley is indeed my father, not some chocolatier turned linen peddler."

He stormed out of the shop, slamming the door behind him.

Gromley stood. "I feel rather badly for him, in spite of his refusal to accept what is obvious."

Mrs. Gromley sympathetically added, "I do hope that he gets over his anger and tries to locate his father rather than spending his time trying to find whatever it is that does not exist here or in Avens."

Scorbion stood and stretched his arms behind his back. "It is his choice."

Thomas rose. "Auntie and Uncle, I'm glad the truth came out. I'll wager Bentine was expectin' to become the heir to your estate . . ."

Yves added, "And live the remainder of his life in grand *confort*."

Billy commented, to no one in particular, "The impact of losing all that appears to have clouded Bentine's mind to the reality of the situation. He is fully not accepting of any of it, is he?"

Calvin accompanied the Gromleys to the door, then scanned the mail that he had placed on the counter in front of his barber chair, and responded to Billy. "That is a problem for him. Not for us, or the Gromleys. Good work, Pignon. I doubt that any of us would have arrived at the proper conclusion with such rapidity. It was enjoyable to witness your processes again."

"Thank you, Calvin. This affair was just what I needed to bring me out of my doldrums. Now allow me to hand you your recompense for the work on my hair and nails."

"I will take no remuneration from you today, Pignon. The excitement and experience of this afternoon—and being in your company again—was payment enough for me. Put your coins away."

Scorbion bowed to Calvin, gave Thomas a gratuity, donned his suit jacket, and said farewells. He left the shop whistling a merry tune, as Calvin turned the sign on the door back to Open.

While they put the chairs and table back in the storeroom, Billy made a pronouncement. "I *am* going to write about what just took place. I'd wager that Waters—my editor and the owner of the newspaper—will print a story about this case if I write a real dilly of an article."

"I know what you can call it."

"What's that, Yves?"

"The Case of the Bastard Son."

"You could use 'illegitimate' instead. 'The Case of the Illegitimate Son,'" Calvin suggested.

"I fancy 'bastard' b-better," Barnabus offered.

"Me, too," Thomas concurred. "Then it's settled," Billy said. He smiled at the thought of having an article and a byline in the paper. "It will be 'The Case of The Bastard Son: A Mystery Solved by Chief Inspector Pignon Scorbion.'"

After the table and the chairs were returned to the storeroom, Billy left to write the article, leaving the three barbers and Thomas to tidy up anything else.

Within the next ten minutes, two of the shop's regular customers arrived, both informing Calvin that they had come earlier, but with the blinds drawn and the sign saying Closed, they left, hoping it would be open when they returned.

Calvin ushered them in, and as they sat in his and Barnabus' chairs and had barber's capes draped over them, Calvin whispered to Barnabus, "It's been an exciting day already. But now let us get back to our more mundane duties."

Barnabus leaned in so that only Calvin could hear him. "I enjoyed w-what we did here *so* m-much. I hope we c-can do s-something like t-that again soon."

Calvin responded, "As do I. I wonder what affair Pignon will be presented with next. There always seems to be something taking place in this town."

CHAPTER EIGHT

Two days hence, Billy walked into Scorbion's station house. He noticed Scorbion's dark-brown linen suit jacket carefully draped on the coatrack by the door, with not a single crease or wrinkle on it.

Having never before been in a police station, Billy stood next to the rack and surveyed the one large room, with its drab yellowish concrete block walls and flecked dark blue linoleum floor. He thought, *this is rather sparse*, seeing it furnished with but three desks, nine chairs, and two tall wooden cabinets. The walls were adorned only with brass sconces by each desk, a Longcase clock, a Union Jack, a picture of the newly crowned King Edward VII, and a bulletin board that contained three wanted posters and a hand-crafted notice for Haxford's upcoming Town Feast. The two small windows in the room did not let in enough light to adequately brighten the space, so it felt dim despite having three chandeliers hanging from the ceiling. Billy assumed that the single door in the middle of the back wall led to the cells and a private area for Scorbion and his staff.

Billy spotted Scorbion standing adjacent to one of the desks on his left. He approached Scorbion and handed him a copy of the *Morning News*. "I hope you are not dissatisfied with my article about the case. I tried to write it honestly."

Scorbion took the newspaper and motioned for Billy to sit on one of the two chairs in front of the desk. Scorbion sat behind the desk, moved a neat stack of papers from the center of the desktop to a corner, and placed the newspaper in the empty area in front of him. He firmly but carefully pressed on it with both his hands so that it lay completely flat. Only then did he look down to observe it.

Scorbion was momentarily taken aback at seeing his own face staring back at him from the top of the front page. Below Scorbion's "official" photograph, Billy's article ran under the headline, "The Case of the Bastard Son: A Mystery Solved by Chief Inspector Pignon Scorbion." The story took up the entire bottom half of the front page and the entire next two pages.

After recovering from the unexpected prominence and exposure that the paper gave him, Scorbion read the full account that Billy had written.

When he completed the article, Scorbion looked up at Billy—who was eagerly awaiting his praise but dreading it might be scorn—and wagged his finger at the newspaper. "That is very well written. You are an excellent observer and a good reporter."

A relieved Billy replied, "Thank you, Inspector. I was hoping you'd fancy it."

Scorbion leaned across the desk and placed his hand on Billy's shoulder in the same way that a headmaster would do to one of their prized pupils. "I fancy it very much. You may continue to report on these cases, as they occur." Scorbion thought for a moment. "But I must tell you that regarding the affair with Mr. Bentine, I have this—what do they call it?—ah yes, a nagging feeling that I have missed something. Something important. I cannot put a full stop at the end of Bentine's sentence when I am concerned that I missed something. The final statement of this case ends more with an ellipsis, waiting for something else to occur. But what? I cannot place my finger, nor any other part of my body, on it. However, I am confident that the answer will be brought forth into my consciousness in due time."

Billy was surprised by Scorbion's revelation, not anticipating that the case was anything but closed. "What do you think, Inspector? Is it that the Gromleys were conspiring?"

Scorbion released his grip on Billy and leaned back. "That I rather doubt. Cora Gromley delivered Miss Speckler's reports to me as promised, and they confirmed her and her husband's narrative. However, even having said that, I have formed no conclusions at this time. I am only possessed by a feeling in my body and my being that I have missed an important aspect of this affair that is hiding among the rhetoric and the events that we witnessed. But for now that will have to wait, as I have some constabulary work to do, so you must be on your way. And please ask your editor if he might omit my likeness when he publishes your next report."

"I will," Billy replied, "but Waters does what he wants. He's a stubborn old cuss. Especially when he's sotted."

"However, he printed your story, so he must be a good editor who knows a fine reporter when he sees one," Scorbion observed.

Billy blushed. "Waters did tell me that I can train an assistant to help with the presses so that if I need to report on a case that occurs in the morning I can be in attendance. I start training that fellow later today."

Scorbion leaned forward on his desk chair, "That is quite good. I am, in fact, going back to Mr. Brown's establishment in three days for a shave and polishing of my shoes. I will expect to see you there."

As Billy departed, he shouted back over his shoulder, "You will, Inspector. Have no doubt."

CHAPTER NINE

When Scorbion arrived back at Brown's Barber Shop three mornings later, he carefully hung his black pinstriped suit jacket on the coat rack. A moment later, Billy appeared, holding a colored sheet of paper in one hand. "Two fellows are placing these flyers all around Haxford today. They're putting them up next to the ones for the Town Feast. One of the chaps gave me this copy so I could bring it here."

"And what does it say, my young friend?" Scorbion inquired.

"There's a circus coming to town. The one that had a lot of notoriety last year because of that bloke who tried to stilt-walk higher than anyone else ever had."

Thomas walked over and looked at the flyer as he held it. "Me mum and me dad took me to a circus when I was a little lad. The clowns scared the life out o' me, but I couldn't believe all the animals that were there. Oh, I'm goin' to this one."

Calvin took the flyer from Thomas. "I concur, it will be fun to attend a circus again. Barnabus, please tack this up on the wall so that everyone may view it at their leisure. But for now, let me attend to Pignon."

While Barnabus took the paper and did as Calvin requested, Scorbion announced, "Calvin's wife, Mildred, prepared as delectable a meal for me last evening as I would have had at the most splendid eatery in London. She was all that Calvin described—utterly charming and disarming. Calvin, please thank her for me again, and tell her that I look forward to being in her presence in the near future."

"I will, Pignon." Calvin beamed.

Then Scorbion said, "As regards the circus, I too, will enjoy it. But for now, as there are no other clients in the shop, it will be a fine time for me to respond to Billy Arthurson's question about the heritage of my names."

Scorbion sat in the barber's chair. Calvin started lathering him and Thomas began carefully putting black polish on the outside of his shoes.

Billy addressed Scorbion, who turned his whole body toward him. "Both of your names are most unusual. That's why I'm curious how you got them."

Calvin broke in, "He can tell you whatever he wants as long as he doesn't keep turning toward you." He gently spun Scorbion's chair to its proper position to begin working on his neck.

Scorbion motioned with his hand, "All of you, come close. Draw your seats next to this chair that I am perched upon. But stay clear of Calvin and Thomas, so they may do their work. I will tell you the tale of my names as I keep my head just so, while Mr. Brown continues to perform his duties upon me, and my feet stay stationary so that Thomas does not mix the white and black and turn sections of my shoes into grey."

Yves, Barnabus, and Billy moved their chairs as directed, pulling up next to Scorbion, and leaned in to ensure that they would hear every word.

"My father, Jamal Scorbion, grew up in Cairo, Egypt, in near poverty. But being quite bright and handsome, he was able to rise above his station. In Arabic, the name Scorbion stands for extroversion and adventurousness, and a life path that is progressive, pioneering, innovative, rebellious, and opportunistic. My father lived up to all of those qualities. How did he advance beyond his humble beginnings, you might ask? By selling the finest chocolates, that he personally imported from Belgium, to the wealthiest Egyptian families. He was one of the first importers to utilize ice to maintain cool temperatures for shipped goods that were perishable or needed to remain at low temperatures.

Where did he get the money to do that, you wonder? He first started a rent-a-camel service."

Smiles broke across the faces of all the men. Barnabus uttered a low guffaw.

"You laugh! It was not funny." Then considering what his father had done, Scorbion relented. "Well, possibly it is a bit funny in hindsight, but at the time it was quite serious. He made an arrangement with the families of his friends to give him use of their extra camels for a portion of his profits. He hired out the camels to sightseers, archaeologists, and those foolish enough to wander out into the desert. From those camels he gained sufficient capital to begin using the ice to import the chocolates. Those two ventures grew rapidly and generated quite a sizable income. But after a few years, my father tired of both. He yearned to travel, so he sold the pair of enterprises and bought a large, oceangoing sailing vessel, a craft of enormous proportions."

Calvin interrupted. "Please pause your tale so that I don't accidentally nick you. I shall be finished with your cheeks quickly and then you may complete your story."

"As you wish. I will continue when you are done, Calvin."

"Thank you, Pignon."

Barnabus whispered to Yves, "I am in awe of C-Calvin's calling Scorbion by his g-given name. I've n-never heard our head of police called anything other than Chief Inspector or by their s-surname."

"Nor I," Yves agreed.

Calvin completed Scorbion's cheeks and began on his sideburns. "I believe they need to be a bit shorter than I made them a few days ago."

Scorbion continued. "As I was saying, my father purchased that huge floating craft, stocked it with provisions, took on a sizable crew, and named it the *Chocolate Camel*." He paused. "There is that chocolate connection again. I have always been a believer that things come in triplicate, and here we have my father importing chocolates, naming his ship the *Chocolate Camel*, and then we encounter the tale involving Mr. Choc Ross."

Billy asked, "Where were your father and his crew sailing to?"

"Their destination was the Americas," Scorbion responded.

Barnabus gasped. "The Americas? B-blimey, I d-didn't see that coming."

"Yes, the Americas. My father never did anything small. It took him three months at sea, braving storms and heat and disease, but eventually he and his crew made landfall. The coastline they saw before them was so extraordinarily beautiful that they believed they had arrived in paradise. Fortunately, among the crew were men who spoke French and others who spoke Spanish, and once they moored and disembarked, they learned on what country's shores they had landed."

"Can we g-guess where they were?"

"*Merde*, Barnabus, don't interrupt. Let the Chief Inspector continue."

"Thank you, Yves," Scorbion said. "But you don't have to curse—then again, that is the manner in which you communicate, is it not? I will go on . . . Just as Christopher Columbus had done centuries earlier, they had landed on the lush shores of Haiti. They found a Garden of Eden: magnificent rain forests, grand mountains, and luxuriant valleys—a land populated almost exclusively by men and women of African descent. The men in my father's employ felt familiar and comfortable among the inhabitants. In fact, some met the loves of their lives and opted to remain in that idyllic land, while a number of others took Haitian wives back home on the return voyage. My father was among that latter group."

"He brought your mother back from Haiti?"

"Yes, he did, Billy, but please don't rush the tale; I will get to her in a moment. While the majority of his men caroused and engaged in the abundant pleasures available in the towns along the coastline, my father felt the urge to explore. He and a Haitian guide, accompanied by two members of his crew, made a trek inland. They hacked their way through the rain forest and scaled a number of mountains. My father reported seeing birds of colors and varieties he had never before witnessed, and that amazed and delighted his senses. He proclaimed that everywhere he went, he encountered more varieties of bats than he had known existed."

"On their fourth day, they crested the top of one of the towering mountains. Below them, they witnessed a series of gorgeous, vast green valleys. Most were dotted with plantations growing tobacco, sugar cane, coffee, bananas, mangoes, or cocoa, while others contained livestock farms. My father and his men descended into the valley that was sitting at the foot of the mountain they had been standing upon. They entered its main village, and learned that the town and the mountain shared a name in common—the name of the man who founded the town and settled the region in 1699, a French tradesman and a plantation owner named Jean Guillaume de Pignon."

Yves and Barnabus let out small exclamations of surprise—"*oh la vache*" and "well b-bugger me"—not expecting Scorbion to be named for a place.

Scorbion continued. "Yes, my good men, I was named after a town and a mountain named Pignon. Once again you probably ask why. Why was I named for *them*? Because, it was there, in that very remote part of a most foreign land, that my father laid his eyes upon a cream-colored goddess more beautiful than any woman he had ever encountered. She was native to that town and known throughout the valley for her stunning looks and brilliant mind. My father knew in an instant that he wanted to be with this woman for the rest of his life. And that was to be his fate, and hers. That woman, Natacha Papouloute, would later become my mother."

Calvin interrupted, "I have completed your sideburns. Do you want me to emery your nails again today?"

"You may do whatever you think is best, but now that you have assassinated the mood that I had established, might I finish without interruption?"

Calvin bowed his head. "Of course."

"Then I shall. It took my father ten months to win Natacha's love. He vowed to her on the first day they met that he would not leave Pignon until he was departing with her at his side. And he made good on his promise. During those ten months, he engaged in Pignon's athletics, especially running and sprinting. He hunted boar, ducks, and other wild animals with Natacha's father. He began to learn their language and was able to describe in great detail the wonders of the rest of the world to her and her family. Natacha, having an inquisitive and sharp intellect, was thrilled by Jamal's stories and excited to think that, with him, she would have the opportunity to visit those new lands and meet the different peoples he described."

"Natacha's parents insisted on their having a traditional Haitian wedding ceremony in Pignon before they departed for Europe. And that is exactly what they did. The number of people who attended stunned my father, as the invitations were carried only by word of mouth. After many hours of singing, dancing, walking, signing, swaying, sermons, and vows, my father welcomed the chance to be alone with my mother, and she felt the same. They told me from my earliest age that they believed I was conceived on that very first night of their union in Pignon. When I arrived almost exactly nine months to that day, my parents had already sailed to the Continent and relocated in Paris where they reared me while starting a business that offered assistance to those wishing to travel to Egypt. And, as it is said in the fairy tales that enchant little children, 'they lived happily ever after.'"

"That's so *romantique*, Chief Inspector."

"C'mon, you big duff, you're bein' sappy," Thomas teased Yves.

"You mean little d-duff, d-don't you?" Barnabus taunted.

"*Va te faire voir*," Yves responded to the chiding.

Calvin scolded all three. "Let the chief inspector finish the story."

"I would think that the only items I might add to the narrative," Scorbion said, "is that my naming was to my parents a joyous remembrance of their first glorious night together. I have never been bothered in the least by having two family names for my first and last. Now, that is enough about me."

"Thank you, Chief Inspector. That was a formidable story. And very informative."

"I agree with Yves. It was," Billy added.

Scorbion paid Calvin, handed Thomas a sizable tip—which elicited a broad grin—donned his suit jacket, and departed for his station, just as the first customers of the day approached the shop.

CHAPTER TEN

During the following few days, Scorbion was presented with no cases that his underlings couldn't handle, so he had the time to search his mind to find what he thought of as "the key that unlocks the door to the missing piece of Gromley-Bentine puzzle."

But he was unable to call up what was nagging him no matter how many times he reexamined the facts of the case. Frustrated by that inability to conjure up that which was concerning him, Scorbion told Sergeant Adley that he was headed to the local bookshop, "to see if they might have a volume or tome that could present new ways of thinking and assist me in scouring my mind."

On his walk, he passed the building that housed Haxford's evening newspaper, the *Gazette*. Coming through its front door was Jonathan Bentine, who nearly collided with Scorbion as he hurried out. Scorbion held both of his hands in front of his chest to cushion a possible impact. "Mr. Bentine, I did not expect that you would have remained in Haxford. I rather believed that you would have set out to find your father."

Bentine stopped and stood in front of Scorbion. "I am not departing for another few days. I am exhausting every resource here to prove that Mortimer Gromley *is* my father. I have just met with Faustin Hardcastle, the owner of the *Gazette*, who has committed to assist me in any way he can. After I laid out my particulars to him, he is as skeptical of your findings as I."

"In that case," Scorbion responded sarcastically, "I wish you both the greatest of luck in your quest as you look to uncover facts that do not exist and familial ties that are not tethered in any manner."

"That's your opinion, sir, and it is pure conjecture," Bentine responded. "Pardon me, but I don't care to dally with you any longer." Then he strode away at a quick pace down the street in the opposite direction from which Scorbion had been walking.

Scorbion was aware that Bentine was attempting to discredit his findings so that he could inherit the Gromleys' estate, but he also knew that Bentine's pursuit would end in failure. He was puzzled by Hardcastle's willingness to support Bentine's foolishness, and he made a mental note to ask him about it.

Scorbion then recommended walking to the bookshop. As he did, he passed the town's art gallery, where he stopped to look at the pieces displayed in the windows. Having gained an appreciation of art from his former wife during their courtship, he had become somewhat of an aficionado of certain styles and artists and was pleased that Haxford had such an establishment.

Scorbion's preference ran to English Romantic painters, most especially J. M. W. Turner. While he would normally linger in front of the art gallery to take in all the oils, watercolors, prints, and sculptures on display, he was immediately drawn to, and excited by, the centerpiece of the exhibit, Turner's atmospheric oil painting *Snow Storm: A Steam-Boat off a Harbour's Mouth.*

"What a glorious surprise you are," he exclaimed to the painting. "A gift much more pleasant to view than the works of Picasso or Toulouse-Lautrec."

Scorbion remained in front of the piece for many minutes, contemplating its shimmering, swirling colors and amorphous, turbulent imagery. It drew him in as though he were looking into a reflection of his own subconscious mind, and how he could not see that one definitive answer that he was attempting to latch onto, which had been eluding him about the Bentine case.

His determination intensified to locate a volume at the bookstore that might help him find a new method that would enable him to gain a firmer grasp on his conundrum.

Scorbion reluctantly stopped staring into the tantalizing painting and walked to the bookshop, three doors down the street.

As he entered Books on the Square, a bell attached to the door tinkled, informing the proprietor of his presence. Scorbion closed the door and stood inside, scanning the shop's interior, taking in the many floor-to-ceiling wooden shelves that were crammed full of books, newspapers, and periodicals.

A woman carrying four books emerged from behind one of the stacks, looked at Scorbion, and said, "May I assist you?"

He quickly took in the woman's appearance, which he found to be both pleasing and somewhat unorthodox, as she was attired in billowing, loose-fitting pants—which he knew were not commonly worn by virtually any women at that time. As he studied her, Scorbion judged the woman to be in her thirties, with a remarkably beautiful face, and in spite of wearing a light-blue shawl over her shoulders which partially covered her white silk blouse and obscured her chest, he assessed her to have an attractive figure.

"Ah, madam . . ." he began, but she cut him off.

"Miss, not madam. How may I assist you?" She paused for a beat. "I have never seen shoes similar to those that you are sporting. They are quite unusual, though pleasing to the eye."

"Thank you," Scorbion replied. "May I assume that you assist the proprietor of this establishment?"

"I *am* the proprietor," she sternly replied, before softening her tone. "Are you looking for something in particular? If it interests you, I have just received a copy of a newly published book that is all the rage in London. It is *The Sorcerer's Apprentice* by Hanns Heinz Ewers."

"Thank you, but no," Scorbion told her. "I am seeking a volume that might assist me in unlocking the contents of my mind, and that might aid me in understanding an aspect of human behavior that has eluded me."

"Mercy me," she responded, "I would not have taken you to be looking for a serious tome. A man with your looks and carriage . . . I would have assessed you to be a reader of lighter fare."

Scorbion smiled. "Thank you for your compliment, but I am not in this shop to find a volume that will engage me, amuse me, nor entertain me. Rather, I am seeking something that can educate, instruct, and open a doorway that I presently find closed. A figurative doorway, that is."

The woman walked to a bookshelf near the far side of the store. When she returned, she was carrying a book, which she offered to Scorbion. "I am basing my choice of this book on the assumption that you are attempting to unravel some mystery or enigma whose solution has eluded you, and you are now turning to the thoughts, solutions, and pages that others have written to help you find an answer. Am I correct?"

Scorbion smiled again as he took the book from her hand. "I must say, miss, I do not often encounter people as perceptive as you. You are a breeze of fresh air. Now, as to this tome, let us determine whether you truly have anticipated my needs or not."

Scorbion read the book's title, *The Psychopathology of Everyday Life* by Sigmund Freud.

The woman told him, "Freud has written a number of books recently with observations and information concerning human behavior. He is considered quite radical, but I found the book to be fascinating."

Scorbion was momentarily stunned, "*You* read this book?"

"I did indeed," she firmly replied, "and what is it that makes you believe that I wouldn't have?"

Scorbion paused, thinking how to respond, not wanting to say anything that might antagonize this woman, whom he found very interesting, unusual, and attractive—all things he rather fancied. Once he had his thoughts collected he answered, "It is not a regular occurrence for *anyone* to read a treatise on deviations in everyday behavior. It surprised me that you had an interest in that subject."

She emitted a somewhat derisive laugh as she put her hand on her hip and challenged Scorbion. "Hah. So, my being a woman had nothing to do with your surprise?"

Scorbion smiled back. "Nothing at all, my dear lady, nothing at all."

The bell tinkled, and another customer entered the shop.

"Be with you in a jiffy, or you can just look around," the woman called out to the newcomer, who replied, "I am looking for a particular book, so I will just sit in that comfortable-looking chair by the window until you have concluded your current business."

After he sat down, the woman turned back to Scorbion. "I'm sorry, but I must attend to that gentleman and find the book he is looking for. Do you want Freud's book? Have I estimated your needs correctly?"

A smile broke out on Scorbion's face for a fourth time. "You have indeed, miss. I will purchase it, be on my way, and hopefully be back in the not-too-distant future."

Scorbion paid for the book and left the shop. On his walk to the station, he reflected on how much he had enjoyed the conversation in which he and the woman had engaged and made a mental note to return to the bookstore after he read the book so that he could compare his impressions of it with hers.

CHAPTER ELEVEN

The morning after that, Calvin opened the barbershop half an hour earlier than usual. He spent the time sweeping the floor and tidying up his workstation. When Yves and Barnabus came through the door at their accustomed time, he proclaimed to them in a stern voice, "I want your areas tidied up. This shop should look professional and inviting. And right now, both of your stations are a blooming mess."

He put his hands on his hips and harrumphed. "Barnabus, look at that counter in front of your chair. You've got your paraphernalia— shampoos, soaps, combs, brushes, scissors, razors, jars, and tins—all crammed into that tiny ledge by your mirror. And some are lying on their sides, while others are stacked haphazardly on top of each other. That is *not* inviting."

Yves broke in. "*Pardonnez-moi Patron*, my station is neater than Barnabus's. It is much tidier."

Calvin looked at Yves's counter. "It's a tidier mess, I'll give you that, lad, but it is still a mess, nonetheless."

Billy arrived just then, hoping to spend part of the morning in conversation with the barbers and their clients. He laughed. "Calvin, you are a poet. Bravo."

Calvin blushed, waved Billy off, and said loudly, "I'm serious. Please tidy up your stations *now*. I want that accomplished before the next customer walks through that door."

Barnabus's, Yves's, and Billy's eyes involuntarily went to the front of the shop as Calvin's outstretched arm and finger were pointing at it.

And just as Calvin finished saying, "Use the storeroom for your extra items," to everyone's surprise and delight, Scorbion walked through the door, replete in a fitted houndstooth suit and his signature shoes.

He stopped in the middle of the shop and faced the men, who were utterly silent—stunned that Scorbion was at the shop on as many days as he was in such a short period of time.

Before anyone could learn why Scorbion was there, Thomas came in, quickly walked to his stool, and sat on it.

After he was seated, Scorbion said, with a tone of urgency in his voice, "Yes, my dear associates, it is not my regular day to be in this tonsorial palace, and I have been here very recently, but an incident has taken place that compels me to make an appearance today. I ask that all of you assist me once again to solve a mystery with which I have just been presented. It is a case of murder. Its answer must be determined before the sun sets this pleasant June evening. Fortunately, we will have more sunlit hours than at other times of the year to resolve the affair."

Billy was the first to speak. "Why does it have to be solved by this evening, Inspector?"

Calvin lifted his eyebrows, Barnabus reared back, and Yves's jaw temporarily went slack when they heard Scorbion's surprising answer. "It involves the traveling circus that is setting up on the outskirts of Haxford—the one that has been heavily promoted with poster boards and flyers throughout our area."

Calvin responded, "There is one hanging upon the back wall as we speak."

Scorbion's gaze went to the rear of the store where he spied the handbill. "And as we are all aware, it is not just *any* circus. Just this past summer every newspaper in our land carried the story of this circus and its performer who attempted to set a new height record for stilt-walking."

Barnabus replied, "I b-believe we all know t-that, Chief Inspector. But what d-does the circus have to do with a m-murder?"

"And the need to solve it *aujourd'hui*?" Yves added.

"I will explain," Scorbion told them. "The fellow who built the giant stilts happened to relocate to Haxford within the past year. It was his misfortune to do so as he was found dead behind the main tent at the circus a few hours ago. His head had been bashed in, and in falling, he collapsed into a mound of animal dung. We will eventually ascertain whether he died from the blow or suffocated in the excrement while unconscious, but for now, the exact cause of death is unimportant. The owner of the circus, Henry Hopkins, is concerned that if we do not determine who the murderer is and why the unfortunate chap was killed, there may be more deaths at tonight's performance. He is threatening to cancel the circus's shows rather than risk another member of his troupe being slaughtered."

Billy interjected. "So we have to find out who killed him and why before tonight's performance."

"Or there will be no performance," Scorbion confirmed. "I have dispatched Sergeant Adley to bring Hopkins, the stilt walker, and his wife here so that we may question those who knew the victim most intimately. They should arrive momentarily, so let us swiftly set up our interrogation room once again."

While Yves, Barnabus, and Thomas fetched the furniture, Billy approached Scorbion. "Inspector, have you made any progress with your concerns about the Bentine affair? Have you had any new ideas?"

Scorbion winced and contorted his face slightly. "Unfortunately, no. I have not had a good deal of free time at my disposal to consider what is perplexing me. I am still working through it though. And I assure you, you will be the first to know when my brain reveals exactly what it is that we have missed. But for now, let us concentrate on who killed the stilt-maker and why."

CHAPTER TWELVE

"Get outta the way, you bloody runt!"

Freddy Rumple barely escaped being hit on the head by the back of a ladder that two laborer clowns were carrying at waist level. Dodging under it at the last second saved his head from being bruised, but it did nothing for his ego, especially when they mockingly laughed down at him and called him "gnat," as they went past.

For Freddy, being just over five feet tall at the age of twenty-four was not totally a curse, but being small certainly *was* a curse when he was growing up. The bullying and taunting were so bad that he withdrew from school during Third Form and worked at various menial jobs after that, barely eking out a living.

One ordinary but eventful day, Freddy found a circular for a touring circus that was coming to Eastlake affixed to the side of the barn in which he slept. Freddy's father had taken him to a circus when he was five years old, and that cheerful experience was so ingrained in his memory that from that day forward, he adored circuses. When he saw the notice that there would be three days of performances, he did extra jobs, and with the money he earned he purchased a ticket for opening night.

From the moment he arrived at the circus, the overpowering and distinctive aroma of sawdust, dung, animals, and greasepaint smelled like a custom-blended perfume that was appealing to his senses. When he entered the main tent and saw the snake charmer, the bearded lady, the lion tamer and his cats, the sword swallower, and the other members of the troupe who in a normal setting would be considered misfits or outcasts, he was even more excited and energized.

"I belong here," he exclaimed, and, having said that, Freddy had an instantaneous epiphany that he should join the circus.

Freddy gathered up all his courage, put aside his natural instincts to be invisible, and sought out Mr. Henry Hopkins, the owner of the Hopkins Travelling Circus.

Hopkins wasn't difficult to find—he was also the circus's ringmaster, dressed gaudily in vibrant red and gold.

Quaking with nervousness, Freddy approached Hopkins. "I want to join your circus, Governor, more than anything. I'll work for really low wages doing donkey work. Anything to be part of your troupe."

When Hopkins hesitated, Freddy fell down on his knees and grabbed Hopkins's leg. "Please! Please, guv'nor, have me!"

Partly to get Freddy off his leg, and owing to the fact that he *could* use a low-paid laborer, Hopkins agreed. "All right. All right. I'll find you something, lad. I even have one thing you can do right now to start."

"Anything!" Freddy gasped like an obedient puppy looking to please its master.

"Get up and let go of my bleedin' leg!"

Freddy released his grip and rose. "Thank you. Oh, thank you."

"Let's see if you thank me in a fortnight or two. You're too small to be a laborer, so we'll call you an odd-jobber. Now go and find Reggie Watkins out by the animals, and tell him you're a new worker here. He'll get you set up. He's a giant of a fellow, so you'll have no difficulty finding him. He's a bit rough around the edges and has quite the temper, so make sure you stay on his good side."

Freddy was so elated that he ran to the animal cages. Standing in the midst of them was the largest human being Freddy had ever seen. Nearly seven feet tall, muscular, with wild, unkempt brown hair that appeared to have been shaped by a butcher, and a craggy, horse-shaped face punctuated by deep, penetrating brown eyes, Reggie was pitching hay into the ring where the circus's lone elephant was chained—tossing the pachyderm's food as if it were weightless.

Freddy stopped to watch, but when Reggie saw him, he put down the pitchfork and grunted, "What do you want, shrimp?"

Freddy craned his face up toward Reggie. "Mr. Hopkins told me to tell you I'm a new odd-jobber, and you'd find tasks for me to do."

Reggie turned his back and resumed throwing hay into the elephant's enclosure. He shouted over his shoulder, "What's a pipsqueak like you goin' to do around here? You'll be more trouble than help. You're too small to be any good for anythin'. You should be in the tent with the little people—the freaks. What're you, three feet high?"

Freddy would normally have shied away from any confrontation, but he wanted to be with the circus so badly that he once again summoned up his courage. "A bit less than five feet, if you don't mind. And I can do things: tidying up, carrying water for the animals, sweeping. Maybe I can't do everything you do, but I can do other chores."

Reggie's intelligence didn't match his physical size, and he wasn't used to people contradicting him. He snorted. "We'll see, you bugger. Just stay out of my way and don't cause any problems for me." He pointed to a shovel, and sarcastically asked, "Think you can lift that?"

Freddy ran to the shovel and picked it up. It *was* heavy, but Freddy was determined to use it for whatever Reggie had in mind.

Reggie bellowed, "Now go over to those horses and pick up their shite with it. Once you've filled the shovel, take it to that barrel over there and drop it in. Keep doin' that until all the shite is gone. Think you can do that, runt?"

Freddy put the shovel down and gave Reggie an aye-aye salute. He picked it up again and struggled as he carried it to the horse area where he started his first job as a member of the circus.

CHAPTER THIRTEEN

A month later, Freddy was neither thanking nor cursing Hopkins. Freddy was taunted by many of the larger performers, and routinely tormented by Reggie, but he fit in. He realized: *I'm less a freak than most of the kinkers. I'm normal, and not bad looking, I'm just undersized. Many of the carnies are freakish, and I'm not.*

Freddy kept hoping he'd get to do more diverse and interesting tasks than just tidying up, shoveling shite, swabbing down, and carrying props around every day. But he knew that virtually every circus act took years of intense training and practice. And those that didn't, like being the assistant who stood with the apple on his head while the sometimes-drunken archer reenacted William Tell, didn't appeal to Freddy. Because he had no other skills, he was only fit to be an odd-jobber, a potential casualty, or a joey—and clowning didn't appeal to him.

"Hey! You! Mate, can you give me a hand?"

Freddy looked around to determine if it was he that was being asked to help, but he couldn't see anyone. He had no idea where the voice was coming from.

"Up here."

Freddy looked up.

Standing a few feet to his side was the tallest person Freddy had ever seen—even bigger than Reggie: a clown who had to be eight feet tall or more. One of his colorful polka-dotted pant legs was hung up about halfway to where his kneecap should have been, exposing a wooden prosthetic device.

"Can you pull down my trouser leg? I'd really appreciate it."

Freddy jiggled the fabric, which fell to where it needed to be.

"Thanks. I'm Percy, Percy Harvey. What's your name?"

"Freddy. Freddy Rumple."

"Hello, Freddy."

"Hello, Percy. I've never seen anyone as tall as you before. I thought Reggie was big, but he's small compared to you." Freddy hesitatingly asked Percy about the prosthetic device. "How'd you end up with a wooden leg?"

Percy gave a small laugh and his face burst into a big friendly grin. "It's not a wooden leg, lad. These are stilts. I'm a stilt walker."

Freddy was intrigued. "How'd you become a stilt walker?"

Percy responded, "I've always been kinda short, and I got tired of people laughing at my size, so I decided to one-up everybody and become the tallest person in the circus."

That resonated with Freddy. "Could you teach *me* how to be a stilt walker?"

"You serious about it?"

"Bloody right."

CHAPTER FOURTEEN

It took Percy five sessions, all at night after the crowds had gone home and most of the other performers were in their tents and trailers, to indoctrinate Freddy in the basics of stilt walking. Following that, Freddy, under Percy's guidance, worked on his stilt walking regularly, and after a year of intense practicing, he had it down cold.

"Freddy, you're ready to show the world what you can do," Percy exclaimed one day.

"Thanks, mate," Freddy responded, "but not yet. I don't want anyone to know about this until I can do it so well that I can run and jump and maybe become the greatest stilt walker of all time."

"That's a pretty lofty ambition, Freddy, me boy, but if that's what you want, your secret's safe with me until you're ready to make your appearance. But, my friend, you *are* ready to audition for this circus."

Freddy responded, "I know you're right, Percy, but I want to do more than just walk on stilts. I want to be the world's most famous stilt walker. So I'm not going to show what I can do to Mr. Hopkins until I have an act. Something unique. Something that will kick some serious arse."

Over the next few weeks, Freddy grew frustrated. "Rubbish," he told Percy, as they practiced jumps, turns, leaps, and balancing on one stilt. "The stunts I'm performing are rubbish. They are not new. They are not exciting. They are not special."

"You're too hard on yourself," Percy responded. "You're the best stilt walker *I've* ever met. You've taken to it like a banker to pounds and shillings."

"I appreciate your saying that, but I haven't come upon what'll make me unique."

"Fire. Fires always please a crowd. You could jump through flames or walk across a line of burning charcoal."

"That's already been done."

"Then what *can* you do that's better, or bigger?"

That sparked an idea. "That's it!" Freddy exclaimed. "That's spot on. I'm going big. Really big."

"And by big, what do you mean?"

"Tall. The tallest stilts anyone has ever walked on. Percy, dare I ask if you know the height of the circus tent?"

"You dare, but I don't."

Freddy sought out Mr. Hopkins.

"Inside it's forty-six feet high," Hopkins explained, "and sixty-six feet outside. What makes you ask?"

"Nothing important." Freddy added, "yet" under his breath.

"Glad I could be of help, Freddy. Whatever it is."

As Freddy walked away, he knew how he would make his mark. "Twenty feet. That's what I'm going to do. *That* will kick some serious arse."

It wasn't as easy to accomplish as Freddy had anticipated.

His problem was finding stilts that tall. They didn't exist. So he borrowed a pencil and used the blank backs of circus posters and started sketching designs that he hoped would be that tall and still be stable enough to hold him upright.

Two evenings later, as was his nightly custom, Freddy was practicing his jumps and turns on standard stilts behind the big top. A trouper was walking around the tent, making sure that every pole and line was secure, and came upon him. Freddy startled the newcomer, who seemed fascinated at how adept Freddy was on the stilts.

Mastering stilt walking had provided Freddy with more courage and confidence than he had ever had before, so he jumped up and down three times and then did a back flip before dismounting from the stilts. "I haven't seen you before," he said. "You must be new here. Allow me to introduce myself. I am Freddy Rumple." He swooped into a deep, flamboyant bow, his hand sweeping across his chest. As he stood up, he said, "I have no idea why I did that, but it felt like the right thing to do."

Freddy realized it felt right to do with *that* trouper. That not very tall, but very pretty, *female* trouper—the one he immediately felt an attraction to as he had never felt with anyone before, man or woman.

"Emily," she said. "Emily Collins, recently hired to run the box office. You're good on those. Really good."

"Thanks. But I'm just an odd-jobber."

"Why aren't you performing? To my eye, you're better than any of the others I've seen."

"It's a long tale . . ."

"May I have the short version?"

"Blimey, that's funny—a *short* version . . . Let me consider how to best do that. Aye. Got it. Here's the short version: I won't perform before a crowd until I'm able to master a stunt that's beyond what anyone else has ever done. I want to burst onto the scene, not be a run-of-the-mill stilt walker. I want to be known as the stilt walker who arose out of nowhere to become the best ever. Literally from nowhere in my case."

"I don't believe . . ."

"Let me finish, dear lass. I plan to walk on the tallest stilts ever. They must be twenty feet tall, and I have to take real steps, not just move my legs up and down. That's the reason I haven't performed yet." Freddy paused. "Do you think I'm bonkers?"

Emily responded enthusiastically. "Rather not. To the contrary, it's a marvelous idea. I don't think you should do anything differently. You could be the main attraction of this troupe. You could *make* this circus. If more patrons don't begin attending, we could all be, as they say, out on our bums. One of the greatest problems is that we don't have a real first-class attraction. That could be you if you're able to do what you're planning."

She paused in thought, a radiant glow spreading across her face.

"Crikey, Freddy, if that happened, you'd *definitely* not be just another stilt walker. I'd wager that our new king, George, would attend your show, the way that Queen Victoria did Isaac Van Amburgh's."

Freddy gasped. "That's brilliant! My friend Percy, who taught me, he thinks I should get started performing *now*. He says it'll begin to get me known, and I'll be earning more money. But I want to kick some serious arse when I debut."

"Don't listen to him," Emily agreed. "What he thinks is nonsense. Take your time and make a grand entrance."

Freddy couldn't believe that this beautiful young woman of his stature understood him so well. He got a sudden urge. "Emily, may I give you a buss on the cheek? As a thank-you for saying that." He hesitated, his face filling with color, and then realized that he probably needed to apologize. "Oh my, I'm so sorry. I don't know why I said that. I just had this desire to kiss you. I must appear so inappropriate."

Emily replied, "Freddy, we just met and I don't know you. That's not what proper English girls do, and I *am* a proper English girl."

Freddy felt the color drain from his cheeks. "I meant no disrespect. My word, I would never want to do anything to offend you. It appears that I have become instantly smitten with you, and that has caused me to act in a very peculiar way that I have never done before."

Emily moved closer to Freddy. "You are smitten with me?"

"I am. I cannot tell you how or why it occurred so swiftly, but it has."

Emily became aware of her own unexpected feelings toward Freddy and she was pleased by his declaration. On impulse, she leaned into him and put her lips on his.

When their faces parted, Freddy declared, "Goodness, that was magnificent."

Emily involuntarily patted down her skirt. As she did, she said breathlessly, "I have never done anything that impulsively before. Ever."

"Me neither," Freddy agreed. "I'm always shy, but you . . . you . . . you're different."

Before Freddy could utter another word, Emily kissed him on the cheek. "And, I'm going to help you with your dream."

CHAPTER FIFTEEN

Freddy and Emily didn't see each other again until the next evening's performances concluded. They met behind the big top, and in spite of their intentions to focus on the stilts, they spent the first quarter-hour focusing on their lips.

After Freddy's practice session concluded, Emily suggested they go to her trailer to discuss the making of the taller stilts.

Inside it, Freddy observed, "This is the nicest trailer I've ever seen."

"When I joined the troupe at the last stand, Mr. Hopkins told me he didn't want me lodging with the performers," Emily explained. "So he purchased this trailer for me."

Freddy looked around the spacious room. "That was very kind of him."

Seated at the trailer's table, Freddy began drawing a sketch of the way he thought the stilts would need to be constructed. Emily leaned over to see what Freddy was sketching and bumped her head against his. "Oh, I'm so sorry," she exclaimed.

Then she looked down at the image he had drawn. "The cross struts should be closer together. They will ensure greater stability if you do that. And the platforms on each stilt should be a bit wider so that you have less chance of slipping off them."

Those suggestions impressed Freddy. "You're more knowledgeable about this than I anticipated. Your ideas will be very helpful."

Emily patted Freddy's hand. "Thank you. It's easy working with you."

"Heavens to Betsy, you amaze me, Emily. I realize I know little about you, and I want to know *all* about you."

"What is it that you want to know?" Emily asked. "I'm quite private."

"How is it that someone as beautiful as you isn't with someone? Other than me, that is."

Emily blushed. "You really think I'm beautiful?"

"I do, indeed. The most beautiful woman *I've* ever met."

"Thank you, Freddy. I needed that."

"Why's that? Don't you know you're beautiful?"

"My fiancé never once said that to me after we got engaged."

The panic in Freddy's voice was obvious. "You're engaged?!"

Emily immediately regretted making her statement without adding an explanation. "No. Freddy, I'm not. I *was* engaged—it ended just over a year ago. I'm sorry if I upset you."

Freddy uttered a sigh of relief. "Whew."

Emily continued, "I wished to see the Continent and be around interesting people—ones with a zeal for life. He fancied that I conduct myself in a very Victorian manner and charm his boring, aristocratic friends. We disagreed and clashed during the entire engagement about that."

"Wasn't that obvious to you both before you became betrothed?"

"It was, but neither of us believed the other was as committed to their thinking as we each ended up being. After two years of constant bickering and fighting—and, finally, screaming—we each arrived at the realization that we weren't meant to be together. So, I withdrew from the relationship and traveled for a year."

"And you ended up in a circus?"

"It was just the right environment for me. It's constantly moving from town to town, and I'm with people I'm comfortable around. Like you."

Freddy's face broke out into a giant grin. "How'd you know you'd fancy the circus life and carny people?"

"I was around circuses when I was younger, as was my sister, Mary, before she died from influenza when she was fourteen. But that's enough regarding me. What about you? Tell me more of your life."

Freddy related the story of how he came to join the circus, hoping it wouldn't make Emily not want to be with him any longer—but to his delight, what he told her had the opposite effect. When he finished, she came so near to him that there wasn't a flea's space between them.

She whispered, "I believe I love you. I cannot truly comprehend I am saying that and this is happening, but I do believe I love you."

After telling Emily that he loved her as well, Freddy and Emily remained together for the night.

In the subsequent weeks, Freddy kept his belongings in the laborer's tent but spent every night with Emily in her trailer.

Freddy and Emily spent much of the next three weeks designing and drawing the plans for the stilts. Freddy told Emily how impressed he was by her conceptual abilities. She told him it was something she'd inherited. "My father's always been able to envision completed objects from concepts."

"May I inquire if he's still alive?"

"He is."

"What about your mum?"

"She passed the year after Mary."

"I'm sorry," Freddy commiserated. "Will I meet your dad someday?"

Emily did not directly answer Freddy's question. "You'll really adore him, as I do, once you get to know him."

"I wager I will," Freddy responded.

Emily hugged him. "But in the meantime, please don't ask me about my past. I spent far too much time with someone who was so consuming and jealous that he had to know what I was doing at every turn, and I need a bit of privacy now. Do you fancy that will be all right?"

Even though he was unsure of exactly what he was agreeing to, Freddy acceded to her wishes. "Relate to me whatever you're comfortable with."

"Don't be concerned," Emily reassured him. "There's nothing

abnormal in my background. There are no Jack the Rippers among my family members. I just require a little time."

Emily looked down at the plans they were creating and put her cheek on her fist while she studied them. Looking back up, she said, "I can't wait for these stilts to be made, so let's return to making them a reality."

CHAPTER SIXTEEN

Two weeks later, Emily and Freddy believed they had the absolutely final, assured-to-work drawings for the colossal stilts. But they didn't possess the money or materials to have them made.

"I know a bloke in Devonshire who does marvelous woodworking," Emily told Freddy. "I'll wager he could construct the stilts. I'll ask him if he'll meet with us when the circus gets there."

"But what about money? Won't he want to get paid for his labors?"

"Possibly not," Emily said, and then held her finger up to Freddy's lips so he wouldn't ask more questions.

Emily and Freddy met Victor Hutchfield the day after the circus arrived in Devonshire.

Snacking on tea and crumpets in Victor's kitchen, Freddy learned what the connection was between Victor and Emily. "Emily and I shared three splendid days and nights together during her travels across England soon after her engagement ended. Mind you, nothing physical transpired between us, but she enchanted and delighted me to no end. We have stayed in touch through the post, but we have not seen each other again until now. And I must say, Emily, you are as radiant and bewitching today as you are in my memory—in fact, even more so."

Emily blushed and gave Victor a small peck on his cheek. Then she said, "Let me tell you about the stilts," and described how they needed to be made.

Victor leaned back from the table and turned to Freddy. "I will build them for you. More for Emily, but for you as well. And I will do so at no cost, to reward the best seventy-two hours I have ever had, bar none. If I am being honest with you, I also wish to be a part of what you are going to accomplish. I want to leave my mark, as well. My life is becoming somewhat tiresome, and I could use a good adventure and some stimulation."

After studying the drawings, Victor contributed a number of changes that he believed would help stabilize the stilts, and Freddy and Emily left the meeting feeling confident that the making of the stilts was in good hands.

When Victor sent a message twelve weeks later informing them the stilts were ready, Freddy and Emily discussed whether they could leave the circus early and rejoin it after its upcoming hiatus.

The next day Freddy happened to be walking by Hopkins's trailer and noticed Emily talking with him. Then Hopkins did something that seemed very odd to Freddy—he hugged Emily. Not a big hug, but a hug, nonetheless.

Later, when Freddy and Emily were together, he related to her what he had seen and asked what had happened to occasion the embrace.

"I did a favor for Henry with one of the aerialists," she explained. "He also told me I'm doing a boffo job in the box office. It was a 'thank you, dearie' hug."

"That's great, but I guess that means we're not going to be heading to Devonshire early now."

"Actually, we are, Freddy. I made the arrangements with Henry."

"He must really like you if he lets you call him Henry. I call him Mr. Hopkins, as every kinker here does."

"We have a first-rate, special relationship." Emily crossed her arms, which Freddy knew meant that she was done with a topic.

"You have a Midas touch, Emily," Freddy observed. "As starters, you get a friend who you've only seen for three days to make the stilts, and for nothing. And then you convince the owner of the circus to let two of his best troupers take a leave. I *am* impressed. That's ace."

"Thank you, m'Lord. Your needs are mine to fulfill."

Freddy grabbed Emily by the waist and pulled her toward him. "Come here, wench. Let us both deal with our mutual desires."

After their passion was spent, they placed their clothes for the excursion into one of Emily's old leather suitcases and then fell asleep, looking forward to their journey to Devonshire the next morning.

CHAPTER SEVENTEEN

When they arrived at Victor's cottage in Devonshire, they couldn't help but see the twenty-foot high stilts rising majestically above its roof. Emily jumped down from the hansom and bolted toward them. "My God, they're beautiful. Beautiful, Victor."

Freddy was more reserved. He thought, *They are beautiful. But tall. Taller than I imagined—my-nose-might-bleed tall. What have I got myself into? Crikey, if some serious arse is going to be kicked, it will be mine if I fall from them.*

To get onto the stilts, Freddy had to climb up an old, paint-stained ladder to the roof of Victor's two-story cottage, and from there go up another ladder that Victor had bolted to the top of the roof. When Freddy reached the part of the stilts that he would stand on, he looked down. Victor and Emily, twenty feet below, more closely resembled large porcelain dolls than a full-sized man and woman. Freddy trembled a bit. *If I fall, I'm dead. Gone. Blimey.*

Freddy saw Emily cup her hands to her mouth and her lips move, but no intelligible sound reached him. The wind prevented him from hearing anything. It was making a loud clamoring in his ears which made his head ring, but worse, it was also tossing him back and forth on the stilts. He held on to them, hoping he wouldn't get thrown off and fall, or that they wouldn't detach from the cottage and get blown away, emulating the runaway arm of a windmill alternately careening along the landscape and lifting into the air for brief "flights" like the Wright brothers in America.

After Freddy descended and reached the ground, Victor and Emily asked him what it was like being up so high. "Windy. Blimey, it was windy," Freddy told them. "No, that doesn't do it proper justice. It was blowing like a giant bellows."

Victor shrugged. "I cannot change the weather."

Emily optimistically said, "This could be good. If you can stay on the stilts in these conditions, walking on them in the big top will be smooth sailing."

Victor grabbed her arm and turned her toward him. "You mean Freddy plans on using the stilts more than once? That is a mad idea."

Emily folded her arms across her chest and responded, "Of course, he will, Victor. This isn't going to be an event that takes place just one time. Freddy's going to walk on those stilts at every performance and become renowned. He'll be the most famous stilt walker ever."

Victor shrugged his shoulders. "I sincerely hope they hold up."

Unfortunately, the wind did hold up. After the third day of gusting, Emily and Freddy decided to rejoin the circus and return to Devonshire when the air was calmer.

They were both disappointed but agreed it would be quite a spectacle when Freddy was able to get up on the stilts and walk on them.

During that conversation, Freddy shared his trepidations about how high they were with Emily, who proposed an idea. "We shall purchase a good number of mattresses so that in the event you fall while you're practicing, you won't get hurt or killed."

CHAPTER EIGHTEEN

As the months passed, waiting for another break in the circus's schedule to get back to Devonshire, Emily remained as secretive about herself, her past, and her father as she was when Freddy first met her—which further fueled his curiosity.

During that time, Freddy was promoted to assistant circus manager. When he told her, Emily kidded, "Thanks for carrying your weight in this relationship."

The one person who didn't appreciate Freddy's promotion was Reggie Watkins, who grumbled, "That half-pint can't hold a pitchfork to me. He don't deserve that, I do."

Two days later, Freddy and Emily received a wire from Victor: *Stilts done. Sold my cottage. Have to vacate next week. Stilts can't remain here. Bringing them to you. They fit on long cart in three sections. Be there next week.*

Emily and Freddy had been keeping Percy advised of all the stilt-building developments, and when they told him this latest news, he sounded very excited. "Gawd. I can't wait to see them! And I'm thinking you need to tell Hopkins. A large cart will be arriving here and off-loading some rather giant-sized stilt pieces—it'll be fairly noticeable."

"As I have that special relationship with Henry, let me tell him about the stilts," Emily suggested.

But Freddy responded, "It's my career, and my idea, so I should be the one to apprise him."

When they informed Hopkins together, he was less stunned by the news than Freddy anticipated. He encouraged them to keep moving ahead and said he'd be fully supportive of their venture. "I'm going to pull out all the stops to get the stunt, and this circus, newspaper coverage when Freddy is ready." Then he turned to Emily, "This could be big. Very big. Way to go, lovey."

Freddy wasn't quite sure why Hopkins was ascribing the credit to Emily, but Hopkins's enthusiasm was unmistakable and welcome, especially when he said, "I'll get things set up on this end for them to be housed and reassembled, so tell me when they arrive. Whatever you need. This could put us on the map."

Hopkins slapped Freddy on the back, hugged Emily, and walked away gaily singing "Shine On Harvest Moon."

When Victor arrived, Hopkins had completed all the preparations he'd committed to. He had a tent ready for Victor; three of the circus's best laborers were assigned to work with Freddy and Emily exclusively; the mattresses were bought; and a sizable area of earth was leveled next to the big top where Freddy could do the walk.

Victor told the laborers in great detail how he wanted the stilts to be unloaded from the cart, and when one of the workers, Jed Pierce, didn't handle them exactly as he was instructed, Victor hurled a slew of expletives at him and had him removed from working with the stilts. Victor also verbally abused two other laborers, Teddy Farner and Shelby Winston, as they assisted him in assembling the stilts when they didn't follow his directions to the letter.

The three laborers met that evening, complaining to each other about how badly Victor had treated them. Pierce spat on the ground. "I hope that shit-face runs into a streak of bad luck." Winston concurred, "Me as well," and Farner added, "Maybe we can make some of that bad luck happen."

Once the stilts were fully erected and raised up, they were held in place by guy-lines that were attached to the big top and to a towering pole that the laborers had planted in the ground.

While admiring the lofty stilts, Hopkins turned to Emily and Freddy. "It took me a bit of time to work out how to get Freddy up on them. I've rented a crane from the seaport a few towns over. It's a large device that picks up cargo from the holds of ships and deposits the containers on the docks, but in Freddy's case it'll lift *him* up and set him down on the stilts. I'm sure it will look like a giant beast of some sort, but this particular crane I've arranged for is one of the smallest they have at the harbor. It will arrive tomorrow."

Hopkins then addressed Victor. "I'll say this for those stilts, they're of considerable size. You did a very admirable job with them, matey. But I do wish you'd be a bit less chippy with my people. It's bad for morale when people are yelled at and condemned."

Victor shrugged and didn't respond to Henry in any other way.

Henry pressed the point no further, and instead addressed Freddy and Emily. "Our final day in this town is in a week. I don't believe I can obtain the same newspaper coverage as I can arrange for here in any of the next five stands we're headed to. If this event is going to be as grand as we're all thinking, it has to take place in a sizable location. Here. Unfortunately, that means you have less than a week to practice and perfect the walk. Do you believe you can be ready?"

As Freddy's mind raced through what would have to be done by then, Emily blurted out, "Of course we'll be ready! Won't we, Freddy?"

Freddy meekly replied, "I guess so."

"That's my lad. Cheerio!" Hopkins thumped Freddy on the back and then walked away. Emily told Freddy she had to go to the box office and left as well.

Victor moved next to Freddy. "You know what that was about, don't you?"

Freddy wasn't sure what the "that" was that Victor was referring to. "No. I guess I don't."

"Hopkins and Emily. You know about them, right?"

"Actually, no. I've surmised there's something between them, but I haven't nailed it down yet."

"Maybe this will help. On one of the evenings Emily and I spent together, she mentioned to me that Collins was her mum's surname. But it was not the name she went by at the time. It is the name she uses *now*, but it wasn't then. The name I knew her by was her father's surname."

Freddy had an instantaneous revelation. "Allow me to wager a guess, could it have been Hopkins?"

"Give the bloke a brass ring!"

By the time Emily had completed her shift in the box office and arrived back at their trailer, Freddy's mind had played out a myriad of things to say to her. But when Emily appeared at the door, he could only focus on the fact that she was the woman he loved and the one who loved him, and all the questions he had and the words he was thinking of saying vanished. He simply muttered, "I love you, Miss Hopkins."

Emily started to say, "Freddy . . ." but he cut her off and put his finger to her lips.

"Ssh. Do you love me? That's all I want to know."

"Of course, I do, silly."

"Then that's enough for me. You'll tell me when you're ready."

Emily hugged Freddy and whispered in his ear, "I'm glad you know. It's hung heavy over me to conceal it from you."

Freddy replied, "I'm fine with it."

"No," Emily said in a firmer tone. "You deserve to know everything. Father has asked me to take over the troupe when he is no longer able to run it, and he wants me to know the circus from the bottom up. I've utilized my mum's surname so the troupe members wouldn't know that I'm Henry's daughter and treat me preferentially. It has worked out well that way. I've been able to just be one of the carnies—which is what I wanted."

Emily continued, "I've worried that if you knew, you might imagine I was using you to make the circus successful." Then she said something that changed Freddy's life forever. "Ever since that first night I saw you behind the big top, I knew we'd be together forever. So, this circus is going to be yours as much as it will be mine."

That jolted Freddy. "You would marry me if I asked you to?"

"Right here, right now. Freddy, was that your odd way of proposing to me?"

"No, but this is—Emily Collins Hopkins, will you be my missus?"

"Yes, I will."

As they shared a kiss, an idea popped into Freddy's head. "Emily, what say we wed when I do my walk? We can make the event a two-for-one. What do you think?"

Emily jumped up and down. "Oh my Lord! Oh my Lord! What a fabulous idea, Freddy. Let's make that happen!"

When they told Henry, he hugged Emily and thumped Freddy on the back. "Now that you're my daughter's husband-to-be, call me Henry, son."

CHAPTER NINETEEN

Hopkins went to the town's newspaper to inform them about the walk and the marriage, and to ensure that they would have a reporter at the event. Then he proceeded to the wireless office and sent a message to *The Telegraph* and *The Times* in London.

The next day, Emily and Freddy were being interviewed by a journalist from the local gazette, which scooped both London newspapers, whose reporters didn't arrive until the following morning.

The day after the London papers printed their stories, their articles were reproduced in every other newspaper throughout England, with the details about Freddy's walk, and his and Emily's wedding, on the front page of every one of them.

The Telegraph's and *The Times*'s reporters remained at the circus until the day the big bash occurred. Additional newspapers from across the country, and from France and Belgium, dispatched their best journalists to report on the events, which had become the main topic everyone throughout England—and parts of the Continent—was talking about.

The practice walks, which took place during the dead of night when all the day's circus-goers had departed and many of the performers were asleep in their tents and trailers, were off-limits to the journalists. However, more than half of the circus troupe came out to help in every way they could. Noticeable only to Freddy and Emily, Percy Harvey didn't come out to assist in any way, nor did Reggie Watkins. Also absent were Jed Pierce, Teddy Farner, and Shelby Winston.

The first few times Freddy stood on the stilts, he was held in place with a harness from the crane—which reassured him and calmed his concern about what *would* happen if he fell down.

On the third day, Freddy jettisoned the harness. Unfortunately, he stumbled as he tried to take even one step, and although the mattresses were laid below him, he still managed to get a number of bruises from the falls he had.

On the fourth day, Freddy made noticeable improvement and was able to move the stilts up and down. But no matter how many times he tried, he couldn't take a step without plummeting to the mattresses.

Finally, on the fifth day, he managed to take a step before he tumbled.

As Freddy was being hoisted to the top of the stilts for yet another try at a walk, Henry was concerned and asked Emily, "Daughter, is this going to take place?"

"Yes," she replied. "There is no doubt in my mind. I believe in Freddy."

Henry paced a bit before responding. "We only have two days until he must walk on the stilts. There are even more newspapermen arriving on the morrow and the telegraph office is establishing an auxiliary location within our grounds for them to utilize. This will either be the extravaganza of the year or an utter failure. And this circus can't afford an utter failure. Plus, darling, I don't wish to see our Freddy fail."

On the last night before the performance was to take place, on the final practice walk on the stilts, Freddy managed to take one step with each stilt without falling. And then another. And another. When he descended from the stilts, he told Emily, "I had this most curious feeling that I could have gone a mile. It made no sense, as I was teetering a bit after each step, but I can't deny what I felt."

CHAPTER TWENTY

On the day of Freddy's performance, the circus grounds were adorned with flags, balloons, flowers, and banners, all contributing to the grandiose impression that a spectacle was occurring.

Over one hundred newspapers were represented, the telegraph office's remote station was fully functioning, and more than thirty times the number of people who could fit into the big top were on the circus grounds, some arriving ten hours prior to the box office opening. Hopkins erected a gaily decorated wooden stage next to the animal enclosures from which the town's band serenaded the crowd with oompah favorites. The music soothed some of the caged beasts while others howled along.

Everyone in attendance was hoping to witness a short man in a gaudy tuxedo set a world record by walking on twenty-foot-high stilts, and then wed a circus owner's winsome daughter under an altar fashioned out of the stilts crossed over each other.

Standing inside the big top, Emily, attired in her wedding dress, reassured Freddy. "If you accomplish this feat, you will become a national hero. And then when we get married I, too, will be known. And Victor, as well."

Freddy beamed and joked, "Emily, you and I will become the Rumple Stilts & Kin act that the tabloids have kiddingly named us."

Freddy didn't tell Emily what he thought would happen if he failed. *I'll probably have to shoot myself. Literally. I'd be spoken about as one of the colossal blunderers of all time. I'd be of no use to anyone. If I fail, it will be best if I just crawl back into that shell I was in before I joined this circus.*

Freddy quickly put those thoughts out of his mind and focused on the feeling he'd had that he could walk clear across the circus grounds on the stilts. The more he focused on that belief, the more he was convinced that he could accomplish that feat, and the braver he became.

Emily left the tent and went outside to join Victor and meet with reporters and the crowd.

Soon after that, it was time for Freddy's performance. Make it happen or die time. Possibly literally.

Henry, decked out in his ringmaster uniform, and Freddy, in his hand-made, form-fitting, but not too-tight-to-stilt-walk powder-blue tuxedo with black satin trim, stood side by side—alone in the tent that Freddy would emerge from to be hoisted to the top of the stilts.

Henry slapped Freddy on the back. "I'm proud of you, lad, and I imagine that you *will* accomplish this feat. I want you to know that you are a splendid partner for my Emily. I will feel that way about you whether you succeed today or fail. But please . . . do try to succeed." A broad smile filled Henry's face as he uttered the last sentence.

"Henry," Freddy responded, "I love your daughter and I *will* succeed today. Have you looked out on the grounds? Emily is dazzling the journalists. She is so beautiful and elegant and charming everyone. Look at her in that wedding dress. Oh my. She's . . ."

Freddy was unable to complete what he was saying, as at that exact moment his name was announced, and the entryway curtain was parted by Victor—the cue for Henry's introduction of Freddy and his grand entrance.

Freddy completed what he wanted to say to Henry before they began walking out to Freddy's destiny. "The stilt walking was initially about me and my aspirations, but now it's no longer just for me; it is for Emily, and you, and Victor, and the entire circus troupe. And I *am* going to kick some serious arse out there today for all of us. I'm going to walk from here to London on those stilts. You just watch."

Henry smiled, "I certainly *will* be watching, my good fellow, but trust my judgment, ten feet will be good enough."

Henry squeezed Freddy's arm and proceeded to exit the tent, ready to begin his welcoming speech to the circus-goers and the press, and his introduction of Freddy.

CHAPTER TWENTY-ONE

Sergeant Adley strode into the barbershop, followed by Hopkins, Emily, and Freddy.

When they entered, Barnabus nudged Yves in his side. "Th-there's hope for you yet my small f-friend. Look at the size of the little chap. The one who d-did that walk. He's j-just about your stature and look what he accomplished." Barnabus paused and smiled. "And he d-didn't need to stand on a box to do his job."

Yves scowled. "He needed something twenty feet high to stand on." Then he made an obscene gesture at Barnabus, ending with "*Éteindre.*"

Calvin glared at his barbers. "Stop squabbling, my two infants. Get the chairs and the table from the storeroom and set them up for another interrogation, please."

Scorbion welcomed the three circus folk, informed them about the role of the barbers and Billy, and asked if they'd mind answering a few questions.

They replied in the affirmative, and once the furniture was arranged, Scorbion asked everyone to sit, pointing out the side of the table for the circus people. Then he went to the coatrack, neatly hung his suit jacket, and instructed Adley, "Return to the circus to discover if there is more to learn there, and please, first make a stop at Dr. Franklin Morgan's home, and ask him to accompany you to the circus grounds so that he might determine what the man's cause of death was."

Adley confirmed that he would do that which Scorbion requested and report back any findings.

Scorbion walked to the table and sat. "We welcome you to Haxford and look forward to attending your renowned circus. At the same time, we are distressed that your visit here has begun under such unfortunate circumstances. I assure you that we will, today, learn who perpetrated this heinous deed, and enable you to go on with your scheduled performances this evening."

Hopkins responded, "I appreciate your enthusiasm and confidence, Chief Inspector Scorbion, but how can you be so certain of that?"

"Because he is *that* good," Calvin replied. "You'll see for yourself."

Hopkins shrugged. "I sincerely hope that is the case."

"Which of you knew the victim for the longest period of time and was most knowledgeable of him?" Scorbion asked.

"I-I guess that would be me," Emily stammered. "I've known Victor—or perhaps, should I say, *knew* him—for many years." She then recounted how she and Victor first met and the interactions with him that led to Freddy's stilt walk.

Scorbion listened intently. When Emily completed her story, he asked, "Do you have thoughts as to who might have committed this act upon Mr. Hutchfield, and why?"

Emily thought before replying. "I don't. I can think of no one who might have done this to Victor."

Scorbion leaned forward. "Might *you* have done it?"

Emily was taken aback. "Me? Me? No. I adored Victor as a dear friend. He made our success, and our present lives, possible."

Freddy leaned toward Scorbion. "I don't have specific thoughts about who may have committed this act, but when I was training for the walk, two members of our troupe, who I thought would have helped out with my preparations, did not. I'm not saying either of them might have killed Victor—and Lord knows, I'd have no idea why they would have if they did—but if you need a starting place, you could begin with them."

"And they are?" Scorbion asked.

"Another stilt walker, Percy Harvey," Freddy replied. "But he taught me how to stilt-walk and has been a good friend, so I doubt it would have been him. Plus, I can't see what motive he would have."

Scorbion inquired, "And the other?"

Emily answered, "Reggie Watkins. He's a laborer, a large fellow, but not the brightest candle on the table, if you understand what I am alluding to. He has always resented Freddy and has taunted him about his size unceasingly."

Scorbion leaned back. "Is that it? Is there no one else we should be considering?"

"Actually there were three laborers who Victor was very unkind to when the stilts first arrived," Emily said. "His words and tone were quite abusive toward them."

Freddy confirmed that. "Oh yes, I remember that. Victor really lashed out at Jed Pierce, Shelby Winston, and Teddy Farner. If I recall correctly, they were exceedingly angry with him, and I'd wager they still are even a year later."

Hopkins added, "The way he treated them was uncalled for. They had every right to dislike him."

"Enough to murder him?" Scorbion asked.

Hopkins responded, "My dear Inspector, it goes without saying, but I will say it anyway. The three of us did not kill Victor. I was not aware that Percy and Reggie did not help out last year, but if Freddy says they didn't, I'm sure he knows what he is saying. Personally, I don't believe either of them would commit a murder, but yes, it's possible that one of them did."

"Another person who might have had a reason was the woman Victor was spending his time with," Emily added. "In a letter I received from him a month ago, he wrote that they began being in each other's company a week after he relocated here, but she had just told him that she wished to end their relationship. He wrote that he was attempting to keep them together, but she is a strong-willed individual, and he thought that his attempts might be unfruitful. Yesterday morning when we met with him at the grounds, he told us she had broken off with him, but he was making one more attempt at reconciliation. He said they were planning to meet last evening to discuss the situation, and he hoped she didn't get too roused up, as she could have a temper equal to his on occasion."

Scorbion nodded. "She is someone we must look into. In the affairs of the heart one often loses one's normal composure, and one's sense of right and wrong." He turned to Emily. "Do you perhaps know the name of this woman, or did he mention anything that would assist us in identifying who she might be?"

"Unfortunately, no," Emily replied.

Freddy added, "He called her 'my sweetie,' but Victor never actually said her name to us."

"Nor was it in the letters," Emily recalled.

Scorbion stroked his chin. "Then we must dispatch someone to inquire of those who live near the deceased Mr. Hutchfield, whether they happen to have seen the two together and can identify her. I will send Adley when he returns with Dr. Morgan's report."

Freddy interrupted Scorbion, "One other thing that might be relevant . . . When we met Victor yesterday morning, he mentioned that he had just had an encounter with someone at the grounds, and he was clutching a few sheets of paper in his hand."

"Did he indicate who it was that he had that prior meeting with? And, by any chance, were you able to discern that which was written on the papers?" Scorbion asked.

Emily responded, "Unfortunately, the answer to both questions is no."

Scorbion thought for a moment. "That encounter and those papers may or may not be pertinent to this inquiry. If they are, we shall uncover whom he met with and what was inscribed on those papers before we have completed this investigation. In the meantime, I have additional questions for those of you here now. To begin with, which of you is most closely acquainted with Mr. Percy Harvey?"

Hopkins spoke first. "I have known Harvey the longest, as he has been in my employ for quite a number of years, working up from a laborer odd-job to a stilt-joey, similar to what Freddy has done. But I believe that Freddy and Emily may have known him more intimately than I. I never had much interaction with the fellow on a personal level."

Freddy sat up straighter on his chair. "I fancy that I knew Percy better than anyone. He introduced me to stilt walking, taught it to me, and helped me excel at it. He even gave me my first pair of stilts—an extra pair of his."

"Yet," Scorbion countered, "he was not there for you when you might have most needed him, at your final practices."

Emily leaned in. "That's true, but I can't imagine Percy doing anything sinister. He's a nice man. Plus, he's short, almost as short as Freddy, so he might not have the strength to kill someone who was a full seven inches taller, like Victor."

Freddy added, "And I have no idea why Percy would have wanted to kill Victor."

"Did they know each other?" Scorbion asked.

"Oh yes," Freddy responded. "When Victor brought the stilts to us, Percy helped unload them, and he met Victor a number of times during the preparations for my first walk."

"And there was no animosity between the two?" Scorbion questioned.

Freddy and Emily looked at each other and then both shook their heads. "Reggie is another story, though," Freddy said. "He taunted me and resented me from the very start. He thought I was too small to be of any assistance and would be more work for him than a help to him."

Emily added, "I heard through others in our troupe that Reggie was angry because Freddy advanced, while Reggie didn't. Reggie's good at what he does, especially with the animals, but he's no Freddy. He doesn't have the same intelligence or ambition. Just the brawn."

Hopkins broke in. "But I must say that I've known Reggie for quite a long time—in fact, he was one of my earliest hires, and I have never seen him do anything that might harm anyone else. To my way of thinking, he is a gentle giant with a front of massive bravado."

Scorbion considered what had just been said. "It is good that you feel neither could have killed your friend, but we must still bring both of them here to question. As well as the other three whom Hutchfield antagonized."

Hopkins immediately responded. "Do whatever you have to do, Chief Inspector. Any—*all*—of my company is at your disposal. As you know I am rather concerned about the company performing without having first identified the person who did this."

Billy faced Freddy, Emily, and Hopkins. "Just so we can take you three off our list of suspects, where were you last night and earlier this morning?"

Hopkins was the first to respond. "I would resent that question, but I am aware that you have to ask it. The three of us shared supper last night before retreating to our respective trailers. This morning I was awakened by a pounding on the door. One of our aerialists had come to inform me about the murder."

Emily spoke next. "As father said, after dinner, Freddy and I went to our trailer. We stayed there until we, too, were alerted to Victor's death. We were together all night."

Calvin pointed to Freddy and Emily. "You both have a solid alibi—each other. But Mr. Hopkins, is there anyone who can confirm that you did not leave your trailer after you three parted company last night?"

Scorbion interjected. "That is a very good question, Calvin, but I cannot imagine that Mr. Hopkins had anything to do with Mr. Hutchfield's death. There was nothing for him to gain from it. Rather, it could hurt sales of tickets if people who attend his circus are concerned for their safety. And in addition, he is the one most forcefully asking us to get to the root of this affair. While Mr. Hopkins's involvement is a possibility, it is a remote one at best, and we will only revisit it if all other paths prove fruitless."

Hopkins turned to Calvin. "That was a fair question, chap, but as the chief inspector has said, I had no reason to harm Victor, and his death is not helpful for us as we prepare for our opening tonight."

Then he added, "My good fellows, if this matter is resolved today and we are able to have a performance tonight, may I leave complimentary passes at the box office for you all? And if you are with companions, there will be passes for them tonight as well."

All the men smiled. Billy said, "That would be marvelous. Thank you. I'm sure we'd all be delighted to attend."

Yves added, "*Oui*, and I want to see this small fellow"—he pointed to Freddy—"as the featured performer. He will carry the flag for all of us of smaller stature, doing something that people of larger size cannot."

"S-something *you* can't do, my height-deprived f-friend," Barnabus teased.

Scorbion broke up the squabbling. "Might you tell me who found Mr. Hutchfield?"

Hopkins responded, "Two of our animal handlers came upon his body during their rounds this morning, while they were making certain that the animal cages were locked and the tent poles were secure. When I got to Victor, it was evident that he was no longer alive. He was lying facedown in a pile of manure, just outside the main tent by Gargantua's area. Gargantua is our elephant. There was a pool of blood where the back of his head appeared to be caved in. It seemed to me that the blows came from the shovel we found on the ground next to his body. There was blood on the scoop, as well as the handle. When I arrived there, I asked the handlers, James and Lionel, if they had touched anything, and they said they hadn't."

Scorbion asked one last question: "Are any of you knowledgeable of where Mr. Hutchfield resided?"

"The address on his letters was Blackberry Lane," Emily responded. "I don't recall the exact house number, but I know I can locate a letter when Freddy and I are back in the trailer."

Scorbion stood up and stretched his back. "That would be extremely helpful, thank you. However, to advance this inquiry with the rapidity necessary to determine the murderer before the sun has set today, I believe we must speak with Percy Harvey, Reggie Watkins, the three laborers, and Mr. Hutchfield's so-far-nameless 'sweetie.' Please return to your grounds and request that Harvey, Watkins, Pierce, Farner, and

Winston venture here straightaway. Before they depart, please provide one of them with Mr. Hutchfield's address so that they might present it to us when they arrive."

Freddy, Emily, and Hopkins stood. Hopkins said, "I will make arrangements so that they are all here within the hour, with the information. It will leave me a bit shorthanded for the remainder of our preparations for tonight, but we will make do. I sincerely hope that the murderer is not any of them, but if one of them did commit that foul deed, then do what you have to, Chief Inspector."

After they were gone, Scorbion addressed the men in the shop. "We *will* solve this mystery today, but it is imperative that we learn who Mr. Hutchfield's lady friend was. I do not believe we have the luxury of waiting until Adley arrives to commence searching for her, so Billy and Calvin, would you please go to Blackberry and rap on doors to determine whether anyone knows her identity, or, absent that, whether someone could proffer a description of her?"

Calvin put his arm around Billy's shoulder. "Shall we be on our way? Happily, we are only four short blocks from Blackberry."

As they left, Billy remarked, "I know I've previously encountered someone who lives on Blackberry Lane, but I can't remember who in the blazes it is. It might come to me by the time we are there."

Calvin replied, "That would be helpful, lad."

None of the men, including Scorbion, had any inkling of the strange twists of fate that lay in store for them.

CHAPTER TWENTY-TWO

While the men in the barbershop waited for the circus people to arrive and Billy and Calvin to return, Adley appeared at the door with Dr. Franklin Morgan.

Scorbion welcomed them warmly. "Ah, Dr. Morgan, I thank you for assisting in this affair, and Sergeant Adley, I look forward to hearing whatever you might have to report."

Adley—slightly overweight, sporting a thin pencil mustache, ten years Scorbion's junior, and dressed in his traditional police uniform, which, much to Scorbion's dismay, seemed always to be in need of a good pressing—reported, "We could find no one who witnessed anything, Chief. The blokes who found the body happened upon it as they walked by. Fortunately, nothing was touched or moved, but there wasn't much to handle in any event. Just Hutchfield's body and a shovel stained with blood."

Morgan observed, "The spade that Sergeant Adley is referring to is definitely the implement that crushed Hutchfield's skull. In my learned judgment, I believe that the man expired as he fell, prior to his face coming to rest in the manure. The posterior of his cranium was bashed inward at least three inches. You cannot be struck with the force it took to do that without it killing you. From the look of the area of the trauma, there is no doubt in my mind but that he was hit at least three times with the implement—most likely twice while he was standing and once as he fell. Based on his body temperature, I am of the opinion that he was killed earlier this morning."

Scorbion thought for a moment, then asked Adley, "Have you removed the body to the morgue?"

Adley confirmed that the town's undertaker had been summoned and had taken the corpse to the funeral parlor. "What else would you like done now, Chief?"

Scorbion considered the question before replying, "Nothing further at this time, Sergeant. I might suggest that you return to the station, so I will know where to find you if an occasion arises that requires me to do so."

Adley leaned in to Scorbion. "Sir, would you mind very much if I remained here instead? I would enjoy seeing how this case unfolds and resolves. And the process you employ. And should you need me, I will be right here."

Scorbion's response was instantaneous: "That is a marvelous idea, Sergeant. You are quite right. I am confident that Constable Pawling will sufficiently man the building during the period when we both are absent."

Scorbion asked Barnabus to get another chair out of the back room, announcing that Sergeant Adley would be joining them.

"It might do you well to have me remain here as well," Dr. Morgan suggested. "You might need my expertise. And purely personally, I would like to witness how you clear up this death."

Scorbion instructed Barnabus, "And one more chair for the good doctor, please."

CHAPTER TWENTY-THREE

As they walked to Blackberry Lane, Billy reiterated to Calvin, "It is bothering me that I know someone who lives on the street, but can't recall who it is."

Calvin told him, "Either it will come to you, or you will encounter them there. Don't fret about it, lad."

When they arrived at their destination, Calvin suggested, "Since the street has only two blocks, shall we each take one?"

Billy agreed. "I'll go to the one on the left."

They split up, and Calvin started knocking on the doors of the homes on the block on the right.

When Billy rapped on his third door of his assigned portion of the street, it was opened by a woman. He smiled at her, and she smiled back in recognition. "Billy, how nice to see you. To what do I owe the honor of this visit?"

Billy responded, "For the life of me, I couldn't recall who lived on this street, but I should have remembered it was *you*. How could I have forgotten?"

"Is there some way in which I may assist you?" the woman asked.

Billy shuffled his feet. "Would you mind accompanying me to Calvin

Brown's barbershop? I believe that Chief Inspector Scorbion would like to speak with you."

The woman asked, "Does it have to do with Victor Hutchfield?"

"It does," Billy confirmed.

"Wait one moment while I retrieve my purse and put on a hat. I will be right back," she said.

As she started to walk inside, Billy called to her, "I have to go across the street for a moment. I'll return shortly and meet you here."

Then Billy went to find Calvin.

As Calvin was knocking on his fourth door, Billy appeared behind him. "I've found her. You can return to the shop and tell them she and I will arrive right after you."

Calvin turned from the door. "I'll do that, lad. Good work."

Calvin left for the barbershop and Billy for the woman's house.

When he got there, she was standing in front of it waiting for him. She put her arm in his and they started walking. "I am looking forward to meeting this gentleman who you have said such marvelous things about to me," she told Billy.

When Calvin returned to the barbershop, Scorbion asked, "Where is Billy?"

Calvin's eyebrows lifted slightly. "He'll arrive shortly, Pignon. Billy found Hutchfield's lady friend and is escorting her here. I believe they will both make an appearance momentarily."

Barnabus was impressed. "Th-That was fortuitous, w-wasn't it?"

Yves's ears pricked up. "*Ça alors*! Barnabus, you know a big word. *Je suis impressionné.* You may only know English, and only speak it hesitatingly, but at least you know a big word or two in your own native language."

"P-Piss off, shorty. That word was longer than you are t-tall. Maybe I should get you a p-pair of stilts instead of that b-box you stand on."

Thomas needled them both. "Maybe you two should live together. You quarrel just like my mum and dad."

Before either could reply, Billy and the woman arrived. She entered first, and Billy closed the door behind them.

All discussion and comments ceased. Everyone stared at the woman.

After a few seconds, Yves shook his hand in front of his chest. "*Ooh là là.* Who might this person of rare beauty be?"

Barnabus threw out another barb. "I guess I'd b-better get you those stilts if you have any d-designs on her."

Yves gave Barnabus his raised finger.

The woman was five feet, six inches tall, with long auburn hair that flowed from under her large black hat and cascaded over her shoulders and down her back; a slightly tanned, flawless complexion; and a curvaceous figure that was evident under a dress that reached to her knees and elevated her ample chest above its square-cut top.

She removed her hat and placed it on the coatrack next to Scorbion's suit jacket. She took hold of one of its sleeves and ran the fabric between her fingers. "Very nice material. Whose is this, might I ask?"

Scorbion approached her, and she observed, "You! We meet again. It is *your* jacket. It matches the trousers you are wearing. You have excellent taste in clothes." She paused and looked Scorbion up and down. "And, there are those shoes again. I have never seen any like them. They are custom-made, are they not?"

Scorbion was keenly aware that this was the owner of the bookshop, and he found himself enamored with her beauty and impressed by both her powers of observation and her knowledge of fashion. "Yes. I have them crafted for me by the finest shoemaker in all of the Continent. He happens to reside in Liverpool, but his skill is unsurpassed, anywhere."

Billy interrupted their repartee. "Chief Inspector Pignon Scorbion, I would like to introduce you to Miss Thelma Smith."

CHAPTER TWENTY-FOUR

For the first time since the men in the shop had met him, Scorbion was speechless. When he recovered his voice, he said to Thelma, "It is my sincere pleasure to meet you. Again. Our mutual friend Billy has told me much about you, and sings your praises highly. I believe I rather agree with him, and am of the opinion that I would enjoy making a deeper acquaintance with you, but for now, that is inappropriate. We are in the midst of a murder investigation, and that takes precedent over any personal matters. I—"

"Actually, Chief Inspector Scorbion," Thelma broke in, "I am here as a part of your inquiry. When Billy came to my door and told me who and what he was looking for, I related to him that he need look no further."

The men hung on every word spoken by the gorgeous woman.

"You see," she continued, "I am the woman you are seeking. Victor Hutchfield and I had a relationship that I fully ended last evening at supper—one that I had been attempting to terminate with him for well over two fortnights. I rather believe that over the course of that time, he most likely considered me cold-hearted, tempestuous, and insensitive."

Scorbion carefully weighed her words. Only he knew how conflicted he was. On one hand, Thelma was *exactly* as Billy had described her—alluring, observant, erudite, cultured, independent—yet she was also one of the primary suspects in the case, and a possible murderess.

As Scorbion was deciding how to proceed, Adley walked over to Thelma, introduced himself, and asked if she would mind accompanying him to one of the chairs by the table so that they could question her about Hutchfield.

"Of course," she replied, "is that not why I am here? Which chair shall I sit upon?"

When Adley held out the middle chair on the interviewees' side of the table, Thelma added, "I see you are expecting others as well. May I know who they might be? And, additionally, whom everyone else here is."

Once she was seated, Calvin sat down. "I am Calvin Brown, the proprietor of this establishment."

"Yes. Billy told me about you as we walked here," Thelma replied.

One after the other, the men introduced themselves and sat down.

When Franklin Morgan presented himself, Thelma said, "I have heard of you, Doctor, but fortuitously, I have not yet had the need to avail myself of your services. Are you in attendance in case I faint or suddenly have an attack of some sort under the intense and microscopic questioning that I assume I am in for? I assure you, I will be quite fine."

Scorbion was the only one left standing, and he sat on the unoccupied chair directly across from Thelma, stared into her dark-brown eyes, composed himself, and began. "In spite of this being an unorthodox environment for a formal inquiry, this is one nonetheless. I ask that all the answers you give to questions any of us ask of you, or any information you relate to us, be factual and truthful. May I count on that?"

Without hesitating, Thelma replied, "Well, of course, Chief Inspector Scorbion." Then she smiled and added, "But then again, you are taking my word for that, are you not?"

Scorbion let out his own smile, enjoying the manner in which Thelma thought. "Yes, that is true. However, you will find that I am quite accomplished at rooting out truths. Similar to the way ferrets seek out and then get to rats and other food."

"Since I am neither a rodent nor a liar, I assure you that you will only hear candor and honesty from me," Thelma said. "Please ask whatever suits your fancy."

Scorbion realized that he had never before been in a similar situation: a witness who could have committed murder, but who was also a bewitching female that he felt extremely attracted to, was intrigued by, and wanted to know better on a personal level.

He quickly put those thoughts aside. "The additional chairs on either side of you are reserved for the circus folk who will be joining us shortly. Now, to begin, am I correct in believing that Billy has told you about Mr. Hutchfield's murder?"

Thelma quietly replied, "Yes."

"Then, please tell us whatever you think might be relevant about you, and to this affair."

Thelma responded, "By affair, do you mean this case or my relationship with Victor? Or both?"

"Both, please," Scorbion affirmed.

"I am a woman of thirty-seven years," she began. "I have lived in Haxford half a decade, and prior to that I resided in London. I consider myself somewhat unconventional—as I assume you consider yourself, Chief Inspector—and I rail at hard and fast rules. For the majority of my adult life, I was a librarian, but for the past four years I have owned and run the bookshop in this town. Having not made prior acquaintance with any of you, except for Billy, I believe that none of you other than Chief Inspector Scorbion have visited my establishment, Books on the Square, but I welcome you to do so in the future. I stock both current publications and antiquarian tomes. I have no animals in my home and spend the majority of my time reading, working, solving puzzles of varying sorts, and championing women having the right to vote—as a member of the Women's Social and Political Union. I have never been betrothed, and at my current age, I find it doubtful that I ever will. But one never does know what life has in store." She stared directly into Scorbion's eyes. "Does one, Chief Inspector?"

Scorbion smiled. "You are correct, dear lady. No one can accurately foretell the future."

"Except possibly Nostradamus," she replied. "And I do happen to possess a reprinting of his book, *Les Prophéties*, in my shop, should you ever desire to read it."

Yves nudged Barnabus. "He was a Frenchman, you know."

"I am aware of th-that," Barnabus responded. "D-Do you think I'm uneducated?"

Yves retorted, "I will not comment on that."

Billy addressed Thelma. "Would you tell us about your relationship with Hutchfield?"

"I'm still in shock that he's been killed, but I have no other feelings for him. The emotional aspect of our relationship ended many months ago, and in the ensuing time, I have been attempting to get him to be my friend, rather than my beau. Unsuccessfully, I must add, until last evening, when I declared to Victor, in no uncertain terms, that whatever had been between us at some point no longer existed. To borrow a Germanic word, our relationship was kaput."

Yves declared proudly, "Actually, mademoiselle, it was originally a French word that the Germans borrowed."

Thelma smiled at Yves. "I did not know that. Thank you for the education, my dear fellow."

Yves beamed.

"How were your protestations of disinterest in continuing with Hutchfield accepted by him?" Scorbion asked.

"Not particularly the way either of us would have desired. I must confess that it became quite loud. Neither he nor I conceal our emotions behind soft rhetoric well. However, I am far less acerbic than he."

Scorbion rubbed his cheek. "In that case, I must do my best to stay in your good graces so I avoid your wrath and do not have a similar experience as Mr. Hutchfield. That said, I do wonder how far your fury went, and if it might have culminated in more than just verbal assaults, and rather ended in physical conflict."

Thelma looked Scorbion directly in the eye. "The only harm I wish to cause another is through my tongue, not my limbs. I do assure you, Chief Inspector, our jousting ended on the field of words, not of battle."

"If that is indeed the extent of how you manifest displeasure, then please tell us what Mr. Hutchfield was like, beyond his temper. It would be helpful if you could give us some insight into the totality of his personality and manner."

Thelma considered Scorbion's question. "Victor could be very charming, but under his calm demeanor, he did possess a raging volcano and was truly subject to violent outbursts at times. Not physical ones that could cause bodily harm, but rather he had a rapier-like tongue and could shred a person with his strident words. He was *quite* talented, but of late he had not utilized his woodworking or design skills. He mostly fretted about the remainder of his life, as he told me his zest for those things that had pleased him in the past had dissipated. A significant portion of why I parted with him was his growing morose, stubborn, negative, and verbally abusive. He lost interest in discourse of any meaningful nature. He stopped reading and working, and the word 'joy' had escaped from his vocabulary and his being."

Scorbion replied, "I am most sorry to hear that. Poor chap. Please tell us about your meal with Victor Hutchfield last evening. Not what you consumed, but rather what you and he discussed."

Before Thelma could answer, the shop's door opened, and five scruffy men appeared in the doorway. One was almost exactly the same height as Yves, another was a giant of a man, and the rest were burly and of significant stature.

Scorbion stood and addressed the shorter man first. "You must be Percy Harvey, and you," he said to the larger man, "Reggie Watkins."

The men confirmed his assumptions, then each of the others identified themselves, and Harvey handed Scorbion a sheet of paper. "This is that poor Mr. Hutchfield's address, as you requested."

Thelma piped up. "You could have asked me. I certainly know where he lived."

Scorbion put his hand to his head and nodded. "Quite right. My oversight."

Thelma smilingly kidded Scorbion. "You make mistakes? That is *not* what Billy has said to me."

Calvin came to Scorbion's defense. "Pignon does *not* make mistakes, my dear. This is the first I have ever witnessed, and I have known him for over a score of years."

Billy added, "And I wouldn't call that a mistake as much as a lapse."

Thelma smiled at each of them, while Scorbion looked at the paper and motioned to Adley to come to him. "Please proceed to this address on Blackberry Lane and enter Hutchfield's home. Determine if there is anything within his premises that might relate to this affair. When you return, you may rejoin the proceedings here."

Adley took the paper and departed. Scorbion invited the five men to sit on either side of Thelma, and then introduced them to everyone before addressing Thelma again. "May you answer my previous question, and also one last query, before I move on to these gentlemen? Where did you go last evening after your dinner with Hutchfield, and what were your whereabouts this morning?"

Thelma responded without hesitation. "During the meal we spoke of maudlin things that had no significance, filling the time until we reached the central reason we dined together—Victor's desire to reunite. I made it perfectly clear that that was not going to happen. I believe that my statement, which I uttered with an air of cruel finality, had the effect I desired, and Victor, at last, realized that our relationship was unsalvageable and terminated. He raised his voice, as did I in response. He then described me with a few choice words that I shan't repeat here, and straightaway told me he wished to end the meal and depart. Having just finished our tripe and onions, that was acceptable to me.

"Victor paid the tab, and we walked together in silence to Blackberry Lane—it had been convenient that we lived less than a block from each other when we were in each other's company. He saw me to my door and left me standing there. I undressed, went directly to bed, and read a bit more of E. M. Forester's *A Room with a View* until I fell asleep with it upon my lap. This morning, after I awoke and bathed, I dressed, prepared my breakfast, and was consuming it when Billy's knock sounded upon my door."

Scorbion challenged, "So in actuality, you have no alibi for either late last evening or this morning before Billy arrived at your door."

Thelma grinned like the Cheshire Cat. "You are quite right. No alibi."

"Gentlemen," Scorbion said, turning to the circus men, "I will address you as Harvey, Watkins, Wilson, Pierce, and Farner. Is that acceptable?"

"Whatever suits you, sir," Watkins said. The others confirmed their agreement as well.

Scorbion rubbed his hands together. "Excellent. Mr. Watkins, let me commence with you. Where were you last evening and earlier this morning?"

Even sitting, Watkins towered over Harvey. "I did what I always do when we come to a new stand. Last night I helped put up the tent, checked the locks on the animal cages, fed Gargantua—she's our elephant, and she's very sweet—and I watched Walt Robbins, our newest laborer, shovel her shite. After he was done, we left to help set up the tightrope. Then he and I went to our tents. I fell asleep as soon as my head touched the pillow."

Thomas asked, "What did you do with the shovel?"

"We left it as we always do, leanin' against the shite barrel," Watkins answered quickly.

"And this morning—?" Scorbion inquired.

Watkins slouched down a bit. "I met up with Robbins to feed the animals. I'm trainin' him, so he goes where I go most of the time. After that, we went to set up the crane in the stilt-walk area. Once we were done, we hosed down Gargantua, and then we went into the tent to spread sawdust and hay on the ground. That's about when Hutchfield's body was discovered. Our lion tamer, John Parks, and our bearded lady, Sabrina, saw him lying in the shite pile as they went to the cages."

Billy said in a somewhat accusatory manner, "I understand that you don't much like Freddy Rumple."

Watkins became defensive. "Who told you that? The little pipsqueak is annoyin'—always has been—but he did what he said he was going to do, and it's helped the circus." Watkins stopped to think. "Yeah, I don't much like the runt, but he's married to the gaffer's daughter, and he's mostly why people come to see us these days. So I put up with him."

Barnabus asked, "Wh-What about Hutchfield? D-Did you know him?"

"Not much," Watkins responded. "He hung around when Rumple was settin' up and preparin' for that first walk, but I didn't have much contact with him. Me an' Percy helped him unload the stilts from his cart when he first brought 'em. He was demandin' and rude, and I didn't particularly like him. After that, I didn't see him hardly at all."

Scorbion asked, "We were told that you did not assist in any way when Freddy Rumple was doing his final preparations. Is that accurate?"

"It is, governor," Watkins replied. "Like I said, I don't fancy him very much and didn't think he deserved all the attention he was gettin'. I mean, they were makin' a big deal about him, and he hadn't even done nothin' yet. I really thought the little fool was gonna fail, and I didn't wanna have anythin' to do with that."

Calvin turned to Watkins. "You're a big man. Very large. You'd certainly have the strength to hit someone with a shovel and bash their head in. What do you say to that?"

Watkins was indignant. "I say that's shite. I didn't strike no one. I been with this circus for fifteen years and never had no problems."

"Watkins may be correct," Dr. Morgan confirmed. "In my medical opinion, Hutchfield was hit from behind, not from above. If Mr. Watkins had struck the blows, they would have come from above and behind. Which they didn't."

"I appreciate that, Doc. Like I said, I didn't hit no one."

Scorbion observed, "But, Dr. Morgan, is it not possible that if Watkins crouched down, he could have struck the blows at the proper angle?"

Morgan thought about Scorbion's question before replying. "Yes, it is possible. But not the most likely scenario, in my opinion."

Scorbion turned toward Harvey. "And now to you, sir."

Watkins, relieved that the questioning of him was concluded, sunk down further on his seat. "Yeah, now it's this other stilt-walking pipsqueak's turn. The only way him and Rumple can feel like they're men is to get on those stilts. Otherwise they're just runts."

Scorbion ignored Watkin's barbs. "Mr. Harvey, I am going to ask you many of the same questions I just asked Mr. Watkins. Where were you last night and this morning?"

Harvey leaned forward. "If you're asking if I have an alibi, I don't. I was practicing on my stilts last night and then went right off to sleep. This morning, I stayed in the tent until I heard the commotion outside. When I poked my head through the flap, one of the joeys told me someone had been killed. I went to look and saw that Hutchfield's head had been bashed in."

Thelma addressed Scorbion. "It's probably improper, but may I ask a question?"

Scorbion pondered her question for a moment and then replied, "It *is* highly unusual to have a possible suspect interrogate another, but I am curious as to what it is you would like to know. Please proceed with your query."

Thelma thanked Scorbion, and swiveled to face Harvey. "Weren't you jealous of Freddy when he accomplished his walk? I know if I were good at what I did and then taught someone who ended up doing it better, and they received all the kudos, I'd be upset."

Harvey hesitated. "I think anyone would be a little envious, but I was Freddy's teacher, and I'm glad he's done well and brought so much attention to stilt walking. I—"

Scorbion interrupted, "Then why did you not assist with his final preparations and practices?"

Harvey answered belligerently, "Who said I didn't?"

"Mr. Rumple told us that you and Mr. Watkins were not at any of his practice runs just prior to his first walk," Scorbion answered. "Was he mistaken?"

Harvey sat back. "I was hoping Freddy didn't notice. He's correct, I wasn't there."

"Why was that?" Calvin asked.

"I'd taught Freddy everything I knew," Harvey responded. "There was nothing I could add by then. He was way beyond me. I figured I'd just be hanging around and getting in the way."

Billy asked, "How well did *you* know Hutchfield?"

Before Harvey could answer, Scorbion added, "And if you knew him, how would you describe him? Not his appearance, but more his manner and personality."

Harvey responded, "I knew the bloke casually. Like Reggie said, I helped out when he brought the stilts and had one or two conversations with him. Not a lot of interaction." After pausing for a breath, Harvey continued: "He seemed like a decent enough chap. Mostly we had superficial conversations, although I do remember that when two of the stilt sections didn't fit together as he thought they should have, he got very frustrated and cursed at Teddy and Shelby, who were assisting him. I offered to help, but he told me to bugger off. I didn't offer any further aid after that."

Scorbion addressed both Watkins and Harvey. "Do either of you have any idea why Hutchfield was at the circus this morning?"

Watkins shrugged his shoulders. "I don't."

Harvey agreed. "Nor I."

The two seemed visibly relieved when Scorbion turned his attention to Jed Pierce. "You're the fellow who Hutchfield first had a row with when you were uncarting the stilts, were you not?"

"Yeah, dat was me," Pierce confirmed. "I wanted ta sock him in da mug. Awful bad. Da bum had no right tawkin' to me da way he did."

Yves turned to Barnabus. "What kind of an accent is that, *mon ami*? I couldn't understand anything he just said."

Barnabus shrugged, but Calvin answered. "While we probably expected these circus folk to be from the Continent, this bloke appears to be American. A few years ago, I met another fellow who spoke as Pierce does, and learned that they say 'da' for 'the' and 'dat' for 'that' in New York."

Thelma concurred. "I had contact with an American who had that dialect when I was in London, and Calvin is absolutely correct, it is a way of speaking that is peculiar to New York." She turned to Pierce. "Mr. Pierce, a question—"

Pierce cut her off. "A babe as gorgeous as you, honey, can ask whatever you want. You can call me Jed."

Undeterred, Thelma continued. "Mr. Pierce, may I assume that we are correct in that you hail from the New York area?"

"Da Bronx," Pierce responded, "and since I been sittin' here an' listenin' to all youse, I got to tell you, you all tawk funny. This whole friggin' country does."

Everyone in the room laughed, except Yves, who agreed. "*Oui. Je suis d'accord.*"

Pierce challenged Yves. "What'd you just say, froggie?"

Thelma whispered to Scorbion, "He is such a disagreeable and vulgar sort, is he not?"

Barnabus defended Yves. "You have n-no right calling him that. Only I m-may insult him."

Pierce turned to Barnabus. "Spit it out, you big lug. I ain't got all day."

Scorbion slammed his palm on the table. "Let us cease this taunting and these coarse, derisive insults. Mr. Pierce, we have been told that Hutchfield screamed and cursed at you, and then dismissed you from the work you were doing for him. Is that not accurate?"

Pierce neither denied nor confirmed. "Whatever you say. Da man was an arsehole. He shouldn'ta said any a' what he said to me. No siree."

Scorbion asked, this time more sternly, "Did Hutchfield scream at you, curse at you, and dismiss you, or did he not?"

"Yeah. He did. Da schmuck."

Calvin asked, "So you had disdain for him, and a reason to dislike him, and possibly to want injury to befall him?"

Pierce swiveled to look at Calvin. "Can you repeat dat in plain English?"

Exasperated, Calvin replied, "Did you want him dead?"

"Sure," Pierce confirmed, "wouldn't you? But I didn't whack da guy. I may be dumb, but I ain't stupid. And, I ain't no killer."

"We'll see about that," Scorbion said. "And may I ask what your whereabouts were this morning?"

"You mean where was I? I was all around the area-r. I went to da store for Hopkins for a couple a hours. Then I fixed da freakin' trapeze riggin'. All sorts a thin's."

"So then," Scorbion asked, "may I assume that part of the time you were alone and in other instances you were with others?"

"Yeah," Pierce confirmed. "Dat's right."

Billy turned to Thelma. "Does everyone from New York talk that way? He's the first I've ever actually met."

Thelma let out a small laugh. "Fortunately, no. Most are much more erudite and civil, but our Mr. Pierce is quite the persona, is he not?"

Scorbion spoke again. "Mr. Pierce, I will potentially return to you to determine the veracity of your statements, but for now I desire to question Mr. Farner and Mr. Winston."

Pierce leaned back. "Whatever you say, boss. I guess I ain't goin' nowheres right now."

Scorbion turned to Farner and Winston. "You were both berated by Hutchfield during the assembly of the stilts. Is that not a correct statement?"

Farner answered first. "Yes, sir, he was horrid to us."

"Ghastly insulting," Winston added.

Picking up on a question Scorbion had asked Pierce, Thomas asked, "Was he bad enough to kill him?"

Winston responded first. "Not on your life. He was a mean customer. A sour sort if I ever met one. But I've met others like him before and I know that the best way to deal with them is to say nothing and get out of their way as fast as you can. So that's what I did."

Thelma opened her purse, took out a hankie, and softly blew her nose. She closed the purse and asked, "And where were *you* this morning?"

Farner answered, "He was with me. We've been thick as thieves all day, from just when the sun came up to this very minute."

"Haven't been out of each other's sight," Winston confirmed.

Thelma observed, "Then your only alibis are each other. That is rather convenient."

Farner answered, "Convenient or not, it's the truth. And like Shelby said, the fellow was a nasty sort, but I will grant that he built some first-rate stilts. Best I've ever seen—"

Barnabus interrupted. "B-But you still might have wanted to k-kill him for how he treated you."

"And what reason would we have to do that?" Winston responded. "If I murdered every bloke that ever yelled or cursed at me, there'd be a trail of bodies longer than Mary Ann Cotton's."

Billy stood up and stretched. "We've sat on these chairs a lot recently. Calvin, might I implore you to get more comfortable ones if we are going to keep doing these interrogations?"

Calvin replied sarcastically, "I'll get them when I get a telephone."

"That would be grand as well." Billy turned to Scorbion. "It appears we have six possible suspects, all with limited motives, and only one, Watkins, with a solid alibi that can be confirmed. Are there others we should be questioning?"

Scorbion stood and stretched as well. "Calvin, I am in complete agreement with Billy about the telephone and these plain, wooden chairs. If you do purchase new, more comfortable ones, I will arrange to have my men transport them here. And Billy, we very well may be summoning others from the circus here, but—"

Before Scorbion could continue, Adley walked through the front door carrying a bunch of papers. "I expect you should look at these, Chief."

After examining the papers thoroughly, Scorbion asked Adley, "Did you take notice of the date on the bottom right corner of the reverse side of the second sheet?"

When Adley sheepishly reported that he had not, Scorbion told him, "it is written quite small, but it does fix them as being from two days past."

Scorbion handed the papers to Calvin to share with the rest of the men.

After they each got a look at the sheets, Thelma inquired, "Do we get to see them too?"

After Billy, Scorbion, and Adley sat down, Scorbion answered her. "Yes, especially you. When they come to you, would you confirm if they are in Victor's handwriting?"

Barnabus handed the papers to Harvey, who winced slightly as he looked at them. He passed them to Watkins, who said, "Looks like drawin's of stilts to me. Nothin' I've ever seen before."

Watkins then gave them to Thelma, who studied the writing and the drawings. "These do not look like Victor's at all. His penmanship is much finer than what's written on these papers. Plus, he always wrote in cursive, while these words are printed."

Thelma passed the papers to the other laborers, and Adley confirmed what she had said. "I searched Hutchfield's place extensively, and all the other correspondences and papers I found *were* written in script."

Scorbion asked, "Did you discover or learn anything else that might be of importance while you were there?"

"Unfortunately, no, I did not. His flat was rather sparse. These were the only items of consequence I found."

"Then let us attempt to determine their significance," Scorbion stated. "If Hutchfield had given up fabricating wood, why would he have someone else's drawings of a pair of stilts? Ones dated quite recently?"

"Sergeant," Scorbion said to Adley, "would you please return to the circus grounds and show these papers to the Rumples? Ask if they are theirs, or if they can shed any light on whose they might be or what they might signify."

Adley departed, and Thelma asked, "Might I use the loo?"

Calvin quickly replied, "You may, miss, but as we rarely have females in this establishment, allow me to examine it before you enter. I would like to tidy it up if the men have left it a total mess . . . as they do their stations."

Calvin returned a few minutes later. "I think you'll find it satisfactory now."

Thelma thanked him, went in, and closed the door.

While she was indisposed, everyone stood and stretched.

Watkins asked Scorbion, "Do you still need me, governor? I've work to do and I'm fallin' behind every minute I'm here."

"A fair question, sir," Scorbion responded. "Regrettably, I believe I do still require your attendance. Believe me, I will detain you no longer than necessary."

Harvey lit up a cigarette. Watkins walked to the window and looked out at the street. Pierce, Winston, and Farner went outside and loitered on the pavement in front of the shop. Thomas asked Dr. Morgan his thoughts about the case, and Calvin exhorted Yves and Barnabus to finish the straightening up of their stations.

Billy asked Scorbion, "Do you have any idea who killed Hutchfield?"

"I have an inkling. When Sergeant Adley returns, what he tells us will either strengthen my conjecture, or I will have to embark on a different thought journey."

"No matter the outcome," Billy commented, "I'll have another article to write."

Scorbion reminded Billy, "Do not forget: no likeness."

Billy shrugged. "Waters does what he wants. I don't hold any sway over him. You might do better than I, asking him yourself. I think he'd listen to you much more than he would me."

"That's a splendid idea!" Scorbion exclaimed, "I shall meet you at your building in the near future, you will introduce me to him, and I will plead my case to your Mr. Waters."

Billy then asked, "May I ask you something totally unassociated with that? Do you think Thelma could have murdered Hutchfield?"

Scorbion did not initially answer. He mused on the question, and then said, "That woman is all that you described, and perhaps more, although I did not fathom that possible. I have never met a female as quick, intelligent, educated, independent, and stunning as she, all in one gunnysack. I have hardly ever encountered a man like that, and never a woman. I am intrigued . . . and attracted to her. That definitely surprises me. And to answer your question, while I am not fully decided yet, if my suspicions are correct, she will have taken no part in this murder. However, nothing has been confirmed."

"I hope she's innocent," Billy said, just as Thelma emerged from the toilet.

"Have I missed anything?" she asked.

Scorbion replied kindly, "Nothing at all, Miss Smith. We were all taking some relaxation while you were indisposed."

Thelma put her hand on Scorbion's arm. "Please, call me Thelma."

Scorbion, in spite of wanting her to continue touching his shirt sleeve, replied, "Once this affair is over, and assuming that you are not complicit in it in any way, I will gladly call you that. However, while you remain a suspect, duty compels me to address you in a less familiar manner."

Thelma removed her hand. "I understand." Then she added playfully, "However, assuming I am not involved in any way, what may I call *you* at *that* time, Chief Inspector Scorbion?"

Scorbion became a bit flustered, never having been asked that question before. However, he quickly responded, "At that time, you may call me Pignon, as my dear friend Calvin does. Nothing would please me more than to hear that emanate from your lips. So let us both hope that today we prove your innocence by ascertaining another's guilt."

Scorbion asked everyone to return to the table, and, after all were seated, Scorbion asked the circus men, "Is there anyone else at the circus whom you believe we should question?"

Watkins was the first to answer. "Nah. Can't think of no one."

Harvey suggested, "What about Freddy? He knew Hutchfield really well. Emily, too. What about them?"

Everyone turned to Scorbion to hear his reply. "They are each other's alibis, and while what you are asking is possible, it is not probable. They have no motive for the act that was committed, and they were the deceased's friends. I will not rule them out, but I do not include them in the circle of the most likely suspects."

Thelma then surprised everyone by saying, "And that circle is us. The six of us on this side of the table. Is that not correct?"

Scorbion didn't hesitate to reply. "That is correct. However, if what I conjecture occurred, then only one of you is the murderer."

Thelma smiled. "If you are right, then the remainder of us are sitting among, or next to, a murderer." Then she added, "How thrilling."

Scorbion smiled. "Do not fear, Miss Smith. If you are not the murderess, then these fine gentlemen"—Scorbion pointed to his associates—"will protect you. As will I. I assure you, no harm will come to you in that event."

Thelma laughed. "Well, that is reassuring."

When Pierce, Winston, and Farner could not suggest anyone else at the circus who might have had a reason to murder Hutchfield, Scorbion said, "We will hold off further questioning until Sergeant Adley returns with the answer regarding the papers and the drawings. Please return to what you were doing before Miss Smith joined us just now."

CHAPTER TWENTY-FIVE

Fifteen minutes later, Adley walked through the door, followed by Freddy, Emily, and Hopkins. When they entered, Pierce, Farner, and Winston did as well, and everyone stood in the middle of the shop.

Freddy handed Scorbion the papers, but Emily spoke first. "When we saw these, we knew they were not from Victor's hand. He would never print. His handwriting was precise, like an architect's, but the words on these sheets are somewhat haphazard."

Scorbion was intrigued. "Do you know whose printing that is?"

"We do not," Hopkins reported.

"However," Scorbion postulated, "the handwriting may not be the only thing we can learn from these papers. They deal with a design for the building of a pair of stilts. And . . ." He looked through the papers until he found what he had been looking for, ". . . these stilts would be at least two feet higher than the stilts on which Mr. Rumple regularly performs."

Thelma interrupted. "And the only three people who would have an interest in stilts are in this room right now."

"Freddy and Emily Rumple, and Percy Harvey," Billy added.

"Very good," Scorbion complimented them. "You are both correct. Only the Rumples and Mr. Harvey would have a need for a higher pair of stilts. Unless there is another individual at the circus who is furtively practicing the art of stilt-walking."

"There is no such person that I am aware of," Hopkins responded.

Freddy added, "And I have not lent my stilts to anyone."

"For now, let us eliminate that as a path of inquiry to trod down," Scorbion said. "Returning to Mr. or Mrs. Rumple, if it were they who were commissioning even more impressive stilts, why would they keep that a secret? That would be another feat for the newspapers." He turned to Hopkins. "Did either of them tell you about constructing new stilts?"

Hopkins immediately replied, "No. Not at all."

"Therefore," Scorbion went on, "we can most probably deduce that the person who drew those drawings and made those specifications was you, Percy Harvey."

"I'm not saying I did—but if I did, so what?" Harvey asked.

Scorbion answered his question. "I believe that you were attempting to enlist Victor Hutchfield to build a pair of stilts for you that would exceed Mr. Rumple's in size."

Harvey shrugged his shoulders. "Again, so what if I was? Even if I asked the fellow to fabricate some stilts for me, it doesn't mean I killed him. What good would he be to me if he was dead?"

Scorbion answered, "It is my conjecture that you have been jealous of Mr. Rumple. You were the teacher, but he became the main attraction of the circus. I postulate that you didn't assist him because you wanted him to fail. If he did, you would be more valuable to the circus and it would be you, not Mr. Rumple, who would be considered the premier performer of your art."

For the third time, Harvey said, "And even if that is true, so what?"

Scorbion went on, nonplussed. "I further hold that you arranged to meet Hutchfield when the circus arrived at the fairgrounds yesterday morning, and you handed him these drawings and asked him if he would construct the stilts for you, as he did the ones that Mr. Rumple employs."

Scorbion paused to gather his final thoughts. "And you arranged then to meet again early this morning to discuss the stilts, after Hutchfield had a day to absorb the drawings. I can only surmise that today's encounter did not go as you had hoped and that he told you he would not make them."

Thelma butted in. "And I know why you think that. I told you that Victor had stopped making anything at all, and he didn't want to go back to constructing or designing any items. He wanted something new in his life."

"Quite right," Scorbion agreed. "Therefore, I believe that when you and Victor Hutchfield met today, Mr. Harvey, and he told you he wasn't going to help you, it angered you. You could not understand why he would do that for Freddy Rumple but not for Percy Harvey. And then, I suggest, he said he was going to tell Hopkins and the Rumples about your secret plan for the larger stilts and to upstage Mr. Rumple. You could not have that happen, so in your rage, as he turned to leave, you picked up the shovel and struck him. Three times."

The room was quiet. No one stirred until Harvey said, "That's rubbish. You can't prove any of it. Victor *was* going to build the stilts for me, and I *was* going to leave to join another circus when he did— one that would let me compete against Freddy, not just be in his shadow. Victor told me he needed a challenge, and the stilts were it."

Watkins turned to Harvey. "I'm really sorry, small-fry. I've known you a long time, and we never had no problems with each other, but I don't think you're tellin' the truth. I couldn't see nothin' 'cause I was helpin' with the sawdust and hay inside the big top, but I heard voices outside. One feller was yellin' pretty loud: 'You're not gonna tell me what I'm gonna do. I'm *not* making anythin' for you. Not now. Not ever. Now frigg off, pissant.' I remember them words like I just heard 'em. Robbins heard 'em, too."

As Watkins's words sunk in, Scorbion looked at Harvey. "I have no doubt that when we search your trailer, we will find other papers written in your hand. And they will match these drawings. I put forward to you, Percy Harvey, that between those similarities and Mr. Watkins's testimony, you will be convicted easily. You had means, motive, and opportunity."

Harvey broke down. "Hutchfield told me I was at best a mediocre stilt walker, and my greatest achievement would always be teaching Freddy. He refused to make them for me. I pleaded that I needed the help and that I wanted to be more than just an aging clown—an old stilt-walking joey. But he just cursed and said that he wouldn't do anything for me. He told me to frigg off and called me a pissant. When he turned to walk away, I picked up the shovel, stood up on my toes, and hit him with it. I hit him hard. A few times. He deserved it."

The room went silent again.

Scorbion was the first to break the silence. "Sergeant Adley, please escort Mr. Harvey to a cell at our station. And after you have him fully ensconced there, join us at the circus this evening, with your wife. The passes are compliments of Mr. Hopkins."

Adley smiled, nodded his head in acknowledgment, cuffed Harvey, and started to escort him out of the shop. Before they reached the door, Harvey stopped and turned to face the circus folks. "Mr. Hopkins, I do appreciate everything you have done for me, and I'm sorry that I have repaid your kindness in the manner in which I have. But I did not want to spend the rest of my life as a nobody. I'm been tired of being overlooked and insignificant."

Then he addressed Freddy, "You learned well. Too well, I'm afraid."

As he and Adley started out the door, Harvey waved back at everyone. "Cheerio, all."

Hopkins muttered, "A bloody shame. That's what this entire situation is. A bloody shame."

Dr. Morgan approached Scorbion with his hand outstretched. "Congratulations, Chief Inspector. I am altogether impressed—and gratified that I was able to be of some assistance."

Scorbion clasped Morgan's hand. "Your participation was invaluable, Doctor. Do you have a means of transportation home?"

"If there is a telephone nearby, I can call my man to fetch me with my motorcar," Morgan replied.

"Sadly, there is no telephone within this shop," Scorbion reported. He turned to Calvin. "Mr. Brown, Dr. Morgan has a telephone at his home and inquired whether there might be one here that he might use to call there. I told him you did not possess one. But you are considering obtaining one, are you not?"

Knowing well the trap that Scorbion had laid for him, Calvin graciously agreed. "Yes. I will apply for one next week."

Barnabus, Yves, Thomas, and Billy cheered.

Morgan told Scorbion, "It is of no concern. A nice stroll will be good for my constitution. I will look forward to seeing you at the circus tonight, and I would rather enjoy introducing you to my wife, Isabelle. And speaking of her, we are having a dinner at our home this Sunday. There will be an interesting group in attendance, and I would be honored if you would join us. Say at seven?"

Scorbion thanked Morgan and accepted the invitation. Then Morgan left.

Hopkins, accompanied by Emily and Freddy, approached Scorbion. "The tickets will be waiting at the box office for your men and their guests. Tonight's performance would not have been possible had you not found out Percy Harvey. Thank you. Thank you very much."

Watkins joined the group, and when he did, Scorbion told him how important his testimony had been.

Watkins responded, "It weren't nothin', governor."

As the circus people left to prepare for the night's performance, Pierce called to Thelma. "If ya wanna get tuhgether after da show, I'll be in my tent by da wagons."

Thelma politely declined. "Thank you, but I have other plans for the evening, Mr. Pierce,"

Billy looked at her inquisitively. "You do?"

"I hope to," Thelma responded as she walked to Scorbion. He turned from the door just as she reached him and put her hand on his arm. "What is it that I may call you now? Pignon?"

They both laughed, and then he said, in a more serious tone, "You may call me anything you wish when we are in private together. You may place your hand upon me in any manner you choose, under those same circumstances. And while I wish to make your time with me most enjoyable for you, it is important that my personage, and the dignity and integrity of my position, be maintained when I am among others in public. I am Chief Police Inspector Scorbion to them, though I may be Pignon to you. I can never be seen as a fool or a lackey, under any circumstances. I am not built for levity, but I will do my utmost to bring pleasure to you when we are together. I would understand if that does not appeal to you, but my position demands it, or I cannot be effective."

Thelma didn't hesitate before responding. "Pignon, I would have you no other way. You are who you are, and you are your one-of-a-kind black-and-white shoes, your custom-made suits of the finest fabrics and beautiful colors, your unique mind and mental skills, your standing . . . and the warmth that lies beneath your exterior—warmth that I believe few are allowed to experience. *That* is who you are, and that is who I want you to remain. But does that mean I cannot place my hand on your arm in public?"

Scorbion beamed. "You may, Miss Smith. Any time at your leisure."

Scorbion took his jacket off the coatrack and put it on. Thelma lightly tugged on the hem to straighten it, and Scorbion was delighted when she did. He took Thelma's hat from the rack, handed it to her, and she placed it on her head.

Thinking that Scorbion was leaving, Billy ran over. "I want to make sure we meet up at the circus tonight, Inspector." Then he addressed Thelma. "May I escort you there from your home? Say, when the clock strikes six?"

Thelma looked at Scorbion. "That depends on what the chief inspector is thinking."

"I have some papers I must attend to at the station, and then I will make my way to my home and change into something more fitting for a circus," Scorbion told them.

Thelma teased him. "You have other clothes besides these gorgeous suits? Has anyone ever seen you in anything else, or will this evening be a first of its kind?"

"I will keep you guessing," Scorbion retorted, with a laugh in his voice. "You will see that for yourself tonight. Let me join up with you and Billy at the box office at a quarter past six. Then we may spend the remainder of the time in each other's company."

"All of us?" Billy asked lightheartedly.

Thelma was quick to respond. "We'll see how the evening develops, but to start, yes, it certainly does include you. However, the ending may occur without your participation. Now, I'm off to purchase a new ensemble for tonight's festivities. I will see you at six, Billy. And you shortly after that, Chief Inspector."

CHAPTER TWENTY-SIX

Thelma, Scorbion, and Billy had a marvelous time sitting together in the stands at the circus, especially enjoying the lion tamer, the trapezists, the tightrope walker, the horseback riders, and Freddy's antics on the stilts.

During the performance, Thelma leaned over to Scorbion and said, "There must have been an incident in my childhood that caused me to be afraid of clowns. I don't find them comical at all, but rather frightening."

Scorbion gently put his hand over hers. "Fear not, dear damsel. I will protect you from them should any happen to come closer than they presently are in the middle of the ring."

Overhearing the exchange, Billy said, "My brother's foot was stepped on by a clown the one time my parents took us to a circus when we were both small. He screamed and screamed, and my mum had to take him outside so he didn't ruin the show for everyone else. Ever since, he's been terrified of clowns as well."

Scorbion turned to Billy. "I was not aware that you had any siblings."

"He's the only one," Billy responded. "He's two years younger than I am. He works as a stable boy and is still living at home with Mum and Dad in Sheffield, where we were raised."

Thelma leaned across Scorbion to Billy. "I hope that we'll have the opportunity to meet him."

"I *am* planning to have him visit once I'm a bit more established here. Mum and Dad as well. You'll both meet the three of them when they're here."

Billy remained with Thelma and Scorbion through the last act and Hopkins's thanking everyone for attending, after which Scorbion walked Thelma home. As they were strolling to Blackberry Lane, they made arrangements to dine together twice over the course of the following five evenings.

During those meals they spent the majority of their time sharing more about their lives and likes and dislikes, truly relishing one another's company. At the end of the first supper, Scorbion asked Thelma if she wished to accompany him to the Morgans' dinner party, but Thelma regretfully declined, advising him that she had a prior commitment to attend a suffragette meeting, that she said she, unfortunately, could not ignore.

At the conclusion of their second dinner, after Scorbion had escorted Thelma to her home and then returned to his own abode, he was surprised to find that evening's edition of the *Gazette* on his doormat. When he bent down to pick it up, he was piqued by the headline: "Haxford's New Chief Inspector Mishandles His First Case."

Hurrying inside, he sat down on his couch and read the full story, written by Faustin Hardcastle, the paper's owner and editor, which fully supported Bentine's story and accused Scorbion of incompetence, favoritism, and engaging in pure guesswork.

Scorbion resolved to meet with Hardcastle, to learn why he was besmirching him and what he hoped to gain by promulgating untrue allegations and supporting Bentine's myth.

The following morning he strode into the *Gazette*'s building to meet with Hardcastle, who ushered him into his office.

As soon as Scorbion sat in the guest chair at Hardcastle's desk he said, "I will come to the point of my visit immediately. I am here to learn why you have accused me in the manner in which you have, and why it is that you believe Bentine's story when it is a pure fabrication."

Hardcastle, a rotund and grizzled man who appeared much older than his fifty years, locked his thumbs around his suspenders. "You misunderstand my motives if you think I believe his story. You sold your soul to Waters at the *Morning News* without even the courtesy to invite my paper to the festivities. I am in a war with Waters for the readership of Haxford's residents, and it will now serve my purposes to oppose whatever you do and discredit anything that so-called reporter of his writes. I do not care what the truth may be. I only care to sell newspapers. It is of no concern to me how that affects you."

Scorbion did not expect those to be the reasons behind Hardcastle's support of Bentine's tale. "I am distressed that you are willing to throw veracity and truthfulness under the hooves of horses and allege facts to be beliefs. You are doing a grave disservice to Haxford's citizenry by undermining their trust in me and my men, all of which can serve no good purpose."

"As I said," Hardcastle repeated, "it will sell newspapers. I believe there is nothing further for us to say to each other. You cast your line in with Waters . . ." He paused to consider the humor in his analogy. ". . . And you will suffer the consequences of that. I bid you a good day, sir, I have a paper to run."

Scorbion stood, but before starting toward the door, he admonished Hardcastle. "Your efforts to subvert the truth, and your attempts to emulate the American newspapers' yellow journalism, will not end well for you. Mark my words." Then he turned and left.

That afternoon Thelma closed her shop early and called upon Scorbion at the station. "I am here to learn how you have been affected by the story in the *Gazette* and to lend you support and comfort, should you desire it."

Scorbion told her the details of his meeting with Hardcastle and thanked Thelma for her concern. "The truth will always triumph, and I will not allow an unscrupulous, unprincipled mercenary to influence what I do in any way. Let Hardcastle write what he writes. It will not deter me from doing what I do, and in the manner that I do it."

Thelma smiled and glanced at Adley to make sure he wasn't looking. When she saw that he was engrossed in paperwork at his desk, she hugged Scorbion and gave him a peck on the cheek. "And that is exactly why I like you so very much and find you so truly appealing."

CHAPTER TWENTY-SEVEN

The following Sunday, even without Thelma by his side, Scorbion *did* enjoy a wonderful evening at the stately home of Isabelle and Dr. Franklin Morgan, engaging in interesting conversations with pleasant fellow guests, and dining on sumptuous food. He remained well past the time when the other attendees had departed, slowly savoring a fine brandy with Franklin Morgan, who was describing new advances in medicine that fascinated Scorbion.

Morgan's narrative was interrupted when the clock on the wall of the study they were seated in chimed eleven times. "I am afraid I must take my leave, despite the engrossing discourse we have been having, Franklin," Scorbion reported. "I must be at the station early in the morning and it is well past the hour that I regularly take my sleep. If you will excuse me, I will be off. I hope that we may do this again not too distantly in the future."

Franklin nodded. "I do have one last thing I would be remiss in not asking you before you depart. Have you allowed the *Gazette*'s horridly misguided story to affect you? I sincerely hope that you have dismissed that hogwash without a second thought."

Scorbion appreciated the support. "Prior to my arrival in Haxford, Inspector Benson told me of Hardcastle's ambitions and style of journalism and alerted me to be wary of him. During this past week, I did meet with Hardcastle, and he made it quite clear to me that he is intent on gaining circulation at my expense. And in that regard, unfortunately, he has lived up to all that Benson forewarned me about. That said, I shall be fine, and I thank you for your words of caring."

Scorbion awoke the next morning with a minor headache and arrived at the station house forty-five minutes later than his usual hour. When he appeared, Franklin Morgan was pacing the floor and blurted out, "I did not expect that our paths would cross again this soon, Inspector, but Isabelle and I need your assistance. A crime was committed at our home sometime after you departed last evening, and we would appreciate your personal attention to the matter."

When he related that a prized old American tomahawk that had been in their family for years had been stolen, Scorbion responded, "I saw it last night above your mantel and Isabelle told me the wonderful story about its origins. I will most certainly look into its disappearance."

Pleased with Scorbion's willingness to investigate the matter, Morgan left the station with a lighter gait than the one with which he had entered.

Sergeant Adley rose from behind his desk and approached Scorbion. "George Barlan, our local butcher, whom I do not believe you have met, reported to me earlier this morning that his prize hog was stolen last night. It was to be his donation to the Town Feast." He described to Scorbion the details that Barlan had related about the theft.

After jotting down notes about the incident and quickly sorting through a few papers that required his attention, Scorbion walked to the barbershop to seek the aid of the men there in the solving of the crimes Morgan and Barlan had reported.

On his way, he stopped in front of Toban's Tavern and exchanged words with Harry, the town drunkard, who related to Scorbion an incident that he had seen the prior night, just as the church bell sounded the clanging of midnight. Scorbion thanked him, handed him a few pence, and continued to the barbershop.

As he entered the shop, two customers were paying Calvin and Yves. When they passed they acknowledged Scorbion and left. Once they were gone, he closed the door, and announced to Calvin, Thomas, Barnabus, and Yves, "I am here not for a haircut or a polish, but rather to enlist your aid once again in the solving of a mystery. In fact, two mysteries. To start, I will relate to you a story that will intrigue you all."

Scorbion looked around the shop. "I was rather pleased with Billy's insights and the account he scribed for the *Morning News* regarding the Bentine case. I would prefer if he were here to be a part of these proceedings as well."

At that very instant, the front door flew open, and Billy strode into the barbershop. "Someone told me they saw you heading this way, Inspector, and I didn't want to miss anything."

Scorbion replied, "As I was just telling the others, I was hoping you would be in attendance. Now, let me describe to you all a crime that I have just been advised of, and that we will look into."

Calvin walked over to Scorbion. "Before you begin, do you wish to talk about the story in the *Gazette*?"

Scorbion responded, "Pay no attention to it and give it no credence. Billy is scribing what is accurate and valid, and no matter what the *Gazette* reports, it will not alter the truth. I have already spent too many of my breaths on the matter, so let us move on to the reason that I am here today."

Calvin responded, "Hardcastle has not been welcome in this shop since the time that he attacked Benson with similar untruths, so I am fine never discussing him or anything he does ever again."

Scorbion hung his light-green suit jacket—which contained a perfectly folded four-peak, dark-green handkerchief in the left breast pocket—on the coatrack while Thomas brought over a high stool which he placed in front of Calvin's barber's chair. Scorbion seated himself on the stool while Brown sat on his barber's chair and swiveled it so that he was facing Scorbion. Yves and Barnabus went to the shop's storeroom and brought out four chairs, which they positioned on each side of Brown's chair.

Billy took out his pad, a pen, and a pencil and once everyone was seated, they all fell silent, waiting to hear the details of the crime. However, Scorbion instead began by telling them the story of Sky Bear.

CHAPTER TWENTY-EIGHT

He walked down the pioneer town's dusty two-block-long main street, lined on both sides with false-front buildings. His arms were draped over his two young daughters' shoulders, hugging them close to each side of his body. The rope tied around his bare abdomen strained from the weight of the litter he was pulling which carried the frail body of his sickly wife.

They walked slowly and deliberately.

The sharp edges of stones that protruded from the hard clay of the street pricked the soles of the girls' feet and caused them to wince with every step they took. Calluses that had built up over years of walking barefoot prevented the jagged edges from piercing their father's feet, but he still grimaced in discomfort with every stride.

As the three figures, clad in ragged cloth and leather, and the conveyance that trailed closely behind them made their way along the town's main artery, women pulled their children off the street and into the nearest stores. Men quickened their pace to reach their destinations as rapidly as they could. Shopkeepers checked the loads in their shotguns. Within minutes of their unwelcome arrival, the bustling street had become deserted.

When they reached the white wooden house surrounded by a picket fence that sat just past the second block, he unlatched the gate and began walking toward the front door, dragging the litter. His girls followed closely behind him.

Before they advanced three steps, the door flew open. A woman rushed out of the house toward them. They stopped, not knowing what to expect, the younger of the girls cowering at her father's side.

"You are not welcome in this town."

The man nodded in comprehension.

"But you are welcome here. My husband will be right out. He will assist you." She pointed to the litter. "Is that your wife?"

The man bobbed his head, "Yes."

"I hope we can help her."

The indigenous man, who was mostly unfamiliar with the language of the settlers, reached his arm across his chest and tapped it twice as his way of indicating that he was thankful for not being shunned. He haltingly said, "Thank you."

"Don't thank us yet. I do not know if my husband will be able to heal your wife. But he will try. We are all God's creatures. That is the only thing that matters. Those people . . ." The woman pointed down the empty street. "They hear that on Sundays, and then they forget it."

Her husband, the town's doctor, emerged from the house and went straight to the litter. He quickly assessed the condition of the woman as well as he could without removing the blanket that covered her. "Let's get her into the house. I need to examine her more closely. Do you speak my language?"

The man gestured by holding his thumb and forefinger apart a short distance. "Little."

The doctor answered, "I wish I spoke yours, but I speak none, so you are doing better than I. What is your name?"

"In your words, Sky Bear."

"And her?"

"My wife, Yellow Flower."

Sky Bear loosened the rope. When it fell to the ground deep red welts that were carved into his stomach bled.

"I'm Dr. Adams. We will take care of you after we help her. Take her head. I will hold her feet." The doctor indicated with his hands what he wanted Sky Bear to do.

As they carried Yellow Flower into the house, the doctor's wife turned to the young girls. The smaller one was trembling in fear while the larger girl's body was tensed, her fists were clenched, and her face was contorted into a look of fierce defiance. In a soothing voice, knowing that both girls would understand her tone but not her language, the doctor's wife said, "We will try to make your mother well. Don't be afraid. Come in and I will get you some warm tea and sweets."

Only after their father, calling to them over his shoulder as he passed through the doorway, told them to obey Dr. Adams's wife did the girls follow her into the house.

"Come with me to the kitchen. My husband and your father have taken your mother to the room right next to it, the doctor's place. He will find out what is wrong with her and do everything he can to make her all better."

The girls, who didn't understand her words, huddled together, the smaller one's apprehensive eyes scanning the still-empty street for any trouble that might arise. Only after the front door closed behind them, sealing off the house and creating a sanctuary from the rest of the world, did she let down her guard.

The doctor's wife smiled. "That's better. I'm Eve." Seeing that they did not understand her, Eve poked her chest with her finger. "Eve." Then she pointed to the room in which Sky Bear and her husband had taken Yellow Flower. "Dr. James." She turned back to the girls. "What are your names? What are you called?"

Sky Bear, overhearing the conversation through the thin walls of the house, translated Eve's words to them from the other room.

The older girl said, "Ajei."

That gave her younger sister the courage to speak, but still, she only whispered, "Dibe."

"Those are such pretty names. How old are you?"

Sky Bear answered, "Eight. Six."

Continuing to speak in a calming tone, Eve held her hand up to her mouth in a gesture of eating food while saying, "How about we have some tea and honey and warm cookies I made just this morning?"

Eve tried to take their hands, but the girls resisted until their father told them that they should go with her and that she wouldn't hurt them. Ajei unclenched her fists, and Eve led both girls to the kitchen.

For over an hour, while Dr. Adams was attending to Yellow Flower, Eve tried as best she could to keep two young girls occupied and calm, in spite of the language barrier between them. Finally, Sky Bear came into the room, hugged them, and told them that the doctor had saved Yellow Flower. And she would be going home with them to heal.

When Dibe ran her fingers across the bandage on Sky Bear's midriff, feeling the material, he told his daughters in their language that the doctor helped fix his wounds as well as their mother's.

Dr. Adams entered the kitchen.

Sky Bear walked up to him, again patted his fist on his chest, and nodded. He said in his best broken English, "You good people. Save Yellow Flower. Elders could not. Your medicine strong."

Then Sky Bear said in his own language, "I am in your debt for as long as I walk upon this world. Whatever you request, I will do."

Dr. Adams held his hands outstretched, palms up, and shook his head from side to side, indicating that he did not know the meaning of Sky Bear's words. "I'm sorry, I do not know what you said."

Sky Bear understood the doctor's gesture and tried to find words that he would understand. The best he was able to utter was, "What want for save Yellow Flower?"

The doctor responded, "I suppose asking you to live in peace with the farmers and ranchers here would not be possible?" But he immediately realized that Sky Bear did not know what those words meant, so he spoke one of the few words he knew in their language, "K'é . . . peace." He pointed to Sky Bear, "You," then pointed toward the town, "and us. No more fighting." He pounded his fist into his open hand and shook his head while saying the last word.

Sky Bear got his meaning. "K'é. That what want? So it is."

"It is as easy as that?"

Sky Bear responded in his own language, "Yes. I give you my solemn word. I will live by it through my eternities," before saying "Yes" in English.

He then took his tomahawk from where it was hanging by the side of his leg and handed it to the doctor. "No fighting."

Adams took the hatchet, and once he had a firm grip on it, he turned it over to see both sides. He was fascinated by the implement, as he had never before held an artifact like it.

"What if you are attacked by our townspeople?"

"We fight back. *Not* attack, but defend. Not aim first bow."

"Fair enough. May I tell the townspeople this?"

"I told you and Creator. You tell others."

Early the next morning, Adams summoned a town meeting.

Every member of the town's population jammed into the church. There was a discernible air of excitement and anxiety and anger running through the mass of people.

Preparing to speak from the pulpit, James and Eve were trembling in anticipation as well. They knew how significant the news was that they were about to bring to the townspeople. It meant ongoing peace between the tribe and the townsfolk.

As they reached the pulpit one man started booing from the pews. Then a second, then a third, then a chorus.

James and Eve were stunned.

"Indian lover!"

"Traitor!"

"I would rather die than be treated by you!"

"Me too!"

"And me!"

"Get out of town!"

James waved his arms a number of times in an attempt to calm and quiet the crowd. He was certain that once the townspeople knew of the truce they would feel differently.

The screaming lowered to a soft murmur, and then to silence.

"My friends," he began, "I assure you, you have it wrong! Sky Bear gave me his word that he and his tribe will not harm anyone from this town. Ever. The fighting between us is over."

Eve added, "Yes, it *is* ended. The loss of our husbands and children and Sky Bear's people will not happen any longer."

Voices from the townsfolk rang out in opposition.

"I don't trust him!"

"Me either. The word of a bow bender means nothing."

Trying to be heard above the rising volume of dissent and the chorus of "get out of town," Adams yelled back as loudly as he possibly could. "Believe me! Please. We can all live in peace. Together."

But he could not be heard by anyone but Eve.

That evening, Dr. James Adams and his wife Eve decided that the West was too biased and uncivilized for them. They packed their possessions into their covered wagon, with Sky Bear's tomahawk safely nestled between two petticoats in the middle of the largest trunk. The next morning, they started out toward Sky Bear's encampment to tell him what had happened at the meeting, but no trail led to it that was accessible for the wagon, so they reluctantly turned around and headed east.

Two days later, believing that the truce was in place, and not knowing that the doctor had departed, two families from the tribe were peacefully walking to a spring to collect water for their camp. As they crossed a cattleman's range that was just outside of the town, three ranchers—Samuel Lewiston, John Borlan, and Will Farland—came upon them. They shot and killed the two men, their wives, and their five children. The ranchers dragged the bodies behind their horses and dumped them outside the tribe's encampment.

And with that act, the opportunity for peace, and the chance for the pioneers and the tribespeople to live in harmony, ended as quickly as it had begun.

CHAPTER TWENTY-NINE

"That was a remarkable narrative, Chief Inspector," Yves said, "but what does it have to do with a new case? It appears to have taken place many years in the past."

"Decades ago, if you ask me," Calvin agreed.

"You are both correct," Scorbion confirmed. "The time period involved was well beyond a half-century earlier than today. You have made sound deductions from the information I presented in the tale."

Billy asked, "How'd you learn of this tragedy, Inspector? It isn't an incident one would normally hear about here from so long ago in America."

"I will explain . . ." Scorbion began.

Thomas and Barnabus inched closer to not miss a word of his response.

"Upon reaching the shores of the Atlantic Ocean, the good doctor and his wife made their way to the city of Baltimore, in the state called Maryland. Adams established his practice there and thrived in it for a good number of years until the day that his wealthiest patient, Robert Masterford, a high-ranking official in their federal government, advised the doctor that he and his family were being transferred to London. Masterford asked Adams to accompany him as his private physician, stating that he did not have the same confidence in the healers in England that he had in Adams."

"Did he go?"

"Yes, Billy. Dr. Adams, his wife Eve, and the three children they had sired after returning from the American West, accompanied the Masterfords and lived the remainder of their lives in London."

"I still d-don't see how that relates to a c-case here."

"Have patience, Barnabus. Let the tale unfold and it will become clear to you. Almost immediately, in fact," Scorbion advised.

"S-Sorry, Chief Inspector."

Scorbion continued. "While the Adams family remained in London for the balance of their lives, their descendants did not. One of their granddaughters and her physician husband traveled a great deal. They journeyed through many countries and counties before eventually settling, not in London or Paris, but rather in a charming hamlet that was in need of a doctor. Here. In this municipality of Haxford. The man you all know as Dr. Franklin Morgan is in actuality the grandson-in-law of Dr. James Adams and his wife Eve. Isabelle Morgan is their granddaughter."

That surprised Calvin. "Well, I'll be flabbergasted . . ."

"How did you b-become aware of that, Chief Inspector?"

"Isabelle Morgan related the entire account during a most sumptuous feast that I partook in at their marvelous home last evening. Fortunately, my mind was able to retain every word of the narrative— one that has been recounted within her family from each generation to the next. I am most surprised that to date it has not been committed to paper for posterity."

Billy enthusiastically interrupted. "I can write it. I'll get it into the *Morning News*. After Waters printed my story detailing your case with the Bastard Son he has asked me for more like it. I am in the process of writing the circus affair, and this could be another. Is there a local crime that goes with the story?"

"There most assuredly is," Scorbion replied. "In fact, there are *two* crimes that may be associated with the tale. However, before I reveal them to you, I must add one additional detail to my narrative."

Calvin urged, "Please do, Pignon."

"At the dinner table, during the interval between the soup course and the main course, Isabelle Morgan asked me to accompany her to their library. Once we were in that lavishly decorated, volume-filled room, she directed my attention to an artifact hanging on the wall above the hearth. I approached the object, and quite quickly it became obvious to me that it was the hatchet that Sky Bear gave to Dr. James Adams. Lady Morgan confirmed this to me."

Billy asked inquisitively, "What'd it look like, Inspector? Were you able to hold it?"

"In spite of the hatchet's being quite old, it was in remarkable condition. The multicolored feathers and strap were pristine, yet when I inquired about them, Lady Morgan assured me they were original to the implement. And yes, I was able to hold it and feel its weight and balance. It was a remarkably well-made weapon."

"Was it still sharp or had it dulled over the decades?" Calvin asked.

"It was quite razor-edged, my dear Calvin. I believe that if you were to shave a client using it, you would encounter no complaint."

Billy was anxious to hear more about the crimes the hatchet was tied to. "What was the crime . . . or crimes . . . that were committed? Was the hatchet involved in both of them?"

"It definitely was a part of at least one, and most probably both incidents," Scorbion confirmed. "Last evening, after I dined at the Morgans', the hatchet was stolen. The doctor personally contacted me today. He advised me of its disappearance, and asked me to look into the matter, to see if I might recover the artifact."

"What was the second crime?" Thomas asked.

CHAPTER THIRTY

One of the two people involved in stealing the artifact slipped into the Morgans' library, took the hatchet from its resting place above the fireplace, and secreted it beneath their clothes. The second person waited outside the house until their confederate emerged.

"Do you have it?"

"I do."

Together they harnessed the horse to the cart, where a large sailcloth was stored in the rear. Then they quietly walked the horse and cart away from the house, until they were far enough away that the sound of galloping hooves would not awake anyone inside.

They donned the hooded robes that one of them had secured from a mercantile shop distant enough away so that news of what they were about to do would not be heard about.

The two sped through town on their way to George Barlan's farm, one holding the reins and the other gripping the hatchet next to their leg under their robe.

They knew that at this late hour, in spite of a full moon, Barlan would be sound asleep, and most likely unwakable from the grog that he regularly consumed prior to dozing off, and they could proceed with their plan without any concern of his finding them on his property.

When they reached Barlan's farm, they alit from the cart, opened the barn door, and spread the sailcloth on the floor. One of them fetched Barlan's prize hog from the pigpen and guided it to the barn. Even with two of them, they had a hard time positioning the hog in the middle of the sailcloth due to its massive size and friendly nature, but finally, when it was in place, one of them took the hatchet and slit its throat.

They proceeded to carve the hog into small pieces, and when that task was completed, they wrapped it in the sailcloth so that the blood would not spill onto the barn floor.

The third person arrived, as scheduled, took the hatchet from them, and together they lifted the carcass-laden sailcloth into the third person's cart.

The third person drove off.

Then the two posted a note upon Barlan's barn door. After that, they rode in the cart back to the Morgans' house, groomed the horse, and left.

CHAPTER THIRTY-ONE

Scorbion shifted on his stool to face Thomas. "Also last evening, one of his most prized hogs was stolen from butcher Barlan's farm—the animal that he was saving for the Town Feast. It was to be his pièce de résistance at that upcoming banquet."

Billy interrupted Scorbion, "Wasn't the swine rather large? It doesn't seem that it would be easy to have made away with it."

Scorbion responded, "That is indeed a valid observation, which leads directly to my assumption that it was not stolen, but rather slaughtered in Barlan's barn while he slept. The individual parts of the deceased animal would then have been much easier to transport than a live, squirming beast."

"If it was slaughtered there, would not there have been a lot of blood on the floor of the barn?" Yves asked.

"Indeed, there would be," Scorbion confirmed. "But if you will wait a moment, I will get to why I believe the floor of the barn showed no trace of any fluid of the slaughter."

Calvin leaned toward Scorbion from his barber's chair. "Pignon, why would someone have done such a thing?"

"Ah, my friend," Scorbion replied, "*that*, and who did the deed, are certainly the questions that need answering. And we shall see if the six of us, collectively, can ascertain the truth to the situation as we did with the affairs regarding young Jonathan Bentine and Percy Harvey. However, there was one other aspect to the affair that I have not related to you yet. When Barlan awoke the next morning, he found a note affixed to the door of his barn that read, 'This is the first.'"

Billy asked, "Does Barlan have any idea who might want any sort of revenge against him?"

Scorbion replied, "When he reported the theft, Barlan told Sergeant Adley that he had no sense of who would want to cause him harm."

Yves questioned, "Where do we start, Chief Inspector?"

Scorbion turned to look at Yves. "We begin by summoning Harry to join us here."

The five men looked at each other in surprise, before Yves said what they were all thinking: "Harry? Harry, our town's *ivrogne*?"

Barnabus derided him. "C-can't you speak in English? W-what in the blazes is th-that?"

Yves calmly responded, "Drunkard, you dolt," and then chided Barnabus, "If you had the capacity to speak more than one language, as I am able to, you might have known what I meant."

Barnabus ignored Yves's barb.

"What could Harry possibly know?" Calvin asked. "He sits in his rags soliciting coins, completely inebriated, most, if not all, of the time."

Scorbion scolded Calvin. "My friend, do not always judge people by the attire they sport, nor by the apparent condition of their situation. In Harry's case, you would be—in fact, you *are*—mistaken about who he is and what he does."

Calvin replied, "Well then, Pignon, I think you'd better educate us as to the correct circumstances surrounding Harry." The rest of the men nodded in agreement.

Scorbion stood up. "I will do that once Harry is here among us. But first, my good fellows, as I deputized all of you recently, and you are my associates in crime-solving, it is important that whatever I reveal about Harry remain solely between us and no one else. Ever. Do you all understand and agree to that stipulation?"

The men voiced their agreement.

"And, Billy, this will stay out of whatever you write."

"Yes, sir, it will."

Looking at his watch, Scorbion asked Billy, "Would you mind fetching Harry? He should be on his regular patch of pavement in front of Toban's Tavern at this hour. Please inform him that I am requesting his presence. It should take you no longer than ten minutes to locate him and bring him here."

Billy left to find Harry. Thomas retrieved another chair from the storeroom and placed it next to Scorbion's stool. Calvin asked Pignon if he wanted any services performed while they waited for Billy to arrive with Harry.

"I thank you, Calvin, but I do not want anything to distract my concentration while I am attempting to solve these two crimes. I will wait until after we have resolved these affairs, and then you may perform your duties upon me. My locks, nails, and shoes will patiently wait until these cases are resolved, which I expect might well happen within the next few hours. They will not know the difference, as time has no measurement to those objects."

The men in the shop smelled Harry before they saw him. Calvin remarked, "What is that ghastly foul odor?"

When Harry and Billy opened the front door, everyone turned to see where that most repugnant stench was emanating from.

Calvin pulled Scorbion aside and whispered, "Pignon, is it *truly* necessary to have Harry in attendance? I am concerned that my shop will reek for days, or even worse, the odor will permanently infest the interior of my establishment."

Scorbion kindly but emphatically replied, "I am most sympathetic to your concern, my dear friend Calvin, but I do quite assure you that Harry's presence is most necessary to these proceedings. If such a displeasing aroma as you have described does linger after we depart, I will dispatch the best cleaner in Haxford to arrive here as the sun rises on the morrow. By the time you turn your sign to Open, no trace of any unpleasant aroma shall be detected within these premises by any nose."

Harry shuffled over to Scorbion who directed him to the chair designated for him. Once everyone was seated, Scorbion addressed them.

"Harry is not as he seems. It is true that he imbibes more than most, but he is not at all useless, in fact, he is quite useful. You probably ask yourselves how that can be. I will tell you. Before he departed, Chief Inspector Benson informed me that Harry was one of his most trusted resources. While Harry is ensconced in his various locations within this community, he observes. And he listens. Most people see Harry as a part of the pavement, similar to a fireplug or a lamppost, so they talk freely around him, forgetting that Harry has eyes and ears. Benson used Henry's knowledge to keep abreast of the happenings in this community, and I am now employing Harry to do the same for me."

Obvious surprise lit up the faces of Calvin and the others, that being not at all what they expected Scorbion to say.

"Harry reports to me daily, everything that he has heard or seen the previous day and night that may be of interest to me. Anything suspicious or out of the ordinary is noted and recounted."

Billy remarked, "You could strike me down with a bubble. I never expected anything like *that*."

The other men nodded and muttered in agreement.

Scorbion turned to Harry. "Would you please tell these gentlemen what you reported to me regarding last night?"

Harry drew himself upright on the chair, tugged on his tattered shirt sleeve so that it fell down to his wrist, stroked his stubbly chin, and began his story, telling it with slightly slurred speech.

"I wazsh preparing to sleep for the night on the corner where Water and Redmond streets meet. It wazsh quite late. I had nothing to tell the time, but I would guessh that it wazsh a few minutes past midnight as the tavern was closed, the church bell was ringing, and the full moon wazsh high in the night heavens above me. A small horse-drawn cart turned onto Redmond, with two figures seated upon it. I couldn't tell who they were, or whether they were male or female. They both wazsh covered in dark hoods and cloaks. But just as the cart passed me, one wheel went into a large rut in the road, and it wazsh so badly jolted that it lifted into the air. When it fell back down, the robe of the passenger closhest to me opened at their knee. Ash that occurred, I shaw the moonlight glinting off a metal blade of some sort of ax that they were holding next to their trouser leg, and there appeared to be a colored decoration on the handle. I alsho noticed that the rear of the cart contained a very large blanket or sailcloth."

Calvin turned to Scorbion. "May I ask Harry a question?"

Scorbion twisted on his stool. "Of course you may."

"Harry, did you watch the cart as it passed you on Redmond Street?"

"I did, indeed."

"And how far did it go?"

"Two streets further and then it turned left onto Ormond."

"Which leads out of town . . ." Billy observed.

"Toward Barlan's farm," Yves added.

"You are both correct," Scorbion confirmed. He shifted on his stool to face Harry. "Is there any other detail or incident you recall that might be germane to this inquiry?"

"No, Chief Inspector. I wish there wazsh, but there isn't."

Yves gently waved his hand at Scorbion. "*S'il vous plaît*, may I ask a question?"

"Certainly."

"Were there any defining features of the horse that pulled the cart?"

Harry thought for a moment. "No, there wazshn't. It wazsh a very dark animal. I couldn't fully tell if it wazsh of the deepest brown or black, or some combination of the two. But it had no distinguishing marks. It wazsh devoid of any white, or rust, or other color that I wazsh able to see."

Scorbion stood. "A good question, nonetheless, Yves. Now, unless anyone has further questions for you, Harry, you are free to return to your post."

Calvin folded his arms. "I do not have another question, but I have an observation."

Scorbion was intrigued. "I am delighted by a good observation, so please proceed."

"I have noticed my reaction to Harry, and it is not what I anticipated," Calvin reported. "He is much more erudite than I would have imagined. He is not the illiterate drunkard I expected him to be."

Droplets of beer-tinged spittle flew out of Harry's mouth as he replied, somewhat unsteadily, "Jush becaush I drink a lot doeshn't mean I'm stupid or uneducated. I jush choose to occupy my waking hours differently than you. But I sincerely do appreciate your compliment."

Scorbion asked again if there were any other questions for Harry, and when no one offered any, he thanked Harry and handed him five coins. "You have earned these."

As Harry exited the shop, Billy commented, "So we have a stolen hatchet, that could very likely be the one Harry saw the person with in the cart . . ."

Barnabus continued, ". . . A c-cart that was headed toward Barlan's farm last night when his p-prized hog was stolen, or as the Chief Inspector believes, was s-slaughtered."

"That is a very good summation of the details we now know, with the exception that the ax Harry saw was absolutely the hatchet stolen from the Morgan's residence."

Thomas asked, "Why're you so convinced of that, Chief Inspector?"

"It is too much of a coincidence not to be so. As I related to you during the affair with Mr. Bentine, when something appears to be the obvious answer or solution to a problem or situation, it most likely is. Additionally, I have seen no other ax decorated in any way in this town on any previous occasion. Therefore, I must conclude that the implement that Henry observed in the cart was the stolen hatchet."

"Pignon, you said earlier that you have an explanation for why there was no blood on the floor of Barlan's barn."

"Yes, Calvin, I do. I believe that we will find that the sailcloth or blanket that was in the rear of the cart will be stained with blood. I postulate, gentlemen, that it was laid out on the floor of the barn and the hog was slaughtered upon it. Then the blood was collected from it into a container of some sort and ultimately disposed of."

Thomas asked, "And what d'ya think the note meant?"

Scorbion replied, "I can only surmise it indicated that the taking of the pig was the first in what will be a series of actions directed against Barlan. But to what purpose, we know not yet."

"Shouldn't we b-bring B-Barlan here?"

Before Scorbion could answer, Yves responded to Barnabus's question. "*Mon dieu,* to what purpose? Didn't Barlan sleep through the evening? I can't see how there's anything he could add that would be useful."

Scorbion waved his hand. "No. No. You are incorrect, Yves. It makes no difference what butcher Barlan's state of sleep or consciousness was last night. He is one of the victims. He must be heard. We must determine if the man is aware of any enemies who might have done such a deed, with the promise of more."

Thomas asked, "D'you want me to fetch Barlan?"

"That would be quite good of you," Scorbion replied. "Please do so. If his house is empty, check the Green Door tobacco shop. I have been informed that he is regularly at that den smoking cigars with the proprietor. After we ask our questions of Barlan, then the most interesting part begins—we must identify and summon here the two persons who were riding in the cart that night. The ones who stole the hatchet and slaughtered the hog."

Yves was confused. "But how can we summon them if we don't know who they are?"

Scorbion positively asserted, "By the hour that we conclude this procedure, we *will know* who they are. Harry has given us information with which to start, I believe Barlan will add to that, and from there we will commence building a picture of the crime—I group both the theft of the hatchet and the pig together as one crime with two acts. That picture will lead us to the identities of the perpetrators. However, consider this as well: Conversely, if we can deduce why the pig was stolen and slaughtered, it will most certainly lead us to who desired it. Either path will lead to the same place. The same conclusion."

Billy said, "No matter who did it, or what their motivation, the pig was slaughtered. That would make *me* think that someone wanted to eat it. Otherwise, why would they kill the swine rather than just take it?"

"That is sound reasoning," Scorbion acknowledged. "My presumption agrees with your conclusion. You have a keen mind for the solving of problems."

Thomas left the shop to find Barlan.

Calvin propped a chair against the front door to keep it open. "I'm going to sweep that smell out of this shop. Right out into the street."

Scorbion suggested, "Might I propose that additionally you remove the lids from the jars that sit on your counters; the ones that contain your antiseptic alcohol and liniment. The odor from those acerbic fluids should overtake and eradicate any of Harry's lingering smell that remains prior to Thomas and Barlan's arrival."

Calvin did just that, and by the time the two men returned there was much less trace of Harry in the shop.

CHAPTER THIRTY-TWO

Barlan, a ruddy-complexioned man of sizable proportions, dressed in overalls and a sweat-stained burlap shirt, was directed to sit on the chair that Harry had occupied. As he approached the seat, Barlan commented, "There is an odor that is faintly similar to my manure pile. I did not smell it as much near the door."

Once he and everyone else was seated, Scorbion thanked Barlan for coming on such short notice and explained to him the role of the men in the barbershop. Then he asked, "Will you confirm that as you slept last night when your prized hog vanished, no sound woke you up?"

"That is so, Chief Inspector. I'd drunk a few too many tankards and fell into a deeper sleep than is typical for me. If a nubile, amorous wench had been sitting upon me and ripping off my clothes, I don't believe I'd have awakened."

"Then we must not waste our time asking anything more about last evening. Instead, I ask you, are you aware of anyone who might have wanted to harm you by taking your hog, as well as what *you* make of the note left on your door?"

Billy eagerly jumped in, "Do you have an enemy you know of?"

Barlan replied without hesitating. "No. No one who would wish me harm, at least not that I'm aware of. I fancy myself the sort who gets along with everyone. I've lived here all my years and never had troubles with anyone ever before."

"What about your parents?" Calvin asked. "They lived here, did they not? Could they have made enemies?"

Barlan answered, "My mother and father met in Scotland a number of years after my father's family sent him there from somewhere in the American West to live with his maternal grandparents. My father was a very young child when he went to Scotland, but later, while he was studying at the academy, he met my mother, and after he graduated, they married. They left Scotland and moved here. He became the town butcher, and I learned my trade and inherited the farm from him. Unfortunately, they both passed away by the time I reached my twenty-fifth year, but I do not recall either of them having any issues with anyone in the village."

Scorbion asked, "Is there any other situation in your life that may be out of the usual, or that may have any connection to the swine? No matter how remote a possibility it may be."

Barlan thought for a moment. "My life is quite ordinary. The only thing that's changed is that I've recently sold off some of my pasture-land to my neighbor, Martin Chames—"

Scorbion interrupted. "I met Chames at the Morgans'. He also partook in the sumptuous repast I had at their home last evening, and apparently enjoyed it every bit as much as I."

"Chames is a fine farmer," Barlan replied. "I do find him to be a bit boisterous and loud, but that does not affect his farming. He's raising wheat and other grains, and since I don't need the extra land any longer, I sold him two pastures. He didn't say whether he was going to plant crops or use the land to feed his livestock. It's of no concern to me, either way. Actually, he offered to purchase my entire farmstead, but I told him that two pastures were the most I would sell. I needed the money that the sale of the land brought to cover the cost of the feed for my animals. Other than that transaction, there has been nothing special or different from one day to the next in my life."

Thomas inquired, "What're you doing 'bout the Town Feast? Now that the pig's gone, will you supply somethin' else instead?"

Barlan shrugged in resignation. "Unfortunately, I can't afford to give up another animal. Money is tight and even offering up my hog was stretching for me. The committee for the feast will have to make other arrangements for the meal."

Scorbion stood and asked if anyone had further questions for the good butcher. When no one did, he addressed Barlan. "Thank you for taking the time to join us. It is unfortunate that you have no information to offer about last evening, but it is equally fortunate that you have no enemies of whom you are aware. So now, we must look to find the motive for the act that was committed."

"Whatever you need, Inspector. I hope you find the thief who took my hog and make him pay for it."

After Barlan left, Yves spoke first. "Barlan is obviously hurting for money. Could he have staged the abduction of his own hog?"

"How would that help him?" Billy asked.

Yves responded, "Possibly he could have sold it and used the supposed theft as a ruse so that he wouldn't have to donate it to the feast."

Scorbion addressed both men. "That is something we should continue to consider, and possibly pursue. However, my bones tell me that that is not the resolution we will ultimately find to this situation, chiefly due to the fact that Barlan would not have had to purloin the hatchet to make off with his own hog."

"*Merde*, I hadn't thought of that."

Scorbion continued. "Yves, do not be concerned with your overlooking that. Please continue to proffer ideas. But for now, we must turn our attention elsewhere, away from butcher Barlan, to determine the true culprits in this affair."

Barnabus stood and stretched his back. "I'm n-not as young as I was, and m-my body reminds me of that daily. Chief Inspector, we are at a d-dead end. We have no motive, nor any s-suspects. Where do we go f-from here?"

Scorbion gently cuffed Barnabus on the shoulder. "My friend and associate, we have just begun, not ended. We know there were two perpetrators, that both owned cloaks and hoods, and that at least one had access to a cart and a large sailcloth or blanket."

Standing behind Scorbion, Calvin added, "One or both also had to have, as you just used the word, Pignon, 'access' to the Morgans' library."

Scorbion beamed. "Bravo Calvin! You have pointed out a very important piece of information that we must move to the top of our list of those things that will assist us in identifying the perpetrators. Fewer people in this town will have had access—there is that word again—to the Morgans' home than will own carts and sailcloths or blankets. We must start there."

"Are we goin' to their home to speak with them?" Thomas asked.

Scorbion thought for a moment. "No. We will summon them here. Just as we would anyone else we would question in the course of an investigation."

Yves related that as a patient of Dr. Morgan, on many occasions he had been to the doctor's office in the outbuilding next to their home. He volunteered to bicycle to the house and ask them to come with him to the barbershop to meet with Scorbion and the others.

While Yves was gone, the men brought out the table from the shop's storeroom, along with one additional chair. They arranged the furniture so that Scorbion's stool and their chairs were on one side of the table with two chairs on the opposite side.

Once everything was in place, Billy asked Scorbion, "May I ask you a few questions for my story about this case? I believe that people in Haxford would like to know more about their new chief inspector."

"You may, indeed. Proceed."

"I was wondering if there were any other inspectors or detectives whom you admired or whom you might have gotten some training with."

The corners of Scorbion's mouth turned upward. "I am totally self-educated in the ways of detection, though I have read extensively the exploits and ways of those who preceded me, most especially Sherlock Holmes."

Billy let out an admiring gasp.

Scorbion continued, "Just at the time that I was accelerating my career as a detective I had the good fortune to meet Dr. John Watson. We were both in London attending a meeting that paired those engaged in the art of detection with practitioners of witchcraft, and we became quick friends in the midst of the nonsense that lasted those two days. We regularly stayed in communication until his death. I have read, with great curiosity and attention, all of Watson's accounts of the crimes Holmes solved. I only wish that he and I could have sat down together and shared our views on the solving of intricate crime puzzles. But alas, that was never to be. Neither of us made the time in our schedules to enable such a meeting to take place."

"Sorry."

"Oh, do not be, Billy. I am making plans to travel to London to meet up with another detective I have heard much about lately. He retired from the Belgian police force two decades ago and set up his own practice in that lovely country. However, he recently had to flee Belgium, and he now resides here in England. I have heard that he is exceptional, and I do plan to meet and share ideas with him soon. He has a rather unique name, as mine is—Hercule Poirot."

Billy asked Scorbion to spell Poirot's name just as the front door opened and Thelma strode in. "A customer in my shop mentioned George Barlan's hog was stolen. As I had no other clients present, once she left, I closed up and proceeded here. I fully expected to find Inspector Scorbion in this establishment, beginning an investigation into the theft, and it appears that my assumption was correct."

Thelma placed her black-veiled hat on the coatrack next to Scorbion's suit jacket and energetically bounded over to him. "Do you mind if I join in, Pignon? There's little activity taking place in my shop at this time of day, and I could use a bit of mental stimulation."

Scorbion lightly took hold of her forearm and gave it a soft squeeze. "It is my pleasure to be in your presence, and I look forward to your astute and insightful observations."

While Barnabus went to the storeroom, retrieved a chair for Thelma, and placed it at the table, Scorbion described to her the events that had so far unfurled and advised her that the group was awaiting Yves's return with the Morgans.

Shortly after Scorbion completed his explanatory narrative, a silence came over the shop. Everyone's attention went to Yves as he rested his bicycle against the bench in front of the barbershop and walked inside. He was met with a barrage of questions about where the Morgans were and why they hadn't accompanied him.

Before Yves could respond, the sputtering and clanking of a motorcar was heard. Then the vehicle itself came into view, turning the corner of the cobblestone street and pulling to a noisy stop directly in front of the shop's entrance. First Isabelle, and then Dr. Franklin Morgan, exited the rear doors which their driver held open for them.

Scorbion greeted them as they passed through the doorway, explaining to Isabelle the arrangement with the men and Thelma. Then he invited them to sit upon the chairs that were positioned next to each other on the side of the table opposite Scorbion and the group.

Once they were seated, Scorbion began. "We"—he gestured to the men and Thelma, who was sitting directly to his right—"believe that your hatchet was stolen to be used to carve up a helpless hog whose parts were then absconded with. It is our further belief, as Calvin Brown—the proprietor of this establishment—pointed out to us earlier, that it is highly probable that whoever took the hatchet was a guest in your house or worked in your employ. We do not see any other path that would have led to the hatchet being removed from above your mantel."

Franklin Morgan leaned forward. "That makes complete sense to me. Doesn't it to you, Isabelle?"

Isabelle nodded. "Yes, I agree. But you may remove any of our guests as suspects. No one visiting our home was in the library after you handled the hatchet, Chief Inspector."

Scorbion leaned in. "Then, under those circumstances, if you would provide us with the names of those in your employ, a bit of their backgrounds, and the years of service they have with you, that would be extremely useful."

Franklin leaned back a few inches. "That is no issue. Joseph

Nava"—the doctor pointed to their driver standing next to the black motorcar, smoking a cigarette—"has been working for me for just under one year. He had impeccable credentials and references. In fact, Martin Chames vouched for him."

Isabelle asked Scorbion, "Do you recall that you met Martin at our house last evening?"

"I certainly do. He was an interesting conversationalist, but his voice was a bit thunderous and irksome at the same time. But that is of no consequence, so let us return to Mr. Nava."

The doctor continued. "I was saying that Chames vouched for him after our part-time housekeeper, Katy, suggested him. It seems they all were acquainted with one another in London before they each settled here. Nava possesses quite a colorful background; he told me that his ancestors came from England, America, Germany, South America, and Norway. Looking at him, I cannot determine which side of his heritage influenced his appearance the most, although he does *not* look Germanic or Norwegian. Something about his appearance *is* somewhat foreign, most likely South American with his ruddy complexion and straight black hair. Peru, I might venture to guess."

Scorbion asked, "What else do you know about him?"

Isabelle was about to answer, but Franklin spoke before she had fully composed her thoughts. "Nava sold equipment to Chames for his farm in Tottingham, and because he also repaired the machinery, he went to the farm numerous times. Nava and Chames became friendly over the course of those encounters."

Isabelle continued, as if relating some important gossip. "I don't think many people know this, but Katy, our house cleaner, is Chames's niece—and when she started training Chames's horses and taking care of his house, she and Nava met and became fond of each other. I know they parted company after a while, but I believe that Katy was in love with Nava, and that she suggested him to us as a driver and mechanic after Chames told her that Nava was looking for something new to do, hoping they would get together again if he relocated here."

Yves turned to Isabelle. "And, madame, have they reunited?"

Isabelle quickly replied, "Oh yes. After they both came to town, they started accompanying each other again. Franklin and I are not always privy to the private goings-on of our staff, but I believe they still are involved—though I am not totally confident about that."

Thelma sighed mockingly. "Ah, young love. It can be magical or tragic. And, alas, it is occasionally both."

Scorbion moved the proceedings along. "That is indeed often true, and thank you for that insightful observation, Miss Smith. Now, Dr. or Madam Morgan, what of the others in your employ?"

Isabelle related that their cook had been with them for a year as well. "Charles Emerlin is a *wonderful* chef. He is so much better than his predecessor. We were so very fortunate to find him. I do not know his ancestry at all . . ."

"Nor do I," Franklin added.

"But," Isabelle turned to Scorbion, "you tasted his masterpieces at our home. You were witness to his exceptional culinary talents."

"I was indeed," Scorbion confirmed.

Thelma addressed Isabelle. "I truly regret that I was unable to accompany the inspector last evening, as I would have enjoyed being in your and your guests' company, as well as partaking in that sumptuous meal. But I had committed myself to a suffragette meeting, and a commitment is a commitment."

Isabelle responded, "We would have been delighted to have you among us, but I do understand that one cannot be present in two locations at the same time. I, myself, am not active regarding voting rights, but I am sympathetic to your endeavors."

Thelma responded, "If you should ever change your mind and wish to help propel rights for women, it would be my great pleasure to introduce you to others who are energetically engaged in that cause."

Billy didn't wait for Isabelle to comment further. "Mrs. Morgan, might I inquire how you came to be aware of Chef Emerlin?"

Isabelle responded, "Shortly before our former cook left for Africa, we attended the funeral for Samuel Gray." She turned to Scorbion. "I don't know if you are aware of him. Before you arrived in Haxford,

Samuel, who was a farmer and a friend, died in an accident when his cart tumbled over onto him." Then she turned back to Billy. "At the wake, his wife, Florence, overheard us mentioning that our cook was leaving, and she told us that she knew of an exceptional chef who was looking for a new position. She put us in touch with Emerlin the next week."

"Are there any others in your employ who regularly attend to your house?" Scorbion inquired.

The doctor answered. "Our man Warvis assists in the kitchen and handles an assortment of additional needs of ours. He has been a member of our home for well over fifteen years. He is English through and through, and I swear he must have been born to be a professional servant."

"There are no others?"

"Isabelle has already related that Katy does our cleaning. You would have met her when you were at dinner, but she had been down with a nasty illness for a fortnight prior to that gathering. Fortunately, she returned to help tidy up just after we finished dining, and in spite of her still not being fully recovered, her assistance was immensely valuable."

Isabelle added, "While you and Franklin were in the study, Katy was clearing the table and assisting Warvis and Emerlin in the kitchen with the postmeal chores. She has been so helpful to us during the past year. We are quite fortunate that she gave up working for her uncle to come with us. Warvis and I had to maintain the cleanliness of our home in her stead. Thank goodness she's returned."

That raised another question for Scorbion. "Who introduced you to Katy?"

The Morgans hesitated as they attempted to recall how they met her. Then Isabelle answered. "It was a bit convoluted in a way. Florence Gray first mentioned Katy to me. She told me about Katy's connection to Ben Chames and she also mentioned that Katy had a farming background. Her father owned a chicken and pig farm, as well as stabling a number of steeds." Isabelle paused. "And if I recall correctly, Chames sold food to Emerlin at his restaurant, the Cork and Plate, and mentioned that his relative, Katy, was looking for steadier employment than she had working with the horses and wanted a new environment after her relationship with Nava ended."

"And Emerlin told that to Samuel and Florence Gray, who then told you about her," Thelma deduced.

Isabelle was impressed. "Quite right, Miss Smith. That *is* how we learned of Katy."

Thelma smiled. "Isabelle, please call me Thelma."

Thomas broke in. "Can I ask a question please? 'Bout somethin' else."

"Of course," Scorbion affirmed.

Thomas addressed Franklin. "Do you have a cart?"

"I do."

Barnabus followed, "D-do you own a l-large sailcloth?"

"Again, I say I do. Why do you ask?"

Scorbion answered the doctor's question. "We believe that your cart was utilized to transport the thieves and the hog, which was slaughtered upon your sailcloth. Have you seen the sailcloth recently?"

Morgan thought for a moment, and Isabelle shook her head. "I cannot say that I have. But it is not anything that I would regularly see. Possibly once a year or less, especially now that we have this motorized transport. I rarely utilize the cart any longer."

"Please search out the sailcloth when you return to your home and advise me as to whether you were able to locate it, or not. If you do come upon it, please examine it for any bloodstains."

"I will, Chief Inspector. I will also give the cart a thorough going-over. I am curious about both and will report to you what I find. Or don't find."

"Excellent. I look forward to learning what you discover, although I would wager that you will find nothing out of the ordinary with your cart and that your sailcloth will be missing."

Barnabus turned to the doctor. "Has your c-cook, Emerlin, made d-dinners of p-pork for you recently?"

Billy added, "Or are there any pork dinners scheduled in your home in the near future?"

Isabelle shifted in her chair. "We knew that we would be consuming pork at the Town Feast, so we did not ask Charles to prepare it for us between now and then."

"Yes dear," Franklin interrupted, "but if you recall, Charles told us earlier today that since now there would be no pork at the feast, he would prepare us some for tonight's supper."

"That's right, Franklin, I forgot. I wonder where Charles obtained the meat on such short notice."

"I am sure he has an explanation, Isabelle. Probably from some other farmer or butcher. I will ask him when we return home."

Scorbion and the others spent the next fifteen minutes asking the Morgans numerous additional questions regarding their staff and the night that the hatchet was taken, but they learned nothing that they didn't already know. Once the questioning was completed, Scorbion sent the doctor and his wife on their way, with Franklin promising to contact Scorbion regarding the cart, the sailcloth, and the pork.

Just as the Morgans' car turned the corner and was lost from sight, a foul odor began to seep into the barbershop again. Thelma noticed it first. "What is that horrific smell? It is like fermenting rubbish. Is the loo malfunctioning?"

She had her answer when Harry, running as fast as his inebriated legs would carry him, appeared at the shop's front door.

Wheezing and panting when he entered the shop, Harry could only manage to gasp out, "Uh . . . uh . . ."

Scorbion walked to him. "Please wait to breathe my friend. Then you may tell us what matter of such obvious urgency and importance has brought you here in such haste."

Harry gulped a few more breaths, and then blurted out, "Barlan . . . Barlan's dead. Stabbed with the hatchet. It's sticking out of his back."

A collective gasp arose from everyone in the shop, except Scorbion. "Where did this occur?"

"Douglas Alley, just near the Green Door. It musht have happened right after he left here."

"Did anyone see the attack?"

"No one that I know about. Sergeant Adley and another of your men are queshtioning people now."

The room went silent as everyone considered this new development. Each looked like they had been struck by a thunderbolt.

As they recovered from the news, Billy turned to Calvin. "Well, that surely lets Nava off. He couldn't have been with the Morgans, and then here, while committing the act. Something about his demeanor and looks made me consider him, but now, it's moot, isn't it?"

Calvin replied, "It appears that way."

Scorbion moved between the men. "Let us cease this line of discussion and attend to the matter at hand: Barlan's murder. Whether Nava is involved in any way or not shall become clear to us by the time we conclude this inquiry. While I agree that he could not have committed the murder, he most assuredly could be an accomplice to the person who did. We certainly have an unexpected development of the first order, do we not?"

Scorbion handed Harry some additional coins, thanked him for bringing the news, and sent him on his way. Then he turned back to the others.

"We must bring each of the Morgans' staff here for questioning. Immediately. They appear to have among them at least one of the perpetrators—and possibly the killer. Yves, as you have already demonstrated your ability to retrieve persons from the Morgan household, please go and fetch the cook, Emerlin, the manservant, Warvis, and Nava. Do not relate anything to them about Barlan's murder. When you return here, have them all wait outside, and bring in Emerlin first. During the time that you are absent, the rest of us will go to this latest crime location to determine what we can see for ourselves. We will rendezvous back here in one hour."

CHAPTER THIRTY-THREE

Yves set out on his bicycle, Thelma donned her hat as Calvin closed the shop, and they both joined Scorbion and the others on their walk to Douglas Alley.

When they arrived, Scorbion was greeted by Sergeant Simon Adley and his underling, Constable Roger Pawling, who informed Scorbion that they had been unable to learn a single fact of any import from the local residents. No one appeared to have witnessed the killing.

With a twinkle in her eye, Thelma teased Scorbion, "I am beginning to wonder how safe it is to be in your company. People end up with their skulls bashed in by shovels and with tomahawks in their backs."

Scorbion laughed. "You have no cause to be alarmed, fair lady. I had no hand in those events, which all took place prior to my involvement. I am not a magnet for death but rather an inquisitor into the whys and hows of its happening. You are as safe and secure in my presence as you would be in the vaults of the Bank of England."

"Thank you for the reassurance, as I much prefer being protected by you than being locked away for safekeeping as was Rapunzel," Thelma quipped.

After laughing a second time, Scorbion began scrutinizing the area. He first looked at Barlan, whose sprawled body looked at rest except for the hatchet sticking out of his back and the circle of blood on his light-blue shirt surrounding it from where it was protruding.

He bent down to take a closer look at the tomahawk, comparing its decorative feathers with those that he remembered seeing on the one above the Morgans' fireplace. He determined, to his satisfaction, that it was the same implement.

Then he scanned the alley.

He noted that there were few doors near where Barlan was killed, but most of the entrances to the buildings on the street were at its opposite end. He stood up and walked down the street and back, occasionally looking at the dirt to see whatever footprints and debris he might find that could be relevant to the slaying of Barlan.

Upon returning to the others, Scorbion pronounced, "There is nothing here that gives any hint as to who perpetrated this heinous deed, or the reason. It is most certainly associated with the two acts of theft that we have been examining, but this murder has elevated the gravity of the situation and the urgency of our determining who committed this wrongdoing. Let us return to the shop and question the Morgans' staff."

Before they left, Scorbion asked Adley if he would investigate Barlan's background and report anything that was not already known. Scorbion also requested that Pawling and Adley arrange to have the body moved quickly, and to keep the murder as quiet as possible, "Until I have completed this day's questioning of potential suspects."

On their walk back to the barbershop, the group witnessed Bentine entering the *Gazette* building.

Barnabus stroked his beard. "That troublemaker's p-probably up to no g-good again."

Calvin added, "I wonder if he had a hand in what happened to Barlan. Is it just a coincidence that he is in the area?"

Scorbion identified Bentine for Thelma before responding to Calvin. "I very much doubt that Bentine had any reason or motive to harm Barlan. He is much too preoccupied with attempting to validate his parentage. However, we must never dismiss any possibility until it is disproven."

They arrived back at the barbershop just minutes ahead of Yves and the trio of Morgan employees. Yves told the three men that Scorbion wanted to meet with each of them separately, and asked Nava and Warvis to wait outside while Emerlin was questioned first. After a bit of grumbling, Nava lit a cigarette, took a deep inhale, blew a perfectly formed smoke ring, and then he and Warvis sat down on the bench in front of the barbershop.

As Emerlin entered, Scorbion took Yves aside and asked him if he had told any of the three about the murder. "I did not," Yves confirmed.

Scorbion rubbed his hands together, "Excellent."

Chapter Thirty-Four

Once everyone was seated at the table, Scorbion began with the question that they all were anxious to hear the answer to. "Lady Morgan has informed us that you will be serving pork, on short notice, tonight. Would you please tell us where you obtained the meat?"

"Most certainly," Emerlin replied. "I go to market both in this town and in Brookdale. It is only a twenty-minute ride there in the cart, and I often acquire meats and produce in both locales. In regard to this pork, I was in Brookdale this morning shortly after the shops opened. The butcher there related to me that he had been offered an already-butchered hog by someone he had never done business with before, just hours before I arrived, as he was trimming the meats for the day in his backroom. Knowing that the Town Feast would no longer be a pork dinner—I was advised by Dr. Morgan that Barlan's pig was stolen, who overheard that when he and Barlan were both in the station—I thought that I would cook pork for the Morgans tonight instead. It felt as though good fortune was looking down on me that the swine was available and already butchered—albeit somewhat crudely."

"Did the butcher happen to describe the person who sold him the hog?"

"I *did* ask him if he knew the person who sold him the animal, but he said that he had never before met the man who had appeared at his back door. He described him as being of average height, slightly stocky, and having a less-rugged complexion than he sees on the typical farmer he does business with."

Calvin asked, "He gave no other description? That is precious little to go on."

"He said that the man wore a hat pulled down over his eyes and kept his face out of view as much as possible, but he was clean-shaven. Other than that, the butcher said there was nothing that would distinguish the meat-seller, and he doubted he would recognize the man if he jostled him on the street."

Thelma turned to Emerlin. "It seems quite convenient that this butcher could not better describe the seller to any greater degree than you have related to us."

Emerlin rose up from his chair, indignantly pointing his finger at Thelma. "Are you accusing me of something? Are you saying that I have fabricated any of what I have told you?"

Scorbion tried to calm him. "No, no. Miss Smith is simply expressing all of our frustration that there is not a more full and accurate description of the man. It seems obvious that the seller of the pork was one of the men who stole butcher Barlan's hog and did not want to be identified. And now that Barlan has been murdered . . ."

"He's been *what*?!"

Emerlin quickly sat down, clearly shocked.

"Barlan's been stabbed to death," Billy said. "Less than an hour ago."

Emerlin looked dumbfounded. He fumbled for words and finally uttered, "My Lord. How? Where? By whom?"

Scorbion answered, "He was impaled with the hatchet that was stolen from the Morgans' library. We do not yet know by whom. But I promise you we will learn that, and the culprit will be made to pay for his or her act."

"I assure you, Chief Inspector, it was *not* me. Other than my trip to Brookdale, I have been in the kitchen since early this morning. Warvis can attest to that. He has been assisting me with the pies and cakes this entire day."

"That may be true; however, there are *two* persons involved in this affair. One could be committing the acts while the other provides a sound alibi."

"Again I ask, are you accusing me of something?"

"No," Scorbion answered. "I am suggesting that since there are two individuals involved, the alibi of either does not provide an alibi for both. I do have one further question for you, though. It has been brought to our attention that you were recommended to the Morgans by the widow Gray. How did you come to know her?"

"Samuel and Florence would eat in my restaurant when they made their yearly trip to London to purchase goods they could not acquire easily here. Additionally, Mrs. Gray traveled to London unaccompanied at least three or four times each year, and she would dine at my establishment almost every evening on those journeys. She once told me that she called those her respite holidays. I've never been quite certain what she meant, but I surmised it was to be on her own. After having served them together and separately for a number of years, I got to know both reasonably well. In fact, we became friendly."

Scorbion stroked his chin. "Did Mrs. Gray ever dine at your establishment with anyone other than her husband?"

Emerlin answered quickly. "I ate a few dinners with the two of them together, and some with her alone." He shrugged. "Even a chef has to eat."

Scorbion forced a small smile. "Yes, but did anyone *else* ever join you when you were with them, or even at any time you were not?"

Emerlin cocked his head. "An older woman they introduced to me as a cousin visiting from Germany, on one occasion, and of course, Martin Chames. Not long after the Grays began patronizing my restaurant, he happened to be delivering goods to me one evening when they were to be dining. I had this unexplainable instinct that he and they would be harmonious. When the Grays arrived, I made the introductions, and asked if they would mind if he and I joined them. We four had a splendid dinner—a scrummy meal, if I may say so myself—and some lively conversation. The next day, Chames asked if I would alert him when they were to come dine with me again, and, coincidently, Mrs. Gray sent me a letter saying that she and her husband had truly enjoyed Chames's company and asked me to invite him to dine with them the next time they were in London. After that, they, and especially Mrs. Gray and he, became quite friendly, and they dined together on most every trip either or both of the Grays made to London."

Thelma inquired, "Did Mr. Gray ever come to your restaurant without Mrs. Gray?"

Emerlin responded without hesitation. "Once that I recall. I believe he was meeting with a barrister on that occasion."

Scorbion followed up. "Did he dine with Chames on that visit?"

Emerlin replied, "He did not."

Scorbion turned to his confederates. "Do you have any further questions for Chef Emerlin? I am satisfied that we have learned all that we need to learn from the good chef at this time."

Thelma leaned toward Emerlin. "May I ask why you closed your restaurant and took a position as a private chef?"

"My avaricious landlord informed me that he was going to raise my rent, and the increase was such an ungodly sum that I doubted I would be able to continue to make a go of the restaurant," Emerlin responded. "I debated whether to reopen in a new location, but after considerable consideration, I decided that I had had enough of running a staff, and keeping the ledger, and all the things that go into proprietorship. When the offer came from the Morgans, it provided the answer for me as to what I should do."

Billy asked Emerlin about the Morgans' cart and sailcloth, both of which he expressed knowledge and use of, but nothing further. Before he was excused, Scorbion instructed Emerlin not to disclose to Warvis or Nava that Barlan had been murdered.

Before Warvis was brought in, Calvin asked Scorbion, "Can we be sure he was telling the truth? What if he made all of that up about the butcher in Brookdale?"

Yves responded, "It will be easy to check on his story, *mon ami*. Why would he lie about that, if all we have to do is ask the butcher if what Emerlin told us was true?"

Thelma nodded. "I am in agreement. It is too easy a story to repudiate if it is inaccurate or fabricated, so it is likely true."

When Scorbion concurred with Thelma, Barnabus said with some finality, "So that t-takes Emerlin off our list of s-suspects."

Scorbion turned to him. "Not necessarily. As I indicated, Emerlin could be one of the two perpetrators, just not the one who sold the slaughtered hog to the butcher in Brookdale."

Billy observed, "It would be quite a clever ruse if he were one of the thieves, who then covered his tracks by buying back the same pig that he and his accomplice had stolen."

Scorbion said, "While that is not likely, it remains a possibility. We will maintain this in the filing cabinets of our minds and pull it out again if, and when, it is needed."

Yves had a quizzical look on his face. "I have heard about filing cabinets, but I have never seen one of those inventions. I have no idea what a filing cabinet looks like, or exactly what its purpose is."

Billy related, "We have two at the newspaper office. They're large cabinets with drawers and are very handy to store papers and keep them sorted by topic, date, or person."

Scorbion thanked Billy for his explanation and asked Calvin to bring Warvis in.

CHAPTER THIRTY-FIVE

Once seated, Warvis stated, "I am prepared to assist in any way that I can, but I do not believe that I have anything useful to offer."

"Let us be the arbiters of that," Scorbion responded.

Warvis scanned everyone seated on Scorbion's side of the table. He stopped when his eyes fell on Thelma. "Ah, Madam, I recognize you from the instances that I have frequented your establishment. I have acquired books and other publications from you on numerous visits. If I might be so bold as to say, I could never forget a woman as striking as you. However, I am at a loss as to the reason that you are here."

Thelma responded, "I appreciate your kind words—and I recognize *you* as well from the times you have been in my shop, for which I thank you. However, today I am in attendance not as a bookshop owner but rather as one who can, hopefully, assist Chief Inspector Scorbion in determining the perpetrators of the events that he is investigating."

Scorbion added, "Miss Smith has a keen analytic mind and is a perceptive observer. She was very helpful to me in another crime we recently resolved. I hope that her presence here is not an issue for you."

"It is not," Warvis responded, "It was only unexpected. Carry on."

Scorbion then asked, "Do you utilize the Morgans' cart often?"

"I do. Regularly."

"Is a sailcloth stored in it?"

"Yes, frequently."

"Is it in the cart now?"

"I have no bloody idea, Chief Inspector," Warvis responded. "I do not inspect the cart and its contents save for those times when I employ it—which tend to be only those occasions when I am asked to go into town to procure something that is too large or bulky for me to transport by hand and on foot. Or that the Morgans do not wish to sully their motorcar with."

Thomas leaned in. "Did you use it a few nights ago to steal a pig?"

Warvis leaned in, too, until there was little space between himself and Thomas. "Absolutely *not*. And if anybody says I did, that is complete twaddle." He sat back and addressed Scorbion. "You are chewing the wrong cud if you suspect that I had anything to do with the disappearance of either the hatchet or the hog. I do not have enough free time to commit such acts. I am at the Morgans' beck and call every minute of every day. I rarely get any time for myself. Do not misunderstand, I do rather enjoy my position in their household, but it is bloody all-consuming. You would be much better served questioning Nava and Emerlin."

Calvin was intrigued. "Why Emerlin? We just met with him and there seemed nothing out of the ordinary that we could ascertain."

Thelma added, "And, are you aware of his tale about the butcher in Brookdale? Do you not believe it?"

"I have heard it, and I do not doubt the validity of his story, but the man does procure his foodstuffs from a wide variety of merchants, some of whom appear to me to be less-than-savory characters. Some seem downright rotten. And one who travels in disagreeable circles may be unsavory himself."

Scorbion dismissed that notion. "Or, it may just be the circumstances surrounding food procurement in these times. However, we will uncover what is accurate before we are done. You also mentioned Nava. What about him concerns you?"

"Everything. He is a loner. He seems to have that proverbial chip on his shoulder at all times. He is a haughty, unpleasant fellow—an odd number in a household of even temperaments. It would be him I would look into if it were I, and not you, sitting on that side of this table."

Scorbion asked, "Not Emerlin?"

"Possibly, but definitely Nava."

"One last question . . ."

"Yes, Chief Inspector?"

"Where were you earlier, and what were you doing?"

"And why do you ask?"

"Butcher Barlan was slain today."

Warvis angled back further on his chair. "My Lord! He was slain, you say?!"

"Within the hour it appears," Scorbion replied.

"And you believe that I might have had a hand in that? Oh ho! So I *am* a possible suspect! How utterly inappropriate. I have an alibi solid as granite. I have been assisting Emerlin all day. We were never out of sight of the other. I can only assume that he has told you that same bloody thing."

Before dismissing Warvis, Scorbion said, "He has, but I offer no apologies. Everyone is under suspicion until they are not. However, you are no longer a suspect, sir. Please do not mention word of what you were told, or what was discussed here, to Nava as you pass outside."

After Warvis left, Thomas asked Scorbion if he believed everything Warvis had told them. He also wanted to know Scorbion's thoughts regarding Warvis's comments about Nava and Emerlin.

Scorbion replied, "My instincts tell me that Warvis is not involved in the affair in any way. He was quite believable, including his opinion that Nava and Emerlin should be looked at more deeply. Let us now bring in the possibly unpleasant Mr. Nava."

"What about Emerlin and Warvis?" Yves asked. "May they go, or should they remain here until we have completed our questioning of Nava?"

"Now that you ask, Yves, please inform Warvis that he is free to depart, but ask Emerlin to stay outside, so that we may recall him if necessary. Although I doubt that will be the case."

Warvis informed Yves that he would sit with Emerlin until they both could leave. "The time will afford me a further break from my rather routine duties."

CHAPTER THIRTY-SIX

Nava entered the shop and sat down. He looked at the men sitting across the table from him until, like Warvis, he stopped at Thelma. "Well, you're a fit beauty, aren't you? I'm sorry I haven't made your acquaintance before now. I doubt there's a bint in this town that can hold a candle to you. I could do well right by you if you gave me the chance."

Thelma screwed her face into a caustic smile. "There are no words that you could utter nor any gifts that you could lavish upon me that would entice me to spend one more second than I have to in your presence, Mr. Nava. So please drop all thoughts and remembrances of me from your mind the instant you depart this establishment."

Nava was undeterred. "You are a feisty wench aren't you? So much the better, to my mind."

Scorbion had had enough of Nava's crassness. "Show some respect for the lady, please. That is, if you are capable of it." He paused, cleared his throat, and in his most professional manner continued. "Thank you for agreeing to join us . . ."

Nava looked away from Thelma to Scorbion and grumbled, "As though I have much choice."

"You *do* have a choice, sir. You can answer our questions here, or I can summon you to the station house and you can be interrogated in a more formal atmosphere. It is at your option."

Nava took a cigarette out of his shirt pocket, lit it, and inhaled a deep draw of smoke. "Oh balls. Let's do this now. The faster I get out of this shit-shop, the better."

Calvin winced.

Scorbion was undeterred. "You have made a decidedly good decision to proceed now. So let us commence. I will start by asking you if you were one of the two people in a cart on Redmond Street between midnight and two in the morning last night."

Scorbion scowled when Nava answered, "I was not. I have not ridden in a cart since the Morgans purchased their Mercedes. Carts are transportation for peasants."

Calvin drew himself up and admonished Nava. "I have a cart. I use it every day, and I do not consider myself a peasant. I am a tradesman and a shop-owner."

Nava blew a smoke ring toward him. "You can call yourself whatever you want, but if you're still using a cart, then you're a frigging peasant to me."

Scorbion interceded. "Before this becomes unruly, let us move on to other inquiries we have. Mr. Nava, what is your given name, and what is the derivation of your family name?"

"Joseph. Joseph Nava. My father gave me my family name. It was his name as well. Where do you *think* I got it from?"

Scorbion tried to contain his disdain. "Yes, thank you, but that is not what I meant. From where does your name originate? Which of your forebearers first was known by the name Nava?"

"I think it came from somewhere in the Americas. Maybe North, maybe South. It might even be Indian. But I wouldn't gamble my scant salary on any of that."

Thomas asked, "The Morgans aren't takin' care of you well?"

Nava flicked ash on the floor. "Are you bantering with me? Those skinflints? They don't take care of any of us well. I'm leaving for a much better position in Berlin. I've already given my notice. If anyone says they pay a living wage, that's bollocks."

Scorbion asked, "When do you depart?"

"Monday next. Can't wait to get out of this flea-trap town. It's stifling."

Billy opened his mouth to argue the merits of life in Haxford, but Scorbion held up his hand and waggled his finger at Billy to stop him from engaging in that argument. Instead, Scorbion asked, "Mr. Nava, have you ever held the hatchet that hung above the hearth in the Morgans' library?"

"Once," Nava replied gruffly.

"Only one time?"

"That's what I just said, didn't I? Once."

"How did it feel?"

Nava asked, "What do you mean how did it feel?" and then he added sarcastically, "It felt like a hatchet."

Scorbion went on, undeterred. "Are you familiar with how hatchets feel from a previous experience?"

Nava smiled. "Nah. I just meant it felt like I imagined a hatchet would feel."

Scorbion then asked, "Do you know butcher Barlan?"

"Yes. But not well. I've driven Emerlin to his farm once or twice to pick up some meat."

"What about his neighbor, Martin Chames? Do you know him?"

"Yeah. A lot better than Barlan. I worked for Chames in Tottingham. Since we've both been here, I've met him on a couple of occasions—picked up some wheat from him—also, with Emerlin." Nava paused. "I've smoked with Chames once or twice. At the Green Door. Strictly by chance."

"Do you like him?" Thelma asked.

"He's a decent sort, although he can cause a row at times."

Calvin asked, "What do you mean?"

Nava ground out his cigarette on the floor under his heel. "He's decidedly set in his views and when they're challenged, he's as likely to resort to fisticuffs as he is to talk it out. He lost customers in Tottingham because of how rude and surly he was to them. I even saw him shove one or two."

Barnabus asked, "W-what about W-Warvis and Emerlin? Are they d-decent sorts?"

"Warvis is so stuffy, if he were a couch, he'd be too overfilled to sit on. And he's a stickler for how things are done. He's a real bugger. Emerlin?" Nava shrugged. "He's adequate."

Scorbion stood. "If I recall properly, you said that you did not know Barlan well."

"That's right. Him and me never ran in the same circles. I don't even remember bumping into him at the Green Door—just picking up things from him like I said before."

Scorbion looked around the table. "Does anyone have additional questions for Mr. Nava?" When no one did, he said, "Thank you for coming and answering our inquiries, Mr. Nava. We may have additional queries for you in the future, but for now, we are done. When you exit would you mind asking Emerlin to come inside."

As Nava left, Thelma turned to Scorbion. "Pignon, I appreciate your defending me earlier. You were gentlemanly and gallant in doing so, but I do wish you to know that I am perfectly capable of dispatching coarse advances such as he made on my own. I have dealt with lotharios and would-be Casanovas since the time that my ample figure became evident. And in the same manner that you are unaffected by those who criticize your shoes, so it is for me with philanderers and crude Don Juans who try to woo me or bed me."

Scorbion was surprised by Thelma's unexpected proclamation, and he responded in an almost joking manner. "You most assuredly *are* different from my former wife, Katherine. I will have to adjust my understanding of a male and female relationship accordingly—although how you want to conduct yourself with someone as boorish as Nava does not displease me."

Billy said, "To me, Nava's about as friendly as Bentine."

Calvin contradicted him. "Nava makes Bentine look like a downright gentleman if you ask me."

Scorbion turned to Calvin. "Since you bring up young Mr. Bentine, there remains a missing aspect to his case that continues to bother me, although I still cannot determine what it is."

Yves postulated, "Maybe that Choc was not really his *pére*. Perhaps it was someone else."

"Anything is possible," Scorbion replied.

Emerlin came back in and sat down.

Scorbion told him he had but three additional questions. "First, did you know butcher Barlan well?"

Emerlin answered, "No, I wasn't really that acquainted with him. I mostly met Barlan the times I secured meat from him. I am in the kitchen so much that I rarely get out and about. And when I do venture into town, other than to procure supplies, I enjoy taking in a moving picture. I find the cinematograph that Lumiere devised to be rather enchanting."

Thelma's face flushed with enthusiasm. "As do I. *La Ciotat*, although lasting less than a minute, startled me. The train engine seemed to come right out of the screen toward me."

Emerlin agreed. "Yes, it was quite astonishing."

Scorbion interrupted their conversation. "I hope someday soon to witness that for myself, but for now, I will proceed with my second question—how frequently have you met with the farmer, Martin Chames, since the time that you both settled in Haxford?"

"Not that often. As I mentioned, we did dine together at my restaurant on a number of occasions and I bought wheat and other produce from him." Emerlin paused. "However, I have seen Chames far less since we both relocated here. You should ask Nava about him. He worked for Chames in Tottingham, and he's smoked with him a number of times at the Green Door."

Scorbion acknowledged, "Yes, he has told us that. And lastly, do the Morgans pay a decent wage?"

"Oh, absolutely! More than decent."

"Do you believe that to be true for all their staff?"

"Warvis, Nava, and I don't give each other exact information, but we do speak about that in general terms. My sense is that we all are compensated well. Although Nava never appears to be satisfied with anything—ever."

Scorbion thanked Emerlin and instructed him to tell Nava and Warvis that they were free to go, saying, "I will reach out to those whom I desire to return here at the time I am in need of them."

Then he addressed the others in the shop. "I hope that none of you took offense that I conducted the majority of these most recent interrogations." When there were no protestations, he resumed. "Calvin, might I entreat you to utilize your cart and convey farmer Chames here? I believe the time has arrived to inquire into him and his past."

"I will indeed, Pignon. My mare is harnessed to my cart two streets from here, as you know, so I should be able to return with Chames within the hour. The rest of you, take care of the shop until I return."

Before Calvin could leave, Simon Adley arrived. "Chief Inspector, I looked into George Barlan as you asked me to. I learned that . . ." Adley stopped speaking when he realized that everyone in the shop would hear what he had to report, including Thelma. "May I speak freely in front of all who are here?"

Scorbion responded, "You may, Sergeant. I assume that your concern centers around Miss Smith, but as opposed to when she was on the witness side of this table, she is now part of the interrogation process. So, please do continue with your report."

Satisfied with Scorbion's clarification, Adley recounted one new revelation. "When Barlan's father arrived on the Continent, his grandparents changed his name to match theirs. In America his family name was either Barlin or Borlan—I could not determine exactly which it was—but his grandparents changed it to Barlan."

Scorbion thanked Adley, "for that interesting piece of information," and then asked Calvin, "to proceed with haste to retrieve Martin Chames."

After Calvin left, Scorbion signaled to Adley to join him at the door. "Sergeant Adley and I must make our way to the stationhouse. There are a few things I wish to look into before Chames joins us. I shall not be long."

Thelma also excused herself. "I must return to my shop so that if any of my clientele appear, I can accommodate them."

Then Thelma, Scorbion, and Adley left.

The men who remained animatedly discussed among themselves what had transpired during the day to that point, and conjectured what they might learn from Chames.

CHAPTER THIRTY-SEVEN

Scorbion returned ten minutes before Calvin's cart pulled to a stop in front of the barbershop with Chames. Calvin tied the mare's lead to the iron ring on the pavement, and as he did, Scorbion studied Chames as he alit from the vehicle.

"Gentlemen," he said to the others, "I see nothing unusual or outstanding in regard to Mr. Chames, other than the well-developed musculature of his arms and chest, no doubt a result of the work he performs in the fields tending to his crops and animals. In every other way, I perceive him as nondescript: brown hair— that I must say could use Calvin's shears—farming attire, average stature, sun-weathered skin, and a slightly bow-legged gait, as is most assuredly present in a great number of this community's rural residents."

"And that is important b-because?" Barnabus asked.

"It is important owing to the fact that it does not preclude him from being the seller of the hog in Brookdale. The butcher reported the person to be generally nondescript, and Chames could fit that description as he has no defining physical characteristic which would exclude him from consideration."

Calvin asked, "What motive could he possibly have to steal the hog . . . or murder Barlan? Chames is a farmer, and he's relatively new to this area."

"Let us learn that together."

Chames entered the shop, the men seated themselves at the table, and Scorbion commenced. "We meet twice in two days, after having never met before. Thank you for joining us. To begin, what is your full name?"

In a strong, booming voice, Chames bellowed, "As I introduced myself to you last night, Martin Chames, but most everyone just calls me Chames."

"Fine, that is how you will be addressed. Mr. Chames, do you know why you are here?"

"I assume it has something to do with that swine that I heard was stolen from my neighbor, George Barlan."

"That theft and more, sir. We will get to that in due time, but for now, would you please recount to us the details of your life prior to residing in Haxford?"

"There's not much to tell. My family was originally from Tottingham, but we moved for a few short years near Glouchester, where I was raised until I attained six years of age. At that time my family returned to Tottingham where my parents established the Chames Family Farm. I spent the remainder of my life there until my relocation here."

"If I recall correctly, Tottingham is close to London, is it not?"

"You are correct, sir . . ."

"Pardon, I am Yves. And did you frequently travel to London during your years in Tottingham?"

"I did. Regularly. It's where my family, and then I, sold most of our produce."

Scorbion leaned back on his stool. "Am I correct that you relocated to this town only within the past year?"

"That's so, Inspector."

"Under what circumstances did you come to reside here?"

"Over the course of the last few years, during my selling trips to London, I'd heard a number of times how fine the land is, and how welcoming the people in this town are. In fact, I had become friendly with Samuel and Florence Gray in London, and they spoke highly of Haxford. So just over eighteen months ago I took a rare holiday—you know a farmer's work is never finished, so I don't get to take holiday very often—and I traveled here to see the area for myself. After having spent the majority of my years in Tottingham, I was up for something different."

"I'm Thomas, and I've got a question. What became of your farm in Tottingham?"

"I sold it, prior to relocating. I garnered a decent amount from the sale and began looking for a suitable property as soon as I arrived in Haxford. It was my good fortune, although I am sorry to call it that, that Samuel Gray had his accident just after I came to town. I used a portion of my funds to purchase his farm from Florence. She told me that she couldn't run it alone, nor did she want to. Had Gray's cart not toppled and crushed him, his farm would not have been available, and I would have had to purchase less desirable land farther away from town."

"I concur with your statement—what was a very unfortunate situation for Gray and his widow turned out quite well for you."

"It did, Chief Inspector. I do not deny that."

"And then you recently expanded your holdings by purchasing two pastures from George Barlan. Is that correct?" Scorbion asked.

"That *is* correct."

"And you inquired about securing additional land from him as well?" Scorbion continued to ask.

"I did," Chames confirmed.

"But he would not sell."

"You're correct again. He wouldn't."

"And what, may I ask, were you going to use the extra land for, had Barlan sold it to you?"

"I was going to plant part of it. The parts that are put to pasture. But my grander design was for the remainder of the property."

That piqued Barnabus's interest. "W-which w-was?"

"Timber," Chames explained. "A great deal of Barlan's land is woodland. If he had sold it all to me, I would've started a timber mill and used the forest for that purpose. At present, the closest mill to Haxford is a two-hour journey. I believe I could become quite well-to-do supplying lumber in this region. And Barlan's property was perfect for that venture."

Scorbion looked Chames in the eye. "Are you aware that Barlan is dead?"

Chames's mouth fell open. "My God! How was he killed?"

"I have not said that he was killed, just that he died. What makes you believe that Barlan might have been killed?"

Chames paused. "He seemed to be in perfect health when I smoked with him at the Green Door yesterday. I can't imagine that he died of natural causes."

Scorbion cradled his chin in his hand. "That is a logical explanation, but one that is still troubling to me. I will consider it."

Chames's body stiffened and his voice rose a few decibels. "Are you insinuating that I had anything to do with that? If so, you are baying at the wrong moon."

Billy leaned closer to Chames. "On your trips to London, how often did you and Nava meet up?"

Chames, still perturbed, gruffly replied, "I didn't say that Nava and I ever met up in London."

"But did you?" Billy asked.

"No, we didn't. He sold me machinery. And worked on it. Our encounters were in Tottingham, not in London. It was—"

Scorbion broke in before Chames could finish. "And how many times have you and Nava met at the Green Door?"

"A few times."

"Could you be more specific?"

Chames's voice grew even louder. "No. I really can't. I have not counted how often we've smoked together."

"Did you smoke there with Barlan as well?" Calvin inquired.

Chames calmed down a bit, and his voice softened. "Yes. Once or twice. And I recall that on at least one occasion Barlan, Nava, and I were there at the same time. I believe we shared farming ideas."

Scorbion stood up, stretched, walked around the shop, and sat back down. "Calvin, you really might wish to consider placing a pillow or cushion of some sort on this stool. It gets less comfortable the longer I sit on it."

Billy added, "Or get those new chairs."

Calvin nodded noncommittally.

Scorbion continued his questioning of Chames. "You told us earlier that you learned of Haxford on your trips to London during the time that you resided in Tottingham. Do you recall who it was that first told you about this community?"

Chames paused to think. "I'm sorry, I don't. However, it must have been either the Grays or Charles Emerlin."

"Could it have been Nava?"

"Possibly, but not likely. It's not my understanding that he had been here before his move to Haxford."

"Did you come here alone?"

"Yes."

"You have no wife?"

"No, not at present. But, to be fair and open, I *am* seeing someone. But, I have no idea what that might have to do with Barlan."

"And who is this woman that you are seeing?"

"Gray's widow, Florence."

Calvin's eyebrows rose. "You're involved with Gray's widow?"

"I am. What is so odd about that? We dined together a number of times in London, became friendly, and seemed to be compatible with each other. Florence is a fine woman. She keeps herself well, and I enjoy her company. She's living with her sister in Brookdale at present, but I know she'd be pleased to be able to move back here into the farm house."

"Why did you not have her accompany you to the Morgans' home last night for dinner?" Scorbion asked. "You and I were the only gentlemen lacking companions."

"I asked her, but she had another engagement previously set up."

Scorbion wondered if she had been at the suffragette meeting with Thelma and he made a mental note to ask her.

Chames barked, "I don't really understand what any of this has to do with Barlan or his hog."

"Everything is a piece of the overall puzzle," Scorbion explained. "Some pieces are very small and of lesser importance, while others are of a much greater size and serve to fill in the bigger spaces in the puzzle. Then there are some items that may be so unimportant that they are eventually discarded. But to find the pieces that fit to the greatest degree, one must often go far afield and ask seemingly immaterial questions. One of those questions that I have for you is how much contact you have had with any of Dr. and Lady Morgan's staff since you located here."

"Very little to none."

"With whom have you had that 'very little' contact?"

"Emerlin—last night I thanked him for the scrumptious meal and suggested he contact me to supply his grains—and Nava, who I already told you I have met once or twice at the Green Door. Other than that, no one. I think I may have only been invited to dinner due to Florence's friendship with Isabelle Morgan, who I'd wager wasn't too pleased when I arrived unaccompanied."

Scorbion cleared his throat. "Have you not left out your niece?"

Chames replied curtly, "I rather thought that went without saying."

Calvin was about to ask a question, but Scorbion waved him off. "Please excuse my cutting you off, my friend, but I think we have taken up enough of Mr. Chames's time. Can I assume that, should we require your presence here again, you will return?"

Chames stood. "Certainly, Chief Inspector. Any time."

When Chames started for the front door, Calvin asked, "Do you want me to return you to your farm?"

"No. Thank you, Mr. Brown. I think I'll drop in at the tavern and hoist a pint or two. I'll find my way home later. Florence shouldn't mind waiting there for me for an extra hour."

Once Chames was walking away from the shop, all eyes turned to Scorbion.

"Gentlemen, the pieces of that aforementioned puzzle are falling into place. Let me summarize what we know. The stealing of the hatchet had to be committed by someone in the Morgan household. I have eliminated Warvis as a possible suspect. He is either the calmest and most accomplished liar I have ever met, or the man is truly innocent of anything that has occurred here. He has no motive, and apparently spends so much of his time in the company of the Morgans and the others on their staff that he would not appear to have had the opportunity to have committed these acts. That leaves Emerlin and Nava."

"Or Katy," Billy added.

Scorbion responded, "Yes. We must not forget about her. Especially since she was able to return to work last night when the hatchet was stolen."

Thomas observed, "None of them appear to have any motive. Do they?"

"That is what it looks like at first blush," Scorbion responded. "But I believe that as we more fully assess what they have told us, we will see inconsistencies appear in at least one of their accounts."

"Could s-some of them be in it t-together?" Barnabus asked.

"Possibly. It is a possibility that we have to consider," Scorbion replied.

Calvin firmly stated, "I still say that Emerlin could have stolen the pig, sold it to the butcher in Brookdale, and then repurchased it."

Scorbion put his arm around his friend. "Ah yes, Calvin, regarding that, I am sorry that I did not disclose this before now, but when I went to the station, I telephoned the butcher. Fortunately, he has a telephone in his shop—and we all await the one you will be acquiring for this establishment."

Calvin drew away a few inches. "You know that I have been considering it, and yes, I will obtain one. But I must say that I am at a partial loss to understand what purpose it will serve. I do not accept appointments. I take my customers in the order they arrive. Except for you, Pignon. When you come, you get served. So, what would I truly desire a telephone for?"

"For us to use in the solving of these affairs—if we are to continue doing so in the future in this establishment, a telephone will be of great assistance," Scorbion responded.

There was a chorus of "yes," "of course," and one "*oui.*"

Calvin's shoulders dropped in resignation. "All right. All of you. I will obtain the telephone. I, too, wish to be a part of subsequent investigations. But for now, Pignon, please continue with your thoughts about this case."

"Certainly. Now, regarding my conversation with Brookdale's butcher—after what he related, which confirmed what Emerlin has told us, I remain convinced that the hog was carved up, stolen, and sold to him by the same persons who took the hatchet."

"And aren't they the same men who murdered Barlan?" Billy asked.

"Most probably they are, but not necessarily. As I perceive the situation, one person stole the hatchet, and we have narrowed that down to Emerlin or Nava . . ."

Billy interjected, "Or Katy."

Scorbion's face lit up. "Yes, Billy, once again, you are correct—or Katy. I continue: two persons slaughtered and made off with the pig, whomever stole the hatchet and his . . . or her . . . accomplice. One man sold it to the butcher, most probably the accomplice, and one man stabbed and killed Barlan, again most likely the accomplice, as both Emerlin and Nava were here with us at the time that Barlan was murdered."

"Is th-there anyone we should be qu-questioning other th-than Chames? Or do you believe that he's th-the accomplice?"

"I am still formulating my opinion, Barnabus. It is possible, but not necessarily a given."

Calvin asked, "Why would you believe Chames might be the accomplice, Pignon? He seemed a nice enough fellow—no matter the volume of his voice."

"And I can't see what his motive would be," Billy added.

Scorbion responded, "I will share my thoughts with everyone when they have fully coalesced, but at the present time, I would ask Calvin to utilize his cart once again—this time to transport Florence Gray to us here. She is the person whom we must next make inquiries of. Chames stated that she is presently at his farm, so you needn't travel to Brookdale to transport her here."

Before Calvin walked out the door, he addressed Scorbion. "It's curious that to Nava the Morgans are tightfisted, while the others say they are compensated well."

Scorbion was pensive. "Yes. This case is beginning to fill with numerous inconsistencies."

CHAPTER THIRTY-EIGHT

Thelma returned to the barbershop before Calvin and Mrs. Gray. "This has not been a banner day for my purse. Or, as Freud would say, my psyche. The few customers I have had all were more interested in discussing that *Gazette* article than in purchasing books. It is costing me more to light the lamps in my shop than I am making in book sales, so I have given up on the remainder of the afternoon. Let any customers who do materialize return tomorrow. What is taking place here is far more interesting and invigorating than sitting alone among my stacks or negating the twaddle that story postulated."

After Scorbion and Billy apprised Thelma of the meeting with Chames, mostly focusing on his relationship with Florence Gray and his niece Katy Alby, Scorbion asked her, "Do you have any thoughts about any of that which we have related to you? Or about any aspect of this situation?"

Thelma lightly rubbed her hands together before answering. "To me, there is an air of conspiracy running through what you have told me and that which I have observed myself. This entire affair involves a niece and an uncle, a widow and her lover—who happens to own her home—a scorned woman who is reunited with the man who jilted her, and a chef who brought all of them together. There are far too many interconnections for my comfort, and somewhere amongst them I believe we will find motivations that span the gamut of revenge, jealousy, greed, devotion, cruelty, and loyalty."

Scorbion nodded. "Well thought out and said, Miss Smith. It is now our job to unravel the layers of those connections and ascertain those motivations. And we will next do that when Calvin Brown returns here with Florence Gray."

Ten minutes later, when they arrived, Calvin once again tied his mare to the post in front of the shop, and then he and Mrs. Gray entered the barbershop.

Due to her heavy use of rouge and being attired in finer clothes than the average female in a farm household, as Florence Gray passed through the doorway, Scorbion's immediate impression of her was that she appeared to be anything but the quintessential-looking farmer's wife. He attempted to look past the cosmetics and the garments to determine her natural appearance. He observed her to be of medium height, somewhat sun-weathered, and large-boned. Scorbion took in that her somewhat unkempt, close-cropped brown hair did not fit with the rest of her image. He also detected a sadness in her eyes that he thought most people would not see.

After Calvin announced that he hadn't had to go all the way to Chames's farm to get Mrs. Gray—she was just outside of town walking along the road to the farm—each of the men introduced themselves to her. When it came Thelma's turn, she did more than introduce herself. "Mrs. Gray, I am Thelma Smith, proprietor of Books on the Square, but today I am additionally a member of this investigatory group. I want to compliment you on those lovely boots you are wearing. The bow adds a wonderful touch that takes them from delightful to sublime. Might I ask where you acquired them?"

Mrs. Gray swelled with pride. "Thank you for noticing. They are one of my most recent purchases. I obtained them on my last excursion to London. I'm afraid you will not find any such as these in Haxford, or in any of our surrounding towns, for that matter. The next time you venture to our capital city, I would be more than pleased to provide you with the name and address of the bootery where they are sold."

Thelma thanked her. "I would appreciate that, and I will take you up on that offer at such time as I do go. Calvin just mentioned that he met you as you were walking back to the farm. Were you not concerned that the road would scuff your boots?"

Florence answered, "It was not how I would have preferred to make my way back there, but I can always obtain another pair if need be."

Scorbion waited until Mrs. Gray had responded to Thelma's question before briefing her on what their inquiry concerned—while leaving out any information about Barlan's murder—and then posed his first question.

"Mrs. Gray . . ."

"Please call me Florence."

Scorbion hesitated. "I will attempt to satisfy your request, but I am not accustomed to addressing people by their given name during an interrogation. So please grant me forgiveness if I err at times."

Mrs. Gray made eye contact with Scorbion. "Is this an *interrogation*? My, my, I thought you just had some questions for me. 'Interrogation' sounds so formal, and so . . . intense."

"It is the same no matter what you call it, dear lady. But, do not be put off by the word or the process. We only seek to clarify and learn certain facts about recent goings-on," Scorbion responded.

"What is it that you wish to know from me, Chief Inspector Scorbion? I do not believe that I have any knowledge that would be helpful to you."

Scorbion placed his hand over his chest. "Allow me to be the arbiter of that. To begin with, would you please describe the circumstances surrounding your late husband's accident. I hope that reliving that incident will not be too difficult for you, but it is important that we know what occurred."

"I will do so, but there is not much to tell. Samuel and I were on our way to Brookdale to pick up supplies for the farm. Their mercantile shop has a different selection of goods than we have in this town so we regularly purchased what we needed from both locations. Samuel turned to speak to me just at the moment that some wild animal in the woods on our left let out the most horrifying loud shriek, which caused our horse, Buddy, to rear up in fright. Unfortunately, when Buddy did so, our cart swerved, and the front right wheel bumped against a large rock in the road. I later learned that the impact broke part of the wheel free from the axle, which caused the cart to flip over sideways. I was fortunate to be thrown from the seat to the soft grass of the pasture that abutted the road on our right. Samuel was not as lucky. His foot became tangled in the reins when I let go of them, and they tethered him to the cart. When it fell over, his head struck a sharp rock that pierced his temple. I was told later that it killed him instantly. When the cart turned upside down, it landed on him, and it crushed him as well." Florence paused, her face drooped, and she sobbed. "It was horrid."

Calvin interjected, "I am so sorry, Florence."

"It *was* tragic, but in the year since that happened, I have made peace with it. Selling the farm and moving in with my sister have helped ease the pain of the memory."

Mrs. Gray took a hankie out of her purse and lightly dabbed her eyes.

Scorbion waited until he judged her to be composed again. "We have recently spoken with Martin Chames who tells us that you and he are now accompanying each other, and that you may have plans to marry—and that you are moving back to the farm you sold to him. Is that accurate?"

Mrs. Gray perked up. "It is, indeed, accurate. Samuel and I dined with Martin in London several times, and I have gotten to know him quite well since I sold him the farm. I have become rather fond of him over the course of this past year."

Barnabus inquired, "And you d-don't have a problem moving b-back to the farm, even though it will revive m-memories of your l-late husband?"

"Martin and I are quite in love, and that should more than make up for any sadness the location will instill in me. Additionally, Samuel was incapable of any intimacy for a number of years prior to his death— he was my senior by a few decades and at the time of his death he was semi-infirm."

Scorbion stood up, arched his back, and sat back down. "Please tell us how you initially met Mr. Chames."

"Let me think . . . Ah yes, the first time we encountered each other was at Chef Emerlin's restaurant, the Cork and Plate. That took place about a year before Martin moved here. Emerlin introduced us. He said he thought we would rather enjoy each other's company. We all dined together that night. The next time I saw Martin was on a trip I made to London without Samuel. We had a splendid time together. He was quite the conversationalist. A bit boisterous, but immensely interesting."

Thelma broke in. "Was it your custom to travel to London without your husband? I would believe it could be rather stressful, and possibly dangerous, for a woman to be alone in a city of that size."

Florence shook her head. "Oh no, not, at all. On the majority of my trips there Samuel and I went together, but I did make some excursions to London on my own, and they were enjoyable, not filled with stress or concern. Samuel despised shopping, other than for farm supplies here in Haxford, but I preferred to purchase my clothes—like my boots—and sundries in that more cosmopolitan environment and take advantage of the many additional shops that sold those goods than are present in this region. So when I went to London for that purpose, Samuel remained here."

Scorbion nodded. "Please continue what you were saying before Miss Smith interrupted you."

Thelma gave Scorbion a scornful look.

Mrs. Gray continued, ignoring Thelma's reaction to Scorbion. "Shortly before Samuel's death, Katy Alby and I shared dinner together one evening here in town, and during the meal she asked had anything ever happened to Samuel, if I would want to run the farm by myself. I told her that I didn't think I had the courage or the stamina to do so, and if Samuel were to become incapacitated, or even worse, if he should pass away, I would put it up for sale. Katy mentioned that her uncle, Martin, desired to relocate to Haxford and wanted to purchase a farm. She asked if I'd have interest in her putting him in touch with me. I told her no at the time, but after Samuel's accident, I recalled the conversation, spoke with her, and she connected me with Martin, who had already come here by then but hadn't purchased any property yet."

"And that is the same Katy who tends to Dr. and Lady Morgan's home—"

"Yes, Chief Inspector, it is. She is one and the same."

Yves asked, "Are not she and Chames *de la même famille*?"

Mrs. Gray answered directly. "Yes, they are. She is his niece. In fact, when Martin and I wed, we hope that Katy will join us and care for our farmhouse instead of the Morgans' home."

Scorbion was curious, "Are the Morgans aware of that?"

"I do not believe so."

"But you and Isabelle Morgan are close, are you not?" Calvin asked.

Florence answered, "Yes, we are. Why do you ask that?"

Calvin responded, "I would imagine that if Katy comes to work for you and Chames that would leave a void in the Morgans' staff that they would not be pleased about."

Florence, sounding uncompassionate, responded, "As they say, blood is thicker than water. Is it not?"

Scorbion posed a new question: "How well do you know George Barlan?"

"Having lived next to him for many years, I believe I'm acquainted with him rather well."

"And are you aware of Mr. Chames's desire to acquire Barlan's farm?"

"Yes, I am. Martin has told me on numerous occasions how combining Barlan's farm and his would be quite beneficial and lucrative. Martin has approached Barlan to sell his farm to him numerous times in the past year, but to no avail."

Yves broke in, "Are you aware of what has happened to Barlan?"

Mrs. Gray paused before answering matter-of-factly. "By now I don't think there's a soul who hasn't heard about his hog being stolen."

Yves started to ask her, "But are you—?" but before he could complete the question, Scorbion held his finger up to his mouth.

Instead, Scorbion asked, "Has Mr. Chames ever mentioned his

relationship with the Morgans' driver, Joseph Nava? Or their manservant, Warvis?"

Mrs. Gray thought for a moment. "Not that I can think of. I know Nava sold Martin some farm equipment and had a brief relationship with Katy, but I am fairly sure that Martin and Nava have not seen each other to any degree since Martin moved here. And to my knowledge, Martin has had no encounters with Warvis. His name has never come up in any of our conversations."

Scorbion rested his elbow on the table, put his fist to his cheek, and looked Mrs. Gray directly in the eyes. "Mrs. Gray—"

"Florence."

"Excuse me, yes, Florence, have you ever been mistaken for a man?"

Mrs. Gray appeared flustered, even angry. "Wh-wh-*what*?!"

"Have you ever had anyone address you as 'sir'? It is a straightforward question," Scorbion said, as he leaned back on his chair.

Quickly recovering her composure, she attacked. "Why would you ask me such a preposterous thing, Chief Inspector? What an uncivilized thing to say to a lady."

"I am sorry to have had to ask, madam, but given your stature, your build, and your features, I wonder if—absent your cosmetics and wearing the right garments—someone might mistake you for a member of the masculine gender."

Mrs. Gray responded adamantly, "I have *never* been mistaken for a man. Never. Never. Never. That is preposterous, sir! You have insulted me."

"My intention was neither to insult you nor to upset you, but I do not apologize for asking any question that might be germane to our investigation. Let us move on."

Florence harrumphed. "Please do."

Thelma interjected, "That was a very bizarre question. Inspector, do you intend to ask the same of me?"

Scorbion responded, "As I am questioning Mrs. Gray, and not you at this time, no matter how inappropriate a question I ask may seem, every possible issue must be raised and explored."

Thelma gave Scorbion a half-hearted smile and leaned back on her chair. When she did, Scorbion turned back to Florence Gray. "I have one additional question for you at this time: Where were you earlier this afternoon, until approximately one hour ago?"

Still smarting, Florence grumbled under her breath while her eye twitched ever so slightly. Then she took in a deep draw of air, and after expelling it, composed herself before responding. "I was out doing some errands. I returned an empty elixir bottle to the chemist and stopped in at the milliner to see the newest styles they recently received—a very feminine thing to do, wouldn't you say?"

She waited for a reaction to her sarcastic challenge. When she got none, she continued. "Then I took lunch at the Green Door, after which I dropped into the post office to retrieve a telegram from one of my cousins in Paris. Lastly, I stopped at the village green for a respite before my walk back to the farm."

Scorbion turned to Yves. "Please ask your question now."

All heads turned to Yves. "Mrs. Gray, butcher Barlan is dead. Are you aware of that?"

Then they turned to Mrs. Gray.

Her face contorted before she answered. "Dead? No. I had no idea. When did it happen?"

Scorbion responded, "Very recently." He paused, waiting for Mrs. Gray to ask another question. When she didn't, he stood, thanked her for coming and answering their questions, and then escorted her out of the shop.

When he returned, Billy asked, "Isn't it another inconsistency that Chames said she was at the farm, yet she was here in town?"

"Yes, my friends and associates," Scorbion confirmed, "there are even more inconsistencies, bends in the road of this affair, than we anticipated. However, we shall straighten everything out. Quite soon, I do believe."

Barnabus responded, "Really? S-Soon? I am at a total loss as to w-what's going on. Do you have an idea of who the p-perpetrators are?"

Scorbion replied, "I have a suspicion. Let us review what we know as factual. Someone from inside the Morgan household took the missing hatchet, two people were seen by Harry riding in a cart with a sailcloth last evening when Barlan's hog was stolen, and one of them appeared to have the hatchet on their person. A nondescript person sold a slaughtered hog to the butcher in Brookdale early this morning, which was then purchased by Emerlin. Chames and Florence Gray are a couple and are planning to marry, and Chames has recently attempted, unsuccessfully, to acquire Barlan's farm."

Billy added, "And, we know that Samuel Gray died a bit over a year ago, shortly before Chames purchased his farm."

Calvin chimed in, "Plus, Chames and Katy are related."

"And K-Katy and Nava were in a relationship at one p-point," Barnabus added.

Scorbion pondered for a moment. "And, they may be in one once again. We also know that there are questions and inconsistencies—untruths—in much of what has been told to us. For instance, do Nava and Chames still have any interactions with each other?"

Thomas added, "And do the Morgans pay good or not?"

Calvin joined in. "And where does Emerlin fit into this?"

"And our possible woman-man Florence Gray," Thelma dryly added.

Lastly, Yves inquired, "And is Bentine involved in any way?"

Scorbion held out his right arm and gestured for his associates to hold off asking further questions. "Those are all excellent queries, and we will uncover the answers to all of them in due time, but for now, and to confirm my suspicions, we must interview the only person involved in this affair with whom we have not yet met."

The men looked at each other, wondering who Scorbion was referring to.

Billy sat bolt upright. "Katy. It's Katy isn't it?"

Scorbion turned to Billy. "Very good. Yes. We must bring Katy here and learn what she knows. Do any of you gentlemen know where she resides?"

When no one responded, Calvin stood. "Why don't Yves and I take my cart to the Morgans' home and determine if Katy is there today. If she is, we can return here with her. If she is not, they might know where we can locate her."

Scorbion complimented Calvin. "That is a sound plan. Please do so posthaste."

Before they departed, Scorbion told Yves, "Do not hold out hope that Mr. Bentine is involved in this particular affair. It is unlikely and improbable. However, I remain uncomfortable with the solution that we arrived at in his situation, which I am still attempting to piece together."

When Calvin and Yves left the shop, Scorbion told the others, "I wish to visit Angus Riley. I have learned that he is both a blacksmith and an animal healer, and I am hoping that he will know which wild animals that live in the woods between here and Brookdale would be capable of making such a sound as Mrs. Gray described, that would so startle a horse that it would stop and rear. I will report what he says when I return. Miss Smith, would you like to accompany me?"

Thelma rose. "I very much would enjoy the walk and the fresh summer air—and your company as well."

"May I join you?" Billy asked.

Scorbion did not hesitate to respond. "Please do. We will both enjoy your company as we make our way there and back."

CHAPTER THIRTY-NINE

When Scorbion, Billy, and Thelma reached Angus Riley's blacksmith shop, he was in the midst of pounding a horseshoe on his anvil with a large hammer. His dusty, soot-blackened, converted barn was filled with home-made tools. Near his wood-burning stove, an assortment of hammers and sledgehammers were propped against, or lying on, a table. Tongs and jaws of varying shapes and sizes lay scattered on the ground, while chisels, punches, and drifts hung from the walls—as did a collection of leather aprons.

Riley did not hear them enter as the din from his banging the horse-shoe into shape obliterated any other sounds. When he paused to wipe sweat from his brow, he looked up and saw them standing at his entrance.

"How can I help you?" he asked.

Scorbion took a step forward. "I am Chief Inspector Scorbion. I, and my associates, have come to ask you questions that will assist us in a murder investigation we are conducting. Might we take a few minutes of your time?"

Riley put down his hammer, picked up a stained cloth, fully wiped his forehead, and said, "Roger that, Chief. I could use a break. I'm not as chipper as I used to be. A murder you say? Who is the unfortunate bloke? Or woman?"

Billy answered. "George Barlan. Did you know him?"

"Of course," Riley responded. "Everybody in Haxford knows George Barlan. He was murdered you said?"

Scorbion replied. "Yes. He was stabbed in the back."

Riley asked, "Do you know who did it?"

"Not yet," Thelma answered, "but the chief inspector will determine that before long."

"I hope you do," Riley said as he put the cloth on the table. "Barlan was a good fellow. Now, what do you want to know from me?"

Scorbion moved closer to Riley until he was standing right in front of him. "I have been told that in addition to your blacksmithing, you are an animal healer, and possibly the most knowledgeable person in this region about the species of all local wildlife."

"I am," Riley confirmed.

Scorbion went on, "Then I ask you what manner of beast would there be in our environs that would make a roar or yell so terrifying that it would cause a horse to rear. A sound similar to this—"

Scorbion turned away from Riley and roared as loud as he was able.

When he was done, he turned back toward Riley. "Similar to that, only possibly more ferociously."

Riley laughed. "You just did a credible imitation of a lion. I congratulate you for that. However, there are no lions in this part of England, probably in all of England, except those in a zoo or a circus. And as to any other type of animal that would be capable of making a sound loud enough to frighten a horse, I would wager you'll not find any around here. No wolves, no hyenas—none of any species that I have encountered or heard about. Not since I've been alive."

"That is very helpful," Scorbion told him. "And you are certain of this?"

"As sure as I am that I need to get back to that horseshoe or there will be one lame horse tonight," Riley responded.

Scorbion thanked him for his time, and then he, Billy, and Thelma left.

On the way back to the barbershop, they discussed what Riley had told them, all agreeing that what he said had contradicted what Florence Gray and Martin Chames had reported.

Thirty minutes later, Scorbion, Thelma, and Billy strode back into the shop.

"I see that Calvin and Yves have not yet returned with the girl, Katy," Scorbion observed. "I will fill them in later, but I tell you who are here that Angus Riley told us, in no uncertain terms, that he has never heard nor seen an animal in any area of our countryside that makes such a shriek as Florence Gray described. It is a further piece of the puzzle that does not fit at all."

Thomas sat on one of the barber chairs and sighed. "None of this makes sense to me. I feel so stupid."

Barnabus consoled him. "Don't f-feel bad, lad, none of us can f-fathom what has happened either. You're n-not alone in b-being bewildered."

Before anyone else could speak, Yves and Katy appeared at the front door. Katy, a slender, pleasant-looking, auburn-haired, twenty-three-year-old girl, was wearing her black maid's uniform. Calvin, trailing just behind them, announced, "We were fortunate that today is a day that Katy works at the Morgans'."

Scorbion gently grasped Katy's hand and welcomed her, but she quickly withdrew it to shield three coughs in the crook of her elbow. After she recovered, Scorbion explained the role of those in the shop and the purpose of their investigation, leaving out any reference to Barlan's murder. He led her to the table, and after she and the others were seated, he began.

"Do you know George Barlan?"

Katy immediately replied, "Of course. Everyone in this town knows butcher Barlan."

"How did you first come to be aware of him, please?" Scorbion asked.

Once again, Katy didn't hesitate when answering. "My uncle Martin Chames bought some pastures from him, although I believe I became aware of him at some point earlier than that."

"Speaking of your uncle," Scorbion continued, "was it not he who told Chef Emerlin about you while in his restaurant in London, which led to Emerlin telling Florence Gray, who then related that information to Isabelle Morgan? And was that not how you came to be employed by the Morgans?"

"That is correct, sir. That is the chain of events that occurred," Katy affirmed.

Scorbion then asked, "Did you know Joseph Nava while you and he both resided in the environs of London?"

Katy's face reddened, just a bit. "Yes, I did. He came to Uncle's farm in Tottingham when I was tending to the horses there."

Scorbion leaned closer to her, speaking softly. "Did you and Joseph Nava not have a relationship while you both were there?"

Katy's face filled with a deeper red, as she quietly replied, "Yes, we did. All too briefly."

Billy followed up. "Have you seen each other more now that you both live in Haxford?"

"Yes," Katy replied. "I met Joseph a few times, when he and Uncle were coming out of the Green Door together, soon after Martin relocated here. Joseph was much more social on those occasions, and we have seen each other more than a few times in the past months. I find him to be quite tender." She blushed again, in saying the word *tender*.

Calvin muttered under his breath, "Friendly and tender are not words I would have used, given how he acted in here."

Scorbion posed his next question. "Isabelle Morgan informed us that you had an illness that kept you away from their household for a fortnight prior to the dinner I attended last evening. May I inquire as to the nature of that infirmity?"

Katy quickly replied, "I had a fever and a dreadful cough. Fortunately, it has passed. Except for an occasional cough or two—like the ones you just heard."

"So can we safely assume that by last evening you were significantly better? Well enough to assist with the after-dinner chores?" Scorbion asked.

Katy nodded. "Yes. Yes, you can. I was *much* better by then. Still not fully recovered, but well enough to—" She stopped abruptly.

Thomas looked at her sternly and asked, "To what?"

"Nothing in particular. Just, to help out."

"Are you aware that Joseph Nava plans to leave for Berlin next week?" Scorbion asked.

Katy flinched just enough for it to be noticeable to Scorbion. "N-No. I did not know that. Are you certain?"

"He told us that earlier today," Billy answered.

Katy rubbed her hand across her forehead, apparently shaken. "I was not aware of that."

In a motherly tone, Thelma said, "I would suggest that you and Mr. Nava discuss his plans so that you are clear about them, and how they might affect you."

Katy looked crestfallen. "Yes. I will."

After a moment of silence, Calvin sloped back in his chair. "What types of animals did your father raise on his farm?"

"Chickens, pigs, and horses. That's where I learned horse grooming and training. Do you have any further questions of me? I do have to return to my chores. The Morgans don't enjoy an unkempt household."

"I do have one last question," Scorbion replied. "Do you know how your uncle first met Florence Gray?"

Katy's response was not unexpected. "I believe that somewhere between one-and-a-half to two years ago, while my uncle was delivering produce to Chef Emerlin's restaurant, he told Emerlin of his intention to move here and purchase land. Shortly after that, the Grays dined at Emerlin's, at which time he related to them what my uncle had told him. I believe that on their next visit to London, they, my uncle, and Emerlin all dined together. From that first time, I know that he and Florence enjoyed each other, rather very much. In fact, he told me that she was an utterly charming woman. I believe it was during that initial dinner that they asked my uncle to make certain to see them if he ever visited here."

"May I, therefore, assume that it was no surprise to you that after Samuel Gray tragically died, your uncle and Florence Gray took up with each other?"

Katy coughed, took a handkerchief out of her purse, dabbed her lips, and then said in a raspy voice, "Not at all. I just told you they liked each other from the beginning."

Scorbion changed the line of questioning. "If you would, please describe your uncle to me. What is he like?"

Katy pondered the question before answering. "He has been kind to me, but I am aware that he can be rowdy and loud—you have heard his voice. He is keenly intelligent, but his manner sometimes makes people think otherwise. He is driven to success, and I know there are some who consider him to be ruthless in his dealings. He is extremely knowledgeable about farming, and that has enabled Uncle to outthink his suppliers and clients on many occasions."

Billy leaned in. "Has your uncle ever been in trouble with the law? Was everything on the up-and-up?"

Katy responded indignantly. "Oh no. He never got in trouble for any of his dealings. The only time he ever had any problems were a brawl or two he was involved in a few years ago. I think he might have spent a night in the Tottingham jail after one of them."

Scorbion asked the others if they had anything else to ask Katy. Barnabus leaned in a bit. "I d-do. I have a question. K-Katy, how do the Morgans p-pay? Are th-they cheap or generous?"

Katy tilted her head in thought. "They are fair. Neither tight nor indulgent."

When no one raised any other questions, Scorbion stood and thanked Katy for attending. He asked, "Would it inconvenience you greatly if I asked you to have a seat on the bench in front of the shop. I believe I will want you to rejoin us in here shortly."

"You have more questions for me?" she asked.

"If you don't mind, I will answer that quite soon, but in the meantime, please do take that seat for now," Scorbion responded.

When Katy went to the bench, Thelma sat contemplating everything she had told them, while the men buzzed with questions that mostly went unanswered: "Do you think she was telling the truth?" "Is she very sweet on Nava?" "What do the Morgans *really* pay?"

Scorbion picked up a heavy hairbrush and clanged it against one of the antiseptic jars on the counter. When the room was quiet, he spoke. "You all have questions . . . and you are correct to have them. But I am seeing a pattern through the trail of falsehoods, deceptions, and lies that has been laid out for us, a trail filled not only with misdirections but with omissions and cunning as well."

Thomas scratched his head. "You know who's done what? You figured this out?"

"I believe I have," Scorbion stated firmly.

Billy approached him. "Shall we sit down at the table, so that you can tell us what you think occurred, and so I have a surface to write upon?"

Scorbion put his hand on Billy's shoulder. "We will do that shortly, but not until there are more than the six of us in this shop." Scorbion turned to the men. "I entreat you all to take your bicycles, your carts, and your feet, and fetch all of those involved in this case. Thomas and Yves, would you both go to the Morgans' home and escort Emerlin and Warvis here? And while you are there, would you also ask the Morgans to have Joseph Nava motor them to this establishment, and have all three join us. Calvin, my friend, would you be so kind as to fetch Martin Chames and Florence Gray? Barnabus and Billy, I ask you to remain here with Miss Smith and me and to arrange the chairs to accommodate us and our guests. Once everyone is present, I will unfold to all what I am now certain is the tale of this affair."

Thelma put her hand on Scorbion's arm. "I cannot wait to hear your explanation, as I am as befuddled as all the rest. If I had to wager, I would put my pounds on that horrible man, Nava."

Scorbion allowed a small grin. "Gambling is an unhealthy vice, but you will soon learn if you actually made that wager whether it would have been lucrative or cost you some of your funds."

"I have a brilliant idea," Thelma responded. "If it is Nava, you will buy dinner for me tonight, and if it is not he, then I will pay the tab. Either way, we both win, by virtue of our being in each other's company."

"That is an excellent proposal, Miss Smith," Scorbion bantered. "I accept. But do be prepared to cover the cost of the dinner should you be wrong in your belief of who perpetrated what in this affair."

CHAPTER FORTY

As they departed to fulfill their tasks, Calvin poked Thomas's and Yves's arms. "I am amazed that Pignon knows what has occurred. I haven't the faintest idea, myself. But that's what makes him who he is."

Thomas skipped out of the way of Calvin's lightly striking him again and responded, "I'm confused. I feel like a buffoon."

Yves strode ahead of them both, nodded to Katy, and called back, "We are all *imbéciles*, while the inspector is *un grand génie*."

Billy and Barnabus brought the remaining chairs out from the storeroom and placed them among the chairs that were already at the table. They asked Scorbion, who was donning his suit jacket, exactly how he wanted them arranged. "To begin, we will no longer use this table, so you may return it to its usual resting place in that back room. We will then organize the chairs into a circle so that each person will have a clear view of all who will be in attendance."

Once the table was removed and the chairs were positioned to Scorbion's satisfaction, he told Billy and Barnabus that he was going out, "to take a stroll on the pavement during the time that the concerned parties are being conveyed here so that I might scrutinize my observations and conclusions for any inconsistencies. I will then confirm and finalize my thoughts and determine in what manner I should best present them when all are assembled in this room."

Then he said to Thelma, "I hope you do not mind lingering here with Billy and Barnabus. Your presence would only serve to distract me."

Thelma replied, "I shall take that as a compliment, and I will remain here."

Billy, Barnabus, and Thelma initially shared their opinions about the case with each other. Billy postulated, "I think Chames murdered Barlan," while Barnabus proposed, "I believe it m-might have b-been Emerlin." Thelma disagreed. "I agree with neither as the killer, but I have no solution of my own. However, my intuition tells me that Nava has had his hand in this affair somewhere, and to a great degree."

After they exhausted their theories, they waited in silence until the first of the summoned individuals returned twenty minutes later, when the Morgans' motorcar noisily arrived in front of the shop.

As the Morgans exited the vehicle, Isabelle spied Scorbion, a block away, walking toward the shop and waved to him. Scorbion lifted his hand in recognition. When he reached the Morgans, he opened the shop door and escorted them and Nava inside. Then he poked his head outside the door and asked Katy to come into the shop.

Once she was in, Scorbion hung his jacket on the coatrack, and then joined the Morgans, exchanging pleasantries.

Nava lit a cigarette and blew a smoke ring at Barnabus, who was standing near him. "This is going to be another waste of my time, and I don't relish being back in this shit-shop again." He looked around the room and when he saw Thelma, he winked at her, blew a kiss in her direction, and exclaimed lecherously, "At least it won't be a *total* waste of time as long as you're here, dolly bird." Thelma turned away from Nava and edged closer to Billy.

Ten minutes later, Calvin escorted Chames and Florence Gray into the barbershop, and after another five minutes, Thomas and Yves arrived with Warvis and Emerlin.

When Thomas shut the door, Calvin made sure the sign on the door was turned to Closed and that all the blinds were drawn tightly.

Scorbion directed the group's attention to the circle of chairs and asked them all to be seated.

Isabelle Morgan turned to Scorbion. "Is there a particular place you would like each of us to sit?"

"Please take any chair you choose," Scorbion answered. "It is of no importance which seat each person occupies."

The Morgans sat down first, next to each other, on the chairs that directly faced the front of the shop. Warvis went to the chair to Isabelle's right, while Thomas and Calvin sat next to him. Katy placed herself to Dr. Morgan's left. Florence Gray then sat next to Katy with Martin Chames positioning himself beside her on the left. Barnabus and Yves took the chairs adjacent to him. Emerlin strode to the chair to Calvin's right, while Billy sat on one of the four remaining chairs, which faced the storeroom at the back of the shop, and Thelma sat down next to him.

Nava ground out his cigarette on the floor by Calvin's barber chair and announced, "I'll stand." Then he sarcastically added, "It will give me a head start for this ridiculous game of musical chairs."

Scorbion walked to him, firmly put his hand on his shoulder, and steered Nava toward one of the two unoccupied seats. In his best authoritarian tone, he told Nava, "This is no game, I assure you. This is an official police matter, and if you do not place yourself upon one of those empty chairs, you will instead be forcibly placed in one of the vacant cells in my station."

Nava reluctantly sat, muttering, "Shit shop. Shit town. I can't wait to get out of here."

Scorbion declared, "*I* will be the one who stands as I unfold the facts and conclusions of this affair." He paused and then continued. "It is not always my custom to gather together all those involved in a case. However, this affair has several unusual motivations and circumstances, many of which dictate the necessity of having you all here at the same time."

Every eye and ear in the room focused on Scorbion.

"The most expedient way for me to begin unraveling the mysteries of this case—and for you to understand why specific events occurred and who perpetrated them—is for me to detail the chronology of the events, starting from the very beginning. During the telling of this tale, I believe it will become evident to you who the participants have been, and what each of their motivations were in regard to the purloined hatchet, the disappearance of the hog, and the killing of George Barlan."

There was a gasp from Katy who was not aware of Barlan's murder.

"Yes, for you, Katy Alby, who does not yet possess this knowledge, George Barlan was slain earlier today, by someone using the hatchet taken from the Morgans' library. I intend to unravel the mysteries of all of these events, and who perpetrated them, before this gathering disperses."

Scorbion rubbed his hands together, but before he could begin there was a rapping on the front door that caused all the people in the room to turn and look in that direction. Calvin stood and walked to the door. He opened it just enough so that he could converse with the man standing on the pavement without him being able to see into the shop. After a few sentences, Calvin closed the door and walked back to his seat. "It was a customer looking to have a shave. I asked him to return tomorrow. I'm sorry for the disturbance."

Scorbion was not perturbed. "There is nothing to be sorry about, my friend. It is I who have commandeered your establishment and robbed you of your recompense today. It is I who should be penitent."

Billy placed his pen and a few sheets of paper on the empty chair next to him that Scorbion would have been sitting on had he not been standing, and used the smooth, hard seat of the wooden chair as a writing surface.

Scorbion waited for Billy to set up his makeshift desk, and then began. "Every event that has recently transpired here had its genesis in Tottingham or London, so let me review what we know took place in those locales. We start with the knowledge that Martin Chames owned and ran a farm in Tottingham, and that Joseph Nava sold equipment to him and carried out maintenance and repair work on that machinery. Nava was at Chames's farm on many occasions, and over the course of those encounters, Nava and Chames became well-acquainted with each other."

Nava snorted, "That's some really grand revelation."

Scorbion ignored Nava's sarcasm and walked behind Katy, perching his hands upon the top of her chair's backrest. "Katy Alby, Chames's niece, took up residency at his farm and began training his horses and cleaning his house. While there, she regularly encountered Nava, and at some point, she and Nava started a relationship—the degree of intimacy of their association at that time solely known by them. At some point in time they parted company—I surmise that not being together any longer was more Nava's choice than Katy's. Yet, I must add, that once they were both here in Haxford, they began accompanying each other once again."

Katy turned in her seat to respond to Scorbion, but he lifted his hands off the chair back and put one finger across his lips, signaling her to be silent. "Please do not attempt to deny that, as it is one of the absolute facts of this case. I will speak to what I believe is the depth of that relationship in a short while."

Scorbion then moved behind Charles Emerlin's chair.

"In London, Charles Emerlin was the owner and chef of a most successful restaurant, the Cork and Plate. Chames regularly sold produce to Emerlin at his restaurant and they became friendly."

Emerlin grunted. "True enough."

Scorbion continued. "Florence and Samuel Gray often ate at Chef Emerlin's restaurant when they took excursions to London. The Cork and Plate was also the meeting place for the Grays and Martin Chames. On one of their visits to the restaurant, Emerlin introduced them both to Chames, who happened to be there that particular day."

Scorbion now stood behind Florence Gray. "They dined together, and apparently enjoyed each other's company to such a degree that on almost every future trip the Grays made to London, they supped with Chames at the restaurant. And during the numerous outings that Florence Gray made to London without her husband, she and Chames ate together on every one of those trips."

"Not every one," Florence contradicted.

"Excuse me, madam," Scorbion replied, "I may have misspoken.

There was possibly one such excursion you took to London during which you did not meet up with Martin Chames. But if that is the case, it was the rare exception, not the usual occurrence. I know this from Chef Emerlin, an eyewitness to those encounters."

Still positioned behind Florence Gray, Scorbion continued. "Sometime after Katy and Nava ceased their relationship, Chames told Emerlin that his niece wanted a change in location and asked Emerlin if he knew anyone who was looking to employ either a horse trainer or a house cleaner. Emerlin most probably said that he did not, but suggested to Chames that Florence and Samuel Gray might be aware of someone who was seeking such help here in Haxford. Emerlin proposed that he or Chames should tell them about Katy the next time they came to the restaurant. Emerlin did, in fact, speak about Katy to Florence Gray the next time she dined at the Cork and Plate—before Martin Chames appeared that night. How do I know that? We have been told that it was Emerlin who related the information about Katy to Florence Gray. If Chames had been there when they arrived, *he* would have been the one to tell her, Katy being *his* niece. Florence Gray then repeated what she was told about Katy to Isabelle Morgan, who, fortuitously, *was* seeking a new house cleaner. At some point shortly thereafter, Isabelle Morgan interviewed, and then employed Katy, who relocated to Haxford to start a new life."

Isabelle shook her head in agreement.

Scorbion went on. "At some point after Katy arrived in Haxford, Chames informed his niece that Nava was looking for something new to do, and coincidentally, at the same time, Isabelle Morgan told her that the Morgans were going to hire a driver for their new motorcar. It is my belief that Katy suggested to Isabelle Morgan that Nava could serve as the operator of their vehicle, knowing he was knowledgeable about mechanical devices and vehicles and good at fixing machinery."

Scorbion walked back behind Katy.

"Katy Alby's motivation most assuredly sprang from her desire to rekindle her relationship with Nava, something that she hoped would occur once she and Nava were in the same location. And that *is* what has happened. But I believe it is equally irrefutable that Katy is more committed to Nava than he to her—for a second time. Why do I say that? Mr. Nava disclosed to us earlier today that he is shortly leaving for Berlin, and yet that came as a revelation to Katy when I asked her if she knew of his plans."

Thelma turned to Katy. "Men can be so insensitive and unreliable at times. Perhaps it is part of their genetics, as Mendel posited."

Katy did not respond, maintaining a blank stare.

Scorbion moved behind Emerlin's chair. "Allow me to return to London and Charles Emerlin. After the Cork and Plate's lease was terminated, he decided not to relocate his restaurant, desiring instead to work as a personal chef. He told Florence Gray of his plans when she dined at the restaurant, and she then suggested him to Isabelle Morgan, knowing that the Morgans' cook was leaving their employ. The Morgans, pleased by this fortuitous turn of events, hired Emerlin to be their new chef."

Emerlin confirmed. "True, true."

Franklin Morgan agreed. "Quite right."

Still standing behind Emerlin, Scorbion pointed to Chames. "Now let us return to Martin Chames, who made a resolve to sell his Tottingham farm and move to Haxford. He related to us that his decision was based on his assessment that there was fertile land to acquire here from which he could derive an income that was more lucrative than what he generated in Tottingham. However, after learning that he and Florence Gray are a couple and planning to marry . . ."

Warvis raised his eyebrows in surprise.

Scorbion continued, ". . . I rather believe that he came here to be with Florence. I hypothesize that Florence Gray and Martin Chames had an ongoing relationship—an affair of the heart if you will—during her visits to London, and they became infatuated with each other. Chames provided her with the energy, excitement, affection, and attention which her older husband, Samuel, was no longer capable of."

Florence sat stoically, staring at the ground, giving no indication of her reaction to Scorbion's pronouncement.

"Coincidentally," Scorbion went on, "if it was a coincidence at all, shortly after Martin Chames located here, Samuel Gray died in a mishap on the road to Brookdale. Once that tragedy occurred, the grieving widow, Florence Gray, sold her farm to Chames and moved to Brookdale to reside with her sister, all the while maintaining a relationship with Chames that they both concealed until recently."

Thomas raised his hand. "I've got a question. What do you mean *if* it was a coincidence?"

Scorbion replied, "I will get to that in due course, but allow me to point out one other 'coincidence' before I move on to the crimes recently committed. Chames, Katy, Nava, and Emerlin all relocated to Haxford approximately one year ago, give or take a few months. Is it not somewhat strange, or fortunate, that they all arrived close to the same time?"

Before anyone could respond to Scorbion's rhetorical question he forged ahead.

"Once everyone was living here, key events started taking place. The first was Samuel Gray's death. We have been told by Florence Gray that it was an unfortunate accident occasioned by a wild beast's howl that caused their horse to rear up in fright, which precipitated their cart's wheel to impact a large rock that was jutting out of the road to Brookdale. That prompted the cart to lurch and tip over on top of Samuel Gray. The cart not only crushed him, but a pointed stone also pierced his skull, the result of those occurrences being Samuel Gray's instant death. Florence Gray was propitiously thrown from the cart onto a grassy field. He died, while she escaped unscathed."

Florence opened her purse, took out her hankie, and dabbed her eyes. "Yes. That *is* what occurred. Poor Samuel."

Scorbion looked her directly in the eye and scowled slightly. "Actually, madam, there are issues with that account. First, Haxford's blacksmith, Angus Riley, an authority on animals in this region, has told me that he knows of no feral beasts in this area that make the sort of howl as you described occurring at the scene. The animal cry you reported was closest to that of a wolf, but there have been no wolves in our country for at least two centuries. Another possibility is that the beast was a banshee; however, as we are all aware, that mythical being does not exist."

Florence stopped Scorbion with a wave of her hand in the air, and a curt tone in her voice. "I know what I heard, no matter what you say. And I heard a frightful baying."

Scorbion was undeterred. "I seriously doubt your account, dear lady, no matter how many times you repeat it. But let me continue, as I have a second issue with your account of the so-called accident. In addition to my own knowledge of the road between here and Brookdale from my travel to rugby matches I have recently attended there, I asked my sergeant if he was familiar with the road on which the event happened. He related that he knows it well as he rides upon it weekly to witness cricket and football matches in Brookdale. When I asked him about the road surface, he confirmed that it is generally smooth. He added that while there are minor depressions and stones along the route, he has never come across a boulder large enough to overturn a cart. He indicated to me his embarrassment at having not made the connection of the dichotomy between your account and the actual conditions of the route prior to my asking."

Florence spluttered, "He is wrong!"

Before she could protest further, Scorbion walked behind her chair and said firmly, "If I must make another journey to witness that road for myself, *again*, I will, but for now I rather tend to believe my remembrance and Constable Adley's account over yours. But let us cease speaking about the beast and the road at this time. I will return to the event shortly. At this time, I wish to summarize what we know, or believe, about each of you who are gathered here."

Those in attendance squirmed or turned on their chairs.

"I will begin with Florence Gray since we already know something about her from the event we have just discussed. Her husband, Samuel, her senior by two decades, had become her companion rather than her lover. We learned that from Florence Gray's own account. We also learned from multiple people that she met with Chames for dinner on the occasions that she traveled to London without her husband."

Chames, Emerlin, and Florence all nodded in agreement.

Scorbion continued, "But what we have not been told is what

occurred between Florence Gray and Martin Chames following those dinners."

Florence and Chames exchanged glances and then both wriggled uncomfortably.

Scorbion went on. "For a number of decades, in the course of carrying out my duties, I have studied human nature. The myriad of cases in which I have been involved have given me an expert understanding of motivations and resultant actions, so I feel quite comfortable conjecturing what did occur between Mrs. Gray and Mr. Chames in London. It is my staunch belief that they engaged in more than just dining and conversation, but rather, once they left the restaurant, they went somewhere to have a tryst—most probably to a hotel close to the Cork and Plate. Tottingham was too distant for them to conveniently travel to and from, and I do not believe they went to Mrs. Gray's lodgings, as both she and her husband would be known there by the establishment's staff from all their prior visits together.

"What Martin Chames and Florence Gray engaged in is far from a social norm in our society, and as such, I believe that if we were to travel to London and show both of their photographs to the clerks at the hotels in the vicinity of the late Cork and Plate, staff at one or more of those establishments would recognize them and confirm my postulation. Those London encounters would have laid the basis for their current relationship, which would not have flourished to the degree it has had they only begun being romantic with each other once Martin Chames arrived here. With Florence Gray living in Brookdale with her sister, it is unlikely that they would have had the opportunity to be together on enough occasions for a deep enough relationship to have developed that would lead to marriage, had there been no underpinnings from their London rendezvous."

Scorbion gestured toward Florence.

"I ask you all to take a good look at Florence Gray. Most do not see through her rouge and her apparel, but under the cosmetics and garments, she possesses a pleasant but generally nondescript face which personally I find to be undermined by her short-cropped hair . . ."

Calvin turned to Florence. "I could do wonders for you, madam, if you gave me the opportunity to work with your locks."

She ignored him and turned her attention back to Scorbion who continued his description of her. "Additionally, Mrs. Gray would not be considered voluptuous by any standard, but rather would be described as somewhat stocky and big-boned. She certainly would not be considered shapely—a word that I find to be very descriptive of a woman who has a full figure, which I suspect Florence Gray does not have, probably even when wearing an hourglass corset."

Scorbion ignored Florence's indignant protestations, instead asking Calvin for a glass of water. After satisfying his thirst, Scorbion handed the vessel back to Calvin.

"Now that you have quieted down, Mrs. Gray, let us ask what do we know about Martin Chames? A successful businessman and farmer, he has a loud, boisterous voice that complements his overall large stature. He has been involved in a number of brawls, at least one of which led to a night of incarceration. He has had additional altercations with some of his customers. He has no issues carrying on a romantic affair with a married woman, and he left a somewhat successful farm in Tottingham to move to Haxford—asserting that he had no specific plan as to what land he might acquire here before his relocation. We also know that once he arrived, he purchased the Grays' farm after the accident that resulted in Samuel's demise. He subsequently purchased two pastures from George Barlan, and made an offer, which was turned down, to acquire the remainder of Barlan's farm. Additionally, we know that he and Florence Gray have spent a good deal of time together and are planning to wed."

Scorbion surveyed the people in the room and asked, "Have I left anything out?"

"He knew everyone involved in this affair b-before he m-moved here," Barnabus responded.

Yves corrected Barnabus. "Everyone except the Morgans."

Scorbion confirmed both statements and proceeded. "With regard to the Morgans, Warvis has served them over many years and appears to have had no opportunity or motive for any of the recent goings-on, so I have little to say about him." He turned to Warvis, "In fact, if you wish to depart, I do not believe there is any need on my part to have you remain here any longer."

Warvis shrugged his shoulders. "I'll not be going anywhere, Chief Inspector. This is all too bloody fascinating for me to take leave. I want to hear your full explanation of everything that has taken place."

Scorbion responded, "As you wish," and then moved behind Nava's chair.

"Joseph Nava is a man of seeming contradictions. A good number of us have found him to be obnoxious, belligerent, and crude, and yet he has also been described as friendly and tender. He is in a relationship, most assuredly romantic in nature, for a second time with Katy Alby, yet he professes that he is leaving for Berlin shortly—while not informing his paramour, Miss Alby, of his plans. He has a history with Martin Chames that goes back to their days together in Tottingham, and he alone, out of all of the Morgans' staff, believes that he is being undercompensated."

Franklin and Isabelle Morgan exchanged looks of surprise.

Scorbion placed his hand on Nava's shoulder and gently kept him seated while he kept speaking. "The derivation of Mr. Nava's name and the truth of his lineage both have significant bearing on the events of this case. It was postulated to us that because of his straight black hair and his general appearance, Nava's ancestors likely came from South or Latin America; in fact, Peru was mentioned specifically as the most probable origin of his heritage. However, I submit that those assumptions are erroneous. I have concluded that Nava's family were for the most part natives from the American West. Has no one else observed that when you reverse his given and family names it results in Nava Joe, or, shortened, Navajo? And that creates a probable connection between him and the stolen hatchet, that I will explain shortly."

Scorbion paused for effect. "And one additional observation about Joseph Nava: he has no alibi for the night the hatchet was taken and the hog stolen—and probably slaughtered."

Calvin interrupted. "But he does have an alibi for when Barlan was killed. Us. We're his alibis. He was with us at that time."

Scorbion confirmed, "That is correct. Nava *was* with us, in this shop when George Barlan was murdered. As were the Morgans."

Billy nodded in agreement and asked, "Is there *anyone* who has an alibi for the evening that the hatchet and pig were stolen?"

Scorbion answered, "Most of those in this room do *not* have an alibi as you correctly observe, but some may have had more of a motive than others. Allow me to continue and all will become understandable soon."

Scorbion walked behind Emerlin. "I have already recounted much of what we know about the good chef, mostly from his time in London, but there are a few additional things we have learned about him. For one, he traveled to Brookdale to purchase pork for a dinner for the Morgans this morning. I wonder how he knew there would be fresh pork available there . . ."

Before Scorbion could continue, Emerlin swiveled on his seat and faced Scorbion. "I did not know. I often purchase my meats there, as the butcher cuts and trims his stock better than most. Better than Barlan, for sure. I do not wish to speak ill of the dead, but that is a fact."

"That may well be," Scorbion responded, "but we have been told that you often acquire your foodstuffs from what were described as 'shady characters' and that butcher could be one of them. I am not acquainted with him well enough to know."

Emerlin turned back toward the circle.

Scorbion continued, "There is not much else that we know about Charles Emerlin. His London restaurant was where Chames and the Grays met, the result of which was Emerlin, Nava, and Katy becoming employed by the Morgans, and Chames relocating here."

Scorbion turned toward Katy.

"Now . . . what do we know about Katy Alby? As I earlier noted, she is Martin Chames' niece. Raised on a farm with pigs and horses, she is quite knowledgeable of the care of both species. She had an ailment in the fortnight leading up to the grand dinner at the Morgans' home last evening, but she recovered well enough to carry out her duties after that magnificent repast. I also believe that she is deeply infatuated with Joseph Nava. I ask you, Miss Alby, am I correct about that?"

Katy gently nodded. "I do love Joseph."

Scorbion made a small bow from his waist. "Thank you for that confirmation. And now, it is time to leave the discussion of the participants and summarize what we know about the events. Let us go back to last evening and the Morgans' dinner. We know that during that sumptuous meal, the hatchet was in its usual place of honor above the fireplace in their library. That is indisputable. Isabelle Morgan took me into that magnificent volume-filled room and showed the relic to me between food courses.

"Later that night, the same night that the hog was stolen, two people were observed riding in a cart that contained a large sailcloth in its cargo area. They were leaving the center of town, heading toward Barlan's farm in dark cloaks. One had some sort of implement with a shiny blade aside his or her trouser leg—one that had colored ornaments attached to it, like those on the hatchet. In fact, there is no question but that it *was* the hatchet. And whomever those two hooded figures were, they are, without a doubt in my mind, the ones who killed the hog and most probably carved it up on the sailcloth using the hatchet. Additionally, the note that they affixed to Barlan's barn door—'this is the first'—gives us our motive. It implies revenge. But what was this act of revenge for? And who wanted revenge against Barlan? When we met with him, he told us that neither he nor his parents had any enemies. So, we must look back, past his most recent ancestry to see if there might be a reason for revenge against him for something done by his grandparents or their parents."

Thomas asked Scorbion, "Didn't Barlan say some of his family came from America?"

Billy looked up from the notes he was taking. "He did. I remember writing that down when we spoke with him."

Scorbion concurred. "My memory of Barlan's words matches yours. We will get back to that later. For now, I continue the tale of the events that took place. This morning, after the hog's disappearance, a carved-up swine was sold to the butcher in Brookdale by a person so nondescript that the butcher can tell us nothing about them beyond the fact that the person was stocky, had a ruddy complexion, as virtually everyone who works with animals does, and they were wearing a hat that concealed their face. We must assume this person was in hiding so that they could not be tied back to the hog. There is no doubt in my mind that the pig in question is the same one that was taken from Barlan. If that were not the case, then where did it come from, where did Barlan's hog go, and why was the seller of the carved-up animal reluctant to show themselves to the butcher?"

Calvin said, "That makes perfect sense to me," and most everyone nodded in agreement.

Scorbion moved to the empty chair and sat down after Billy picked up his papers from it. "That brings us to the second act of death, the murder of George Barlan. If anyone here is not aware of what happened to George Barlan, please identify yourself and I will fill in the details of what occurred."

Franklin Morgan spoke. "Isabelle and I just learned about Barlan on the ride here. Nava told us what he knew, which he said came from information he received from Emerlin and Warvis on their way back to our home after you had questioned them earlier."

Scorbion responded, "Since everyone here but Miss Alby knows the circumstances surrounding Barlan's murder, I will not go through it in detail. But due to the fact that Barlan was killed with the stolen hatchet, it is solely possible that only one of two things could have happened. Before we address those possibilities, we must start with a given: the only people who had access to both the hatchet—which resided above the mantel in the Morgans' library—and the Morgans' cart, was someone or multiple someones in this room. Everyone here was at the Morgans' home last night. Therefore, we need to ascertain whether the hatchet thief, or the accomplice, was the person who killed Barlan, or if instead, they passed the hatchet to another individual—the person who would then be our murderer."

Florence Gray rose from her chair and waved her finger at Scorbion. "You, sir," she ranted, "are wrong! Wrong another time. Just as you were wrong about that young Jonathan Bentine, as the *Gazette* has reported."

Unaccustomed to being challenged in that manner, Scorbion was about to rail at her, but he composed himself and instead calmly asked how he was wrong—ignoring the *Gazette* reference.

Florence lectured him. "I was not at the dinner, and I had no access to that hatchet last night. You erred when you said that everyone in this room could have taken the hatchet and cart." She then folded her arms across her chest in a self-satisfied manner.

Thelma said, "Actually, Inspector, I was not in attendance, either."

Scorbion realized they were right, though Florence Gray had not fully absolved herself of any involvement in the night's events. "I stand corrected. Neither of you *were* in the Morgan household last evening. However, that does not preclude you, Florence Gray, from being the other person in the cart. Please be seated so I may continue."

Florence sat back down.

Scorbion resumed. "We must look at all the events and determine if the two acts of killing—George Barlan and his pig—were done by the same person or persons, or by different individuals, or accomplished through a conspiracy that included multiple people with varying motives."

Billy looked up from his papers. "Do you have a theory about all of that, Inspector?"

Scorbion replied, "I have more than a theory, I am sure that I know the facts. And now the time has come for me to share my thinking and conclude this inquiry."

Everyone shifted on their chairs, preparing to hear Scorbion's revelations.

"From what we know, it appears that everything that has taken place centered around George Barlan, and all of the acts are intertwined. It was his hog that was stolen and slaughtered and then he himself was murdered. However, appearances can be misleading. The stealing and slaughtering of his pig and George Barlan's murder were, in actuality, separate acts with distinctly different motivations."

"Really, Pignon?" Calvin asked. "They were not carried out by the same persons?"

"They were not," Scorbion responded.

Calvin then asked, "How do you know that, and who did what?"

Scorbion began, "To understand what happened regarding the hog we must travel back in time to the American West, back to Sky Bear and to Dr. James Adams and his wife, Eve. That was when the hatchet first made its appearance. The location of the American town that the Adams abandoned when the townspeople turned against them, coupled with Sky Bear's tribe living in encampments rather than villages, leads me to the conclusion that Sky Bear's tribe was Navajo. Additionally, if I recall my history of that era correctly, Navajo tomahawks, hatchets, or axes—no matter what they were called at the time—were adorned with feathers and other decorations as is the Morgans' hatchet. When I employ the knowledge that the hatchet came from a Navajo tribe and then turn Joseph Nava's name backward, I must believe that Nava is a descendant of that tribe."

Nava interrupted. "So what? Even if that's true, it doesn't mean I did anything."

Scorbion stood up, walked behind Nava, and countered, "In and of itself, that is correct, but allow me to continue, and we will all see a connection that you indeed 'did something,' as you put it. The other participants in the story that Isabelle Morgan related were the townsfolk, and if my memory is accurate, there were three ranchers—Samuel Lewiston, John Borlan, and Will Farland—who murdered two Indian families and dragged their bodies back to the Navajo encampment shortly after James and Eve Adams left town."

"What many of you in this room lack the knowledge of, is that one of my men did research into George Barlan's family. He learned that a portion of Barlan's ancestors came from America, and that his father's name was changed to Barlan from a similar sounding name when he arrived on our continent. I submit to you that John Borlan was George Barlan's grandfather or great-grandfather, which logically leads to Joseph Nava's wanting to exact some amount of revenge on George Barlan."

Isabelle Morgan gasped. "Oh my."

"D-do you really b-believe that Nava w-would try to avenge

s-something that happened to his family from as l-long ago as that happened?" Barnabus asked.

Scorbion replied confidently. "I most certainly do. Indians of the American West handed their history down through song and story, from generation to generation, which is almost certainly how Joseph Nava came to learn the details of those events. It is my belief that he has committed a good deal of his life looking to exact a modicum of revenge on someone for the tragedy that befell his ancestors. Joseph Nava searched for the descendants of John Borlan and in the process learned of George Barlan, and then plotted to find him and exact revenge on him for that which his grandparent did to Nava's forebearers."

Nava started to rise from his chair, saying, "That's a cartful of twaddle."

Scorbion gently but firmly put pressure on Nava's shoulder to keep him seated. "No, sir, it is not twaddle. It is precisely what occurred, and this is what I postulate took place here recently: Knowing how deeply Katy Alby is infatuated with you, you confided in her your plan to exact a measure of revenge on George Barlan and asked her to assist you. It was widely known that Barlan was donating the hog for the Town Feast, and taking it from him would be the first of a number of unfortunate occurrences that would befall Barlan at your hand. You had Miss Alby appropriate the hatchet as her duties ended at the conclusion of the dinner, after which you and she took the Morgans' cart and sailcloth, donned hooded capes to conceal your identities, and rode out to Barlan's farm. You and Katy, whose father raised pigs and therefore knew how to slaughter them, then killed the hog, carved it up, and wrapped it in the sailcloth. Your last act at Barlan's farm was to post the note on his barn door."

Nava tried to stand, but Scorbion pressed him down onto his seat again.

"Please do not try to leave or protest. It is beyond conjecture that you related your story and your findings about Barlan to Katy and she offered her assistance." Scorbion turned to Katy. "Do you deny any of this?"

Nava shouted at Katy, "Don't say anything. He's just guessing. It's all a load of shite."

But Katy started softly sobbing and shook her head from side to side. Calvin rose up, went to the counter by his barber chair, and returned to the circle, handing Katy a clean cloth to daub her eyes. Once she had partially cleared the tears, she said, "Thank you, Mr. Brown." Then she looked at Scorbion. "Joseph said no harm would befall Barlan, just his livestock. I am so ashamed of what I have done."

Scorbion walked in front of her. "Thank you, Miss Alby, for your confirmation. I know it was hard for you to do so, but we have now unearthed the truth about who took and slaughtered the hog. Next we must determine who transported it to Brookdale and sold it to the butcher, and who murdered George Barlan."

Katy sobbed, "I had no hand in any of that."

Scorbion responded, "I am aware that you did not."

"Chief Inspector, why don't you think Nava and Katy did all those thin's?" Thomas asked. "Didn't he have a motive?"

"And she was in love," Thelma added.

Scorbion replied, "Ah, that is a good question. As I unfold the remainder of the tale, we will learn if anyone else might have had a motive for committing those other acts. Shall I continue?"

"Yes, please," Billy answered. "I can't speak for the others here, but I want to hear everything else you have to disclose."

Scorbion moved and stood in front of his empty chair. "Then I shall forge ahead. I do not believe that it was Nava or Katy who took the hog to Brookdale, nor that they killed Barlan. I have observed Nava to have a quite unpleasant manner, but I have not seen him exhibit any tendency toward violence. Even though he had one of the most compelling reasons for wanting Barlan dead, I do not believe that he killed him. Additionally, Nava's physique and complexion do not match the description we were given by Brookdale's butcher regarding the person who sold the hog to him."

Calvin turned to Scorbion. "Then who did?"

Scorbion succinctly answered, "Florence Gray."

That pronouncement brought looks and murmurs of disbelief from everyone seated in the circle.

Florence shouted, "I did no such thing! I am not a murdereress! How dare you impugn me so. Retract your accusation this second!"

Isabelle turned to Scorbion. "I've known Florence for years. She is one of my closest confidantes. I cannot believe that she is capable of killing anyone."

Scorbion responded in a kindly but stern tone. "I am sorry to have to tell you that she, along with Martin Chames, have killed at least two people that I am aware of. Unfortunately—or more probably for you, Isabelle, fortunately—in your friendship she exhibited no indication of the evil lurking under her calm demeanor."

Scorbion paused and then addressed Calvin. "Would you be so good as to lock the door to this shop, so that no one may leave until we have concluded?"

Calvin did as Scorbion requested.

Once he was seated, Chames spoke. "Chief Inspector, you are absolutely wrong," he insisted. "Did you say those things just to see what kind of an effect they would generate? Well, let me tell you, from me, it has elicited anger. Neither Florence nor I have harmed anyone—in any way. What you have accused us of is outrageous and untrue. You have besmirched us both."

Scorbion walked in front of Chames's chair. "I have done no such thing. In spite of your protestations, I stand by the words I have uttered, and I will now fill in the tale that leads to that conclusion. I have already detailed the liaisons that you and the then-married Florence Gray engaged in while she was in London. You gave her things, emotional and physical, that her infirm husband could not, the result of which was her falling deeply in love with you. I do not know if she is inherently villainous or if her affection for you overtook her better judgment, but whatever the reason, here is what I am certain transpired."

Scorbion walked to his chair and sat, addressing everyone in the room. "We already know that Chames was intent on selling his farm in Tottingham and moving here to find better acreage. That is perfectly understandable. What does not ring true is that he would relocate to Haxford without previously having purchased a farm here. Chames has been described to us as being of high intelligence and immensely skillful in the realm of business, and those two qualities do not lend themselves to taking chances and risking moving from a profitable working operation to something that is totally unknown. Which causes me to consider the probability that Martin Chames knew well what farm he would be purchasing, *prior* to relocating here."

"But he bought Samuel Gray's farm, and Gray died *after* Chames moved here. How would he know he could buy *that* farm?" Yves asked.

Scorbion responded with a nod. "A very good point. The obvious answer is that Chames already knew that he'd be purchasing Gray's farm *before* he moved here. There are two ways that he could have known that. One is that he worked that out with Samuel and Florence Gray as a straight business transaction. But if that were the case, then why did the sale not occur until *after* Samuel died? And why did no one here know that occurred? When the sale went through, Chames and Florence then told everyone he was purchasing the farm. If it had been prearranged, why was it not announced when that arrangement was consummated?"

Isabelle confirmed Scorbion's statement. "Florence told me about selling the farm to Chames after Samuel had died. In fact, she told me about the sale on the very day that she sold it to Chames."

Scorbion thanked her. "I appreciate the corroboration, madam, and now, allow me to continue. I said there were two possibilities as to how Chames knew he would be purchasing the Grays' farm before he located here, and now that we have discounted the first, it leaves the second. The only other way Chames could have known that, would have been to have arranged the sale with Florence Gray without the knowledge of her husband. But what would make either of them certain that Samuel would sell the farm? I will tell you—it is because they planned to murder Samuel."

Warvis gasped. "Blow me over, Chief Inspector, are you saying that Samuel Gray's death was premeditated?"

Scorbion answered, "Yes. That is exactly what happened. I can only speculate on some of the details, while others are known facts, but this is my belief: Martin Chames, knowing that Florence Gray was devoutly in love with him, suggested to her that they could be together for eternity if Samuel were gone and that there was a way to ensure that—to murder him. I do not know if he used that specific word, or rather if he spoke about doing away with him or postulated what would happen if Samuel were to have a fatal accident. The relationship and intimacy Florence Gray was enjoying with Chames was rekindling feelings she had not experienced in many years because of the advanced age of her husband, and I can only imagine that she desired to be with Chames on a more regular basis than just on her trips to London. What he suggested to her created an opportunity for them to be together permanently, and I believe that love blinded her from the righteous and lawful path."

Emerlin shook his head a few times. "This is unbelievable. Are you quite sure of these accusations?"

"What I have related is the only possible situation that rings true," Scorbion replied. "As I stated earlier, I have determined that there are no animals in this region that would make the loud sound that startled the Grays' horse, nor are there regularly any rocks on the road to Brookdale that are large enough to overturn a cart. That leads me to conclude that the boulder was placed in the road specifically for the purpose of upending the cart, and with Florence Gray at the reins, she made certain to have the wheel strike it."

Scorbion then said, sarcastically, "And was it not fortuitous that the area in which this purported accident occurred was adjacent to a grassy field, upon which Florence Gray could safely land while her husband was crushed under the cart? His death was caused by her affixing the reins to his body, prior to her jumping onto the sward. Regarding the howl, either it was Martin Chames portraying a beast—he does have a booming voice—or there was no such roar and it was a fabrication that Florence and Chames conveniently created, and the 'accident' was solely caused by Florence Gray's steering the cart into the rock that Chames had placed upon the road."

Chames rose up and shouted, "I will not stand for this blasphemy and these inaccuracies any longer! This is all conjecture. You have no proof of any of these vile accusations." He turned to Florence. "Say nothing. He is only guessing." Then Chames turned to the others in the group, adding, "He is wrong. Completely and utterly wrong." After that, he sat down with a thud.

Scorbion calmly replied, "Sir, you have a history of brawling, even being jailed for inflicting physical harm on others during at least one of those tussles, and there are other factors that play into my conclusions. For one, is it not an extreme coincidence that you desired Samuel Gray's farm and then he died, and you secured his property, and now that Barlan is deceased, you are in a position to acquire the remainder of *his* farm, most of which he refused to sell you as recently as last week? I am a decent judge of people and their character, and I deem Katy Alby to be a good person who, like Florence Gray, was love-blind. And I rather do believe that when I ask Katy if she had prearranged for you to meet her and Nava at Barlan's farm the night they slaughtered the hog so that you could carry it away for them and dispose of it, that is exactly what she will confirm. It would have been impossible for them to cart the swine away, as they had to return the Morgans' cart before someone noticed that it was missing or had been used. Additionally, Katy had to groom the mare to remove any traces of their excursion from its body. One error that you made, Chames, was keeping the sailcloth rather than cleansing it and replacing it in the Morgans' cart. I am also reasonably confident that you told Nava and Katy that you would take care of the hatchet, after which they handed it to you."

Katy began sobbing softly again into the cloth Calvin had given her.

Scorbion continued speaking to Chames. "I am also of the belief that neither Nava nor Katy knew of your plan to have Florence Gray sell the slaughtered animal to the butcher in Brookdale. Why you did that does puzzle me. Why did you not just bury it, or throw it to wild animals? Possibly you are so hungry for pounds that you could not pass up the recompense that the sale would generate. We may never know, but what I do know is, that in spite of Florence Gray's protestations, without her cosmetics, and wearing a masculine outfit, she could pass for a man when not under deep scrutiny."

Scorbion moved in front of Katy and Nava, while addressing the group.

"The stealing, slaughtering, and selling of the hog are the minor elements in this affair. They are not to be condoned, but they are not of the same importance or seriousness as are the murders of George Barlan and Samuel Gray."

Scorbion turned to face Nava. "Joseph Nava, while I have found you to be a most unpleasant human being, and slaughtering the pig and purloining the hatchet *are* crimes, I am feeling generous today. You, and Miss Alby, are guilty of nothing more, and if you confess to what you have done, I will take only minor action against you. In the event that you do not acknowledge your actions, then I will bring the full weight of my position to bear on you. Should you confirm my accusations, there is one additional condition to my leniency—you have indicated that you are leaving for Berlin shortly, and you must make that so. You must leave Haxford, and not return. Should Katy Alby accompany you, I will do nothing against her. If she remains here, then I will monitor her closely to ensure that she never commits a similar deed. However, I will take no other action against her, as I believe that losing her lover for a second time is enough punishment for the crime she committed."

Nava thought for a moment before responding. "What would you do to me if I confess?"

Scorbion responded, "You will be required to pay a fine equal to the value of Barlan's hog, and you will spend one night in the accommodations at my station."

"Do I have your word that that will be all that is done to me, Chief Inspector?"

Scorbion confirmed, "You have my word."

"Everything you have surmised and spoken is accurate," Nava said. "Katy and I did no more than try to avenge my family's honor, but that did not include killing George Barlan. I was only planning acts of minor revenge and annoyance against him. And, yes, after we killed the hog, we transferred it, the sailcloth, and the hatchet to Chames, who told us he would take care of them so that we could return the cart unnoticed."

Katy added, "Joseph told me what happened to his ancestors, and I went along with his plan because I didn't think anyone would get hurt. It seemed like a minor revenge for what was a terrible act that many years ago. I told Uncle Martin what we were going to do, and he offered to dispose of the hog and the hatchet."

Scorbion turned to Chames. "And what do you have to say to that, Mr. Chames? Do you refute everything that was just said? Do you deny that you were the last person to possess the weapon that killed George Barlan?"

Chames repositioned himself on his chair to be farther away from Florence Gray. "I say that I am not guilty of any murder. I *am* guilty of all that Nava and Katy just recounted, but not a single other thing. It was Florence Gray who killed her husband and Barlan. Not I."

Florence gasped and put her hand to her chest.

Scorbion responded to Chames, "You may not have committed the murder, but you are as guilty as she is, sir. I judge you to be a predator who will stop at nothing to acquire that which you desire. In this case, it was the properties of both Samuel Gray and George Barlan. Your farm in Tottingham was not generating the revenue it once did, and I venture to guess that occurred because your surly nature drove away your customers. We know this from Joseph Nava who related to us how you lost a portion of your clientele due to arguments you had with them. There is no doubt in my mind that you determined that it was in your best interests to sell the farm and purchase better land in a new community. My speculation is that you realized, almost from the moment that you met them, that the Grays' land was exactly what you were looking for, and so you engaged in a quest to have Florence Gray become infatuated with you. And once that was accomplished, you suggested to her that if only her husband were gone, you and she could be together and marry."

Chames harrumphed. "That is absurd."

"I believe not," Scorbion continued. "Samuel Gray was older than Florence Gray by two decades and no longer capable of giving or receiving intimacy. You, Martin Chames, filled that part of Florence Gray that was empty and missing from the lack of close physical relations with her husband. You preyed upon that, and in some manner, at some appropriate time, you suggested to her how she could rid herself of Samuel and be with you. I do not know what Mrs. Gray's initial reaction was. Shock? Relief? Concern? If it had been horror at the thought of killing her husband, she would have conducted herself quite differently than the manner in which she acted. She would have reported you to the officials in London. However, that was not the action she took. Coming from her love for you, and most likely also having some fear of what would happen if she did not go along with you, she acquiesced to your design."

Chames harrumphed again. "That is even more absurd."

Scorbion went on, undeterred. "Let us examine Samuel Gray's purported accident, which we now know was anything but that. I think it likely that there was no accident at all, and that Florence, the driver of the cart, stopped it at the predetermined location of the accident-to-be. Then you, hiding in the woods, pounced on Samuel, struck him with the sharp, pointed rock that he was said to have hit his head upon, and then turned the cart over onto him—positioning the wheel to lay next to a large rock that you previously placed in the road. There was no animal that howled as Florence Gray reported. None. That is a certainty. Also, the large rock should not have been there, and the remainder of the event that Florence Gray fabricated is much too convenient to be true.

"With Samuel dead, you could acquire the Grays' property from Florence. She would move to her sister's house in the next hamlet, and you could continue to see each other, in a clandestine relationship. You would wait until enough time had gone by before you and she would allow yourselves to be seen together. Anything less would seem to be inappropriate for a widow. Then, when you had Gray's land, you wanted Barlan's as well. You yourself told us about your plans for a timber mill on Barlan's forested acreage. The scheme you devised was brilliant. I conjecture that you enlisted or forced Florence's assistance by holding her involvement in Samuel Gray's murder over her, and also by exploiting her deep affection for you.

"Katy's telling you of Nava's plan to steal the hog offered you the opening to acquire a hatchet that could be used to murder George

Barlan, while also throwing the probable blame on Nava. You and Florence Gray were the only two people who had the hatchet, prior to its lodging in George Barlan's back, and due to the fact that you thought that Florence was at the farm when in actuality she was in town, it *had* to be Florence Gray that planted it in Barlan."

Florence started vigorously sobbing and shaking. She bent forward and leaned her chest and head over her legs, lamenting, "What have I done? What have I done?"

Calvin walked to the counter, got another cloth, and handed it to Florence.

Scorbion crouched down and tried to comfort her. "You had something you hadn't experienced or possessed in many years—love and physical intimacy, two of the most intoxicating forces known to humanity. Unfortunately, they can lead people down paths they would not take in any other situation. I am sorry for you, madam, but you did that which you did, and what you did is inexcusable."

Florence sat up, still sobbing. "I'm so sorry. So sorry. I had nothing against George Barlan. Why did I do what I did?" She turned to Chames and pointed. "*He* killed Samuel. Yes, I went along, but he killed Samuel. Exactly as you said. My God."

Scorbion stood and walked back to Chames. "It will be your word against hers as to who murdered Samuel Gray, but in the end, it will not matter, because regardless of how the fatal blow was struck, you and Florence Gray are accomplices and coconspirators in these murders. And, under English law, that makes you equally guilty, no matter who committed the act. I hereby arrest you and Florence Gray for conspiracy in the murders of Samuel Gray and George Barlan, and for committing those acts."

Florence Gray wept uncontrollably, her entire body shook and was racked with tremors. Chames shot up out of his chair, ran to the door, and pulled on the doorknob, trying to open it with brute force. Calvin and Barnabus jumped up from their seats, raced to the front of the shop, and grabbed Chames from behind. Calvin wrapped his arms around Chames's chest while Barnabus tried to remove Chames's hand from the doorknob.

Chames fought back. He swiveled around, dragging Calvin, who was still clinging across his back, and threw a punch at Barnabus's head. Fortuitously, Barnabus had already started to move so the roundhouse missed its mark and grazed off his shoulder.

Seeing Chames attempting to harm his fellow barber, Yves rose out of his chair and ran to Chames. When he reached the scuffling men, he growled at Chames, "This is for Samuel Gray and George Barlan, *meurtrier*!" And then, Yves' right foot moved as fast as a lightning bolt, and he booted Chames squarely in the groin. Chames involuntarily released his hold of Calvin and crumpled to the ground, moaning in pain. Yves bent over Chames and spit on him. "You, *morceau de merde.*"

Scorbion assisted Florence from her chair, and asked Calvin, Thomas, and Billy to accompany him to the station with her and Chames, adding, "Once Chames has recovered sufficiently from that which I did not witness."

Billy winked at Scorbion. "I think we all only saw a barber trying to restrain an accused murdered who was attempting to flee."

In the ensuing minutes, while Scorbion waited for Chames to recover enough to walk again, Thelma joined Scorbion near the front door. "You are masterful, Pignon. I am in awe of the way you process information and see connections that the rest of us do not. I am convinced that your mind moves faster than that steed Lemberg did winning the derby at Epsom earlier this month."

That pleased Scorbion to no end. He thanked Thelma while he removed his jacket from the rack and carefully put it on.

Nava came up to Scorbion, lit a cigarette, and asked, "When must I endure the accommodations in your station?"

"I will expect you to appear there later this evening," Scorbion replied. "After you spend the overnight hours enjoying our hospitality, if I might characterize it as that, and then pay your fine, you will be free to leave—on the conditions that you do no harm of any manner while you are still in my jurisdiction, and that you travel to Berlin as you have planned."

Nava was quick to reply. "I wouldn't want to stay in this shithole town any longer than I have to, so yes, I will be in Berlin within the week."

Scorbion clamped his arm on Nava's shoulder. "And, Miss Katy Alby, will she be accompanying you?"

"Nah. She won't," Nava replied. "But it isn't what you think. She just told me I'm a bad influence on her, and she doesn't wanna chance moving with me. So, she's decided to remain here. She hopes the town won't shun her for what she did to help me."

Scorbion released his grip on Nava's shoulder. "I will do my utmost to persuade the Morgans to retain her as their housemaid, if they have not already made that same decision for themselves. Miss Alby appears to be a decent young woman who strove to show you how much she loved you by going along with your plan of misguided revenge. It is most unfortunate for her that you do not care for her as much as she adores you. Very probably, though, she will end up having a better life here without you than with you anywhere else on the globe. I anticipate that this unfortunate episode will be a part of her past soon enough, and will not carry very far into the future."

Nava shrugged his shoulders. "Whatever." Then he turned back to Scorbion. "I truly hope never to see you again after tomorrow, Chief Inspector." He crushed his cigarette under his heel, then walked to Franklin and Isabelle Morgan and asked if they wanted him to drive them home.

Franklin responded, "What you did was quite irresponsible, and involving Katy in your vendetta was very selfish and uncaring on your part. However, Isabelle and I are not unsympathetic to what happened to your ancestors. We just find it unfortunate that you took it out on George Barlan, who had nothing to do with any of it. You may remain in our employ until you depart next week, so yes, please do prepare our drive back to our home."

Franklin started to walk away, but then abruptly turned around and added, "One other thing, Katy Alby will be in the motorcar with us. That won't bother you, will it?"

Nava gestured with his arms and shoulders in a way that unmistakably conveyed his nonchalance, and after Calvin unlocked the door, he walked out to crank the motorcar.

Katy was still sobbing when she approached Scorbion and Thelma. "What will happen to Uncle Martin? This week has been like a dark, dark dream that scares you awake. I can't believe what I did. I am so distressed and embarrassed about it."

Scorbion took his handkerchief out of his breast pocket and handed it to her. "Your uncle will stand trial for what he did. It will be a jury's decision that will determine his eventual fate." Scorbion paused for effect and then continued, "He is not someone you should emulate or associate with. You have an opportunity to live a good life, do not waste your years on a devious criminal. Go with the Morgans now, and I will look in on you on occasion to check on your well-being."

"As will I," Thelma added.

Katy gave Scorbion a peck on his cheek. "I'm sorry if that's inappropriate, but, thank you. For preserving my life."

Scorbion put his hand to his cheek and smiled. Then he handcuffed Chames and Florence, and before he departed with them, he and Thelma made arrangements to meet later that evening for dinner.

Billy walked over to Calvin. "Don't forget to get that telephone."

Calvin raised the middle finger of his right hand and held it in Billy's direction—while heartily laughing.

Once Scorbion, Gray, Chames, and Thelma had departed, the men put the chairs back in the storeroom, Calvin unshuttered the blinds, turned the door sign to Open, and waited for any late-day customers to appear.

CHAPTER FORTY-ONE

After securing Gray and Chames in cells and recounting his findings to Adley, Scorbion walked briskly from the station, whistling a gay tune as he strode, thinking of how the case had been solved and about how much he looked forward to seeing Thelma that evening—a woman who he considered extraordinary and unparalleled in his life. He surmised she had faults and peculiarities he hadn't as yet discovered, but told himself that he would find a manner in which to deal with them when they came to light. His trilling lasted sixteen bars before he stopped, slapped his right palm on his forehead, and said aloud to no one, "I am a fool."

Scorbion changed direction and sprinted to the inn. When he asked if Jonathan Bentine was still lodging there, the front desk attendant told him, "Jonathan Bentine is in room six. He is not checking out until tomorrow. I believe that is when the train to London arrives, that he told me he plans to be on."

Scorbion walked up the stairs to Bentine's second-floor room and knocked on the door. When Bentine opened it, Scorbion asked him to accompany him back to the barbershop.

"By no means am I returning there," Bentine caustically replied. "I'm preparing to leave this town, and I assure you, I will only return once Mr. Hardcastle and I prove that Mortimer Gromley is my true father."

Scorbion placed his hands on his hips. "Listen to me, young man. You *will* accompany me, now, and your choice is whether you do it of your own volition or in cuffs. Either way, you *are* coming with me."

When Bentine protested further, Scorbion snapped a set of handcuffs on him, pulled him out of the chamber, and closed the door behind them.

There were no customers in the barbershop when Scorbion appeared at the door holding Bentine by the sleeve. When the barbers saw Bentine with Scorbion, they were surprised. Thomas asked, "Is somethin' wrong, Chief Inspector? Why is Bentine with you?"

"And in cuffs," Calvin added. "What's going on, Pignon?"

"It will all be clear in a very short time. But for now, gentlemen, may I entreat you to set out the table and chairs once again? However, in this instance, we need solely one seat on the opposite side for Mr. Bentine."

The men brought the furniture back out from the storeroom, and when everyone was settled, Billy asked Scorbion, "May I write about whatever is about to take place?"

"I insist that you do," Scorbion responded. "It is important that you chronicle the events that are about to unfold and put to rest any doubts that the *Gazette* has cast about the veracity of our findings regarding Mr. Bentine."

Billy grinned. "It will be my pleasure, Inspector. I surmise that you've figured out what was nagging at you. Have you changed your mind about Mr. Bentine's lineage? Shall we request that the Gromleys return?"

"No," Scorbion responded. "I have not altered my thinking regarding Mr. Bentine's parentage. What I will now impart will be of no impact on the Gromleys, and I prefer to proceed with rapidity. The sun will be soon lowering and I am relishing having dinner with Miss Smith. Thomas can relate the details to them at the conclusion of this second hearing."

"I'll do that, Chief Inspector," Thomas confirmed.

Scorbion began. "Shortly after leaving here when we believed that we had concluded the affair with Mr. Bentine, my light-heartedness gave way to contemplation. I could not immediately identify what was niggling within my mind. That led me to a further examination of the entire situation. Something has felt missing, unresolved. And it is my nature to have everything fully settled. Although it took a number of weeks to make itself known, as I was departing from this shop within the past quarter of an hour, that which was unsettling became clear. Fortunately, Mr. Bentine was still lodging at the inn. I expressed to him the need for us both to return to this establishment so that a finality could be set to this affair. He was not given to accommodate my request, so it was necessary for me to escort him here in cuffs."

Bentine rebuked Scorbion. "This had better be important, and fast. My conveyance to London is coming tomorrow."

Scorbion responded, "It *is* important, Mr. Bentine, and I will move with utmost rapidity, although I seriously question whether London will be your final destination."

Calvin looked confused. "I thought he would be returning to Avens. To find proof of Gromley being his father. What is this about going to London?"

Scorbion removed the cuffs from Bentine's wrists, walked him to the chair that was designated for him, and waited until Bentine sat.

Once seated himself, Scorbion looked down the row of men at the table and spoke to Calvin. "Mr. Bentine's final destination will be neither London nor Avens. Doubtless, it will be a city in some other country, where he can be lost from view to those who knew him before he arrived there. A destination that would afford him total anonymity. London will simply be his point of transfer."

Billy asked, "Why would he do that?"

"That is a very intelligent question, Billy. I will illuminate everyone here with the light of my thinking. Finding nothing further in Haxford to substantiate his claim of being Mortimer Gromley's son and heir, even with the assistance of Faustin Hardcastle, Bentine realized it was time to conclude his ruse and move on."

Calvin was again confused. "Ruse?"

"Throughout this entire affair, the central question has been Mr. Bentine's lineage. We have solely concentrated on establishing the identity of his father, which resulted in Mortimer Gromley's being cleared of any culpability in the matter. But as I kept reflecting on the affair, I started to see inconsistencies that none of us had focused on and had missed."

Barnabus asked, "W-What kind of inconsistencies?"

"Inconsistencies in Mr. Bentine's narrative and person. I suddenly recognized that we had been so absorbed in determining Bentine's parentage that we overlooked the man himself. And as I replayed all that was said and that we witnessed, I realized much of it did not fit together."

Yves asked, "Like what, Chief Inspector?"

"To begin, I was puzzled. Why would Mr. Bentine not be rushing to find his true father, rather than attempting to prove that Mr. Gromley was his parent when it was obvious to all that he was not? I concluded that being the heir to Gromley's fortune took precedence over discovering his lineage. That led me to ponder why. I examined my recollections of Mr. Bentine's testimony, and discrepancies began accumulating."

"*Lesquelles*, Chief Inspector? I must have not seen them."

"I submit the following, Yves. First, Mr. Bentine used his left hand for all of his actions. Do you recall that he placed the bag that he brought with him on the left side of his chair? And he removed the materials that were in that bag with his left hand? Yet the child in the photograph he provided held the bear, which Bentine called Belle, in his *right* hand. When I inquired as to the height of his mother, and whether she had used peroxide on her hair for the majority of her life, he equivocated before giving noncommittal responses. The record of birth he produced listed baby Bentine as having brown hair, yet Bentine's is sandy in color. He related to us that his mother was of average height, and from other accounts we learned that Mr. Ross was not a tall man, yet the Jonathan Bentine with us today is towering."

"I know another one," Thomas added. "His mother and that private detective both said Ross was swarthy. Bentine isn't. He's fair-skinned."

Scorbion congratulated Thomas. "Well done! That would have been my next pronouncement, but you made it for me."

Thomas's face reddened in appreciation of the recognition Scorbion had given him.

Scorbion continued, "And lastly, as Gromley stated, when he first encountered Bentine at his front door, Gromley assessed the young man who sits before us to be greater than thirty years of age, yet the record of birth would make Jonathan Bentine no older than twenty-five. Each of these things, taken on its own, may not be enough to form a valid judgment. But taken together, they create a near indisputable conclusion that the young man sitting before us is *not* Jonathan Bentine."

The men sat in stunned silence.

Calvin blurted, "Well Pignon, if he isn't Jonathan Bentine, who *is* he?"

"I do not yet know who he is, but I do know who he is *not*. Additionally, I am rather confident that the fate and location of the true Jonathan Bentine are intertwined, and I have grasped those facts fully."

"And what might they be, Inspector?" Billy inquired.

"I related my conversation with the chief inspector of Avens to you earlier. If you recall, he told of a male and female who had been burned to death, beyond recognition. I tell you now, that one of those charred corpses was the unfortunate Jonathan Bentine. He is in a mortuary in Avens, designated as identity unknown."

Bentine jumped up and cried out, "That's not true. *I* am Jonathan Bentine! You are wrong! I'm leaving!"

"Please, sit down, or I will have to ask these gentlemen on either side of me to force you onto your seat. And I will put the restraints back on you."

Bentine sat down.

Scorbion continued, "I am *not* incorrect. And I will prove it through the chief inspector in Avens, who, without any doubt, will confirm that you were one of Jonathan Bentine's closest companions when I provide him with a likeness of you—one that I will personally commission first thing tomorrow morning. I do not yet know who the female might be— possibly one of Bentine's acquaintances who was unfortunate enough to be present when you committed your deed—nor do I know what nature of a human being the true Jonathan Bentine was. But I am convinced, that you, sir, are a double murderer and a blackguard."

When Bentine started to rise out of his chair again, Billy and

Barnabus rushed around the table and stood on either side of him. Barnabus pushed down on one shoulder while Billy applied pressure to the other, forcing Bentine back onto his chair.

"Thank you, my good men," Scorbion said. "Mr. Bentine, whoever you may be, now that you will not be leaving us, I will tell you what devious plan I believe your distorted mind devised. You had to have been a close compatriot, friend, and ally of Jonathan Bentine or you would not have known in as much detail and specifics the tale his mother related to him on her deathbed. I can only presume that you realized that you and the true Jonathan were close enough in age, and you knew enough about him, to the degree that you could pass for him and thereby collect the inheritance and standing awaiting him here that he most assuredly confided in you. You had to dispose of Bentine in a way that would make identification impossible. Therefore, I put forward that you took a knife to his throat and to that of the unlucky female, and then set them both afire. Once they were cremated, you went to his abode and rummaged through his possessions, looking for items that would establish your identity as Jonathan Bentine. That would be where you secured his record of birth, the photograph, and Gromley's linen sample and trade card."

Bentine squirmed. "That's bonkers."

Scorbion ignored him. "Locating Gromley must have taken a bit of time, but once you uncovered his whereabouts you set off to claim your spot as his illegitimate son and heir, Jonathan Bentine. Whom it turned out was neither. And that is why you were taking your leave of this town. Even as I commenced my stroll back to the station after our previous session together in this shop, and began reviewing the events of the day, I was bothered by an unknown concern. But I could not place a marker on it. Fortunately, I continued to replay the events that transpired, and today came upon the hidden truth. Had I not, you would have long been gone by the time I discovered your ruse. Do you have anything to say? Have I misportrayed your scheme and actions in any way?"

"I'm not saying anything."

"You don't have to, sir. Your actions have spoken for you. I hereby arrest you for the murder of Jonathan Bentine and a yet-to-be-identified female. You will reside in our facilities until you can be transported to Avens for trial. Please stand up."

Bentine stood between Barnabus and Billy. Scorbion clasped his hands, reapplied the handcuffs, and walked the cad to the door. Before leaving, Scorbion said, "Thank you all, my deputies, for your participation. Together we have captured another murderer, the third today. I shall determine his identity, and when I do, I will make it known to each of you so that you can proudly inform your friends and loved ones that you were instrumental in apprehending this villain."

"Th-Thank you for the compliment, P-Pignon, but it was all you."

"Nonsense, Barnabus, you all contributed. You each asked intelligent questions and proffered good ideas. But now I must bid you farewell and take this miscreant to the cell that awaits him."

When Scorbion left with his prisoner, the men in the shop rearranged the furniture once again and commented on how Scorbion had solved the Bentine case twice—an affair of two cases of impersonation, one by a father, and the other by his son's murderer.

CHAPTER FORTY-TWO

After bringing Bentine to the station and handing him off to Adley, Scorbion walked to the *Gazette* and strode into Hardcastle's office. Hardcastle placed his teacup on his desk as Scorbion leaned over it, close to his face. "I have just arrested Jonathan Bentine for a double murder, the account of which will appear in the *Morning News*. While you were busy planting seeds of doubt, I was busy pursuing the truth. I am not foolish enough to anticipate a retraction, but I tell you here and now that neither you nor any person on your staff shall ever be privy to my investigations until after they are completed and fully reported by Billy Arthurson."

Scorbion stood, turned on his heel, and strode out of Hardcastle's office.

As he did, Hardcastle yelled, "You have made a serious error in judgment. You have made an enemy of me, and you will regret that."

Scorbion stopped in his tracks and turned to face Hardcastle. "I seriously doubt that, Faustin Hardcastle. It is *you* who will regret it if you cross *me* again. And now, I must be on my way to meet up with a person who is as pleasant as you are dour."

As he left, Scorbion slammed the door to Hardcastle's office so forcefully that its glass window nearly shattered.

Once he exited the building, Scorbion began to walk home to adjust his wardrobe for the evening. While he strode, he focused his thoughts on Thelma. He couldn't recall a time in his life when his heart had been filled with as much joy as it was now—not since he had first met his former wife, Katherine, at least. He instinctively knew that if Katherine ever did attempt to reconcile with him, as she threatened in her letters, he would want no part of it—she would not lighten his heart the way Thelma did, nor would she enable him to let go of that part of his restrained demeanor that Thelma had penetrated and softened.

When he reached his home, sitting on the entry mat where the *Gazette* had been before was a telegraph envelope.

Scorbion stooped and picked it up.

He put the envelope on the entry table, hung his jacket, removed his shoes, and placed them in the shoe rack next to the coat tree. Then he retrieved the envelope, and as he walked to the couch in the living room, he neatly opened it and saw that it was from Katherine. His heart sank in his chest. He hoped she had come to her senses and eschewed any thoughts of reuniting with him. He read the long telegram inside.

Dearest Pignon,

Biggest mistake in my life was leaving you. It has taken many years to understand that, but I do now. Will absolutely die, or possibly kill myself, if you do not give us a chance to recapture the love we once had. Not waiting for an answer because I do not, and will not, accept the word no.

Arriving tomorrow from London, my lost love, old love, true love.

Until then,
Katherine

Scorbion stared at the telegram. Katherine would be in Haxford the next day. On the train that would have taken Bentine away.

He was momentarily angered by the thought, *she is really coming,* but he quickly regained his composure.

"Bloody hell! I will not let her ruin my life a second time."

He tore the missive into shreds, dropped the pieces into the rubbish bin, and went to the bedroom to change into a fresh shirt, looking forward to his dinner with Thelma—and whatever might transpire afterward.

AFTERWORD

Billy had three articles published in the following fortnight. The first contained the new information about Bentine, another related the details about the killings of the hog and of George Barlan, and the third described the events of the circus case.

During that same period, there were no articles in the *Gazette* that related anything about Scorbion or the murders, other than an editorial that warned Haxford's citizens that their new chief police inspector needed to be closely monitored and held accountable the next time he erred in a case—with no facts or reasons as to why that statement was made.

Billy's editor, Hubert Waters, met with Scorbion and agreed not to run his likeness on the condition that he allowed Billy to report on all of his future cases. When Scorbion readily agreed, Billy was promoted to crime reporter and chief mechanic for the *Haxford Morning News*. Every one of Scorbion's future exploits was reported on and carried in the paper, but Scorbion's face never again appeared on the cover of the paper until Billy wrote Scorbion's obituary years later.

As for Scorbion's wife, Katherine, that is a story for another day.

SNEAK PEEK AT

PIGNON
SCORBION
& THE
BARBERSHOP
DETECTIVES

BOOK 2

It was a perfect Saturday morning for the Haxford Fair, which was over-filled with locals and residents from nearby towns. Under a cloudless July sky, the fairgrounds, which had housed a traveling circus the prior month, was alive with people—some petting and ogling the horses, cows, chickens, pigs, goats, and the additional barnyard animals on display. Others were playing games of chance, with the longest lines at the booth that rewarded rock throwers with a cuddly stuffed teddy bear when they successfully knocked down all six pins. Many fair-goers walked the grounds taking in all that the festival had to offer, a good number eating fish and chips as they strolled, while competitors partic-ipated in the tug-of-war and best cherry pie contests. Most people were congregated near the rides, which included a carousel, Ferris wheel, small wooden roller coaster, and a lively fun house which was next to a small sideshow tent.

The east end of the grounds was reserved for six hot-air balloons. It was where they were assembled, prepared, and then launched. The area had a large tract of grass populated with couples and families sitting on blankets—there to watch the balloons lift off and then witness their flights in the sky.

That was where Haxford's chief police inspector, Pignon Scorbion;

the *Haxford Morning News*'s reporter and printing press mechanic, Billy Arthurson; barbershop owner, Calvin Brown; and Books on the Square proprietor, Thelma Smith, set up the blankets Calvin and Thelma had brought and the food dishes that they each, except for Scorbion, contributed to the morning's gathering of friends. They all anticipated a wonderful Saturday together sharing their picnic repast, drinking Calvin's homemade beer, and watching the colorful balloons as they lifted skyward, soared across the town and nearby countryside, and then returned and settled down in nearly the exact spot from which they had departed.

Between mouthfuls of the salted lamb sandwich that Thelma had made, Scorbion told Calvin, "It is unfortunate that Mildred could not join us on such a glorious day as this."

Calvin replied, "I do believe she would have enjoyed attending this fair and watching the balloons, but my wife felt duty-bound to assist her sister with their mother's care this weekend."

When the bright sun glared off the mirrorlike glass from which Thelma was drinking, she adjusted her large, feathered hat so that it better shielded her eyes. At the same time, Scorbion put down his sandwich and reached into his front right trousers pocket, taking out a pair of colored eyeglasses.

As he put them on, Calvin asked, "Are you afflicted with that dreaded syphilis, Pignon? I have only seen glasses such as those on patients whose eyes are made so sensitive from that ailment that they need the protection those spectacles provide."

Scorbion patted his friend on the shoulder. "Neither you nor Thelma has anything to be concerned about. I am not a person who finds hats to his liking—on you, Thelma, they look wonderful, but on me, they create the appearance of a bumpkin or a scoundrel. So, during the past week, I paid a visit to the optician in Brookdale, Dr. Grodin, and inquired if he had any recommendation as to how I might dim the rays of the sun from overwhelming my eyes, without the use of a head covering. He suggested that I consider these glasses which, as you rightfully observed, Calvin, are utilized by the unfortunate among us who are afflicted with syphilis. I purchased this pair, and found they work astoundingly well for dimming the effects of the sun."

Billy looked concerned. "Aren't you uneasy that people will wrongly assume you have that horrid disease? As Calvin just did."

Scorbion replied calmly, "People will learn that I am not bound by conventional wisdom, thought, or practice. If they leap to that conclusion, it is their issue, not mine."

Thelma reached over and put her hand on Scorbion's arm. "Do the lenses allow you to see the colors of the balloons, Pignon? They are quite beautiful and impressive. I am obsessed with the rainbow-striped one. I have been following its trajectory since it rose from the ground. The yellow one is striking, as well."

Scorbion had been watching an orange one and took off the glasses for a moment to see the full color spectrum of each balloon. Then he put them back on and agreed. "Yes, they are both pleasing to observe and majestic. They are the ultimate expressions of freedom: untethered from the ground, moving whichever way they care to travel. Free as a kestrel soaring on the wind, literally."

Billy interjected, "Does that appeal to you, Inspector?"

Before Scorbion answered the question, he said, "As Calvin and Thelma call me by my given name, and they are the only ones here, it seems unnecessary—and a bit ludicrous—to have you address me by my title. When we are in situations such as this, you have my permission to call me Pignon, and I will call you Billy. However, when we are in the company of others, Inspector would be appropriate."

Billy replied, slightly tentatively, "I'm not sure I'll be comfortable calling you Pignon. I know you as Inspector."

"You will get used to it," Scorbion responded. "Now, to answer your question, being in a balloon both appeals, and does not appeal, to me. I would enjoy witnessing the countryside from the vantage point that being that elevated in the sky affords a person, but at the same time, one of my weaknesses is heights. I am not certain which would win out, my curiosity about the view or my fear of being at an altitude so much higher than my head."

Thelma laughed and teased, "The great Pignon Scorbion has a weakness? A foible?"

"I am filled with foibles," Scorbion replied. "And as to weaknesses, my foremost one appears to be you."

That pleased Thelma, and her face broke into a wide smile. "Thank you, Pignon."

Billy turned to Calvin. "I fancy the green one, although the purple balloon with stripes is attractive too."

Calvin shook his head. "To me, the blue and white one is most appealing, although . . ."

He was stopped by a piercing shriek emanating from a woman standing close by.

They all turned to look at who had made the sound, and their gazes followed the woman's arm skyward, her finger pointing at a red balloon that was dropping at an alarming rate.

As the balloon rapidly descended, more people began to scream. Mothers grabbed their children by the hands and hurried from the area. Every person in that section of the grounds scattered, running from where they thought the balloon might crash down.

Scorbion had the opposite reaction. "That balloonist is in trouble. There is no fire propelling the balloon and keeping it aloft. We must get to where it will land." He stood up and started to hasten to the spot where he anticipated the balloon would touch down. The others quickly followed him.

Seconds later the gondola smashed into the ground with an explosive thud, twenty feet from where Scorbion had positioned himself, the force of the impact rocking him backward.

Billy, Calvin, and Thelma arrived just as the gondola split apart and the body of the balloonist fell out. The red balloon fluttered down and draped over him, the basket, and the surrounding area like a blanket.

Once the material had fully settled, Scorbion took charge. "We must remove the balloon and attend to the person. Assist me in taking away the cloth."

They each took hold of the balloon fabric and together started gathering it and moving it to the grassy area behind the gondola. While they did, Billy asked Scorbion, "Didn't the fellow look dead to you? He just rolled out after it crashed. I'll wager that's what killed him."

Scorbion responded, "Though I agree with your assessment of it being a dead body rather than a live person, I have no opinion as to what killed him yet. That, we shall determine."

Calvin interjected, "And, we're going to have to learn why the balloon fell from the sky."

Thelma turned to Calvin. "It appeared to have exhausted its fuel."

"We *will* discover what occurred," Scorbion reiterated, "but we cannot know anything for certain until we examine the body, the balloon, and the gondola."

Once they had gathered up all the balloon material and placed it behind the remains of the basket, they followed Scorbion as he walked to the body.

Scorbion removed his colored glasses and placed them back in his pocket in anticipation of examining the body. "Calvin, will you take hold of the legs, and Billy, will you assist with the arms? Let us turn this fellow over so that we may see his face."

Calvin and Billy grasped the man's limbs, gently raised the body a few inches, and laid it on its back.

Thelma uttered a gasp of surprise. "Oh my!"

She, Scorbion, Calvin, and Billy stared at the broken shaft of an arrow that was protruding from the middle of the dead man's chest.

Billy was shaken by the sight but confused about how it could have happened. "That's ghastly. But how could he have been shot with an arrow when he was in the balloon, high above everything, and with no other person in the gondola with him?"

Scorbion clapped Billy on the back. "That certainly is an appropriate question, and I believe that we have found our newest mystery that needs solving."

ACKNOWLEDGMENTS

Over the course of the years that I have been writing articles, columns, books, songs, and short stories, and working in both the music and publishing industries, a great number of people have been supportive in ways that helped me and made my creative endeavors much better. I want to thank them here, and if I inadvertently left someone out who should have been included, I apologize in advance.

At the top of the list is my wife, Deborah Morgan, for her never-ending love, support, and encouragement. After that are my sons, Ben and Jon; Ben's wife, Kate; my granddaughters Sophie and Penny; and Jon's fiancé, Karl—all of whom have shared in the excitement of my undertakings and publications. Plus, I would be remiss not including Gracie, our wonderful Havanese, who has given Deborah and me millions of licks and thousands of hours of joy and laughter.

They say it often "takes a village" to make something be the best it can be, and it was certainly the case for this book. First and foremost are my fantastic agents (and wonderful people) Nicole Resciniti and Julie Gwinn of the Seymour Agency whose numerous insights and edits vastly improved the book, Haila Williams who read the book for Blackstone and provided a number of outstanding observations and suggestions that made it much stronger, my good friend Michael Levine and Michael Carr who both offered invaluable insights and advice. The book's editor, Jason Kirk, pushed me to make the book even better than it was when he became involved with it and absolutely made me a finer writer. Included also are Kate Scholl who fine-tuned the final version, Ed Battistella who gave many invaluable suggestions along the way, and my former writing group, Ashland's Write On Collective, who helped me hone my craft—Bruce Barton, Nancy Bringhurst, Peggy DuVall, the late Ralph Temple, Jeannie Green, Sara Paul, Sidney Copelow, Paul Nyland, and John Fisher-Smith.

Another part of that "village" who I want to recognize and thank are those people who read all or parts of the book to assure its accuracy, compassion, and historical correctness. That most especially includes Christopher Toyne; Nick Jones; Kay Renfrew; Jason R. Couch, MFA; Muskogee Creek; and Thomas M. Yeahpau, Kiowa/Apache.

I must especially thank Craig and Michelle Black, who hired me at Blackstone and have been outstanding owners and friends, and Josh Stanton (Blackstone's visionary CEO) for believing in this book and for creating a wonderful working relationship and environment that I have now been a part of for over a decade and a half.

I want to thank the bestselling and award-winning authors who read this book prior to its publication and thought enough of it to write wonderful endorsements for it.

I also want to recognize those friends and relatives who have been important in my life, and supportive of me and the things I've done. David and Patti Lang, John Kase, MaryKay Feely, Don Robinson and Barb Specker, John Ralston and Leslie Harachek, Patti Wood, Lisa Horwitch, Alan Thomashefsky and Hillary Best, Beryl Patner and John O'Brien, the late Denis Kellman, Bill and Anne Stahl, Pete and Jane Jones, Bill and Debra Berger, Gary Toms, Karine Eberlin, Jacqueline Ambrose, Elly Lessin and Jay Leslie, Maurice "Bugs" Bower and Kathryn Podwall, Mark Cope, Christopher and AnneMarie Morgan and their sons Carter and Sawyer, Sharon and Paul Gerardi, Paula Sendar, Dr. Irene Cypher, Ralph/Phyllis/Debbie Chicorel, Christopher and Bunny Toyne, Terry Currier, Al DiNoble, Jeff Rinkoff and Janis Rosenthal,

Charlie "Chucker" Brown, Len Rokosz, Myra and Ron Silverman, John Luongo, Kevin Kelly, Jack/Mary/Alexandra Climent, Fritz Mars, Mike Dungan, Julie Schoerke, Barbara and Kevin Talbert, Rosemary and Paul Adelian, Sara Brown and Paul Steinele, Jacqueline Schad, Steve Plotnicki, Carol Morgan, Matt Messner and Neil Sechan, the late Lou Maglia, Clive Davis, Curtis Hayden, Herb Rosen, and Jason Couch (including for the wonderful photographs he took of me, one of which adorns the cover of this book).

Next, I want to address and acknowledge everyone I have joyously worked with during my time at Blackstone, most especially my fellow employees, but also the agents, authors, and attorneys I have dealt with. There are far too many people to list—that would comprise a book of its own—and I'd be really concerned if I left someone out who I shouldn't have. Every one of you should know you have a special place in my heart; how much I respect, admire, and enjoy working with you; and that this acknowledgment is for each of you individually.

And lastly, I want to acknowledge my respect for, and love of, all the independent booksellers and music stores, and librarians, whose existence and passion make literature and music, and their dissemination, so much better and much more experiential.

ABOUT THE AUTHOR

Rick Bleiweiss is an award-winning author, publishing executive, music producer, rock musician, record company senior executive, and educator.

Prior to moving to Ashland, Oregon, in 2003, Rick spent his life in New York City in the music industry. He was a rock performer and songwriter; produced over fifty records, including a Grammy-nominated album; and was a senior executive at major and independent record companies helping to launch the careers of Melissa Etheridge and the Backstreet Boys. He also worked on the records of Kiss, U2, Whitney Houston, Britney Spears, and many other superstars, and specialized in marketing and selling major film soundtracks, including the first three Star Wars films, *Saturday Night Fever*, and *Grease*, to name a few.

He has lectured at multiple universities on the business of entertainment and cofounded a sports and entertainment marketing program at Baruch College.

Writing under a pen name, Rick had a number one e-book in Politics and Humor on Kindle which won the New Apple Literary Society Award as the best independently published Short General Fiction e-book of 2016, and received a Readers Favorites award.

Rick has written articles for magazines and newspapers, contributed stories to a number of anthologies, and is a member of the Pacific Northwest Writers' Association and Mystery Writers of America.

Since 2006, Rick has been an executive at Blackstone Publishing where he has acquired works by many incredible authors, including James Clavell, Leon Uris, Gabriel García Márquez, H. P. Lovecraft, Pablo Neruda, Rex Pickett, P. C. and Kristin Cast, and Nicholas Sansbury Smith, and cocreated a book/audiobook series to preserve the wisdom, humor, stories, and life experiences of First Nation elders.

Rick has a BA in film and an MA in communications from New York University, and completed an accelerated business leadership program at Harvard University.

Visit Rick's website at www.RickBleiweiss.com